Gods of the Deep

Drew Montgomery

ISBN: 9798828506293

Cover design by: David King
www.kingsizedcreations.com
Printed in the United States of America

CONTENTS

1

She awoke to the silent room, stirring beneath the woolen blanket, blinking her eyes as if it would do any good against the near total darkness around her. The morning was still, no sign of wind or rain, just the occasional creaking of the old stone and wood house as it settled.

Getting out of bed was always the worst part, the cold evident even through the thick blanket. The temptation to remain beneath the covers was as strong as it ever was, day in and day out, but just like always, she knew there was no choice. She drew in a silent breath, counted to three in her head, and threw the covers off, quickly sliding into her clothing for the day, woolen breeches and seal skin boots and a fur parka that fit over the thin shirt she wore to sleep, all of it still smelling of sweat and sea from the day before. The parka was the lighter of the two she owned, this one more attuned to the relative warmth of summer, enough to fend off the chill of the sea while not overheating her as she worked.

A shiver passed through her as her skin gradually warmed against the clothing, and she rubbed her arms to speed the process as she stepped from the small bedroom to the living room. Her steps fell quietly on the fur rugs that covered the wooden floor, making her way to the iron stove that sat in the corner. The fire had long since burned out, leaving behind only ashes, and as she always did before leaving, she filled it with wood and kindling, striking flint on steel to draw a spark with practiced motions and start the blaze that would heat the home.

"Aunt Kirima?"

The voice came in a whisper, but it was the whisper of one still learning how to control their volume, hardly silent and certainly not secretive. She forced away the smile that came and turned toward the loft that sat atop the two rooms, seeing the small head that poked up, light hair tied back in a pair of matching braids, bright eyes reflecting the light given off by the fire.

"Shouldn't you be asleep, Meriwa?" she asked, her own voice quiet.

"I wanted to see you leave."

"It's nothing exciting, no different from any other day. Now get back to bed, you'll wake your brother."

"He's already awake."

"I am." Hanta's voice didn't even come in a whisper, the younger of the two speaking as if there was no reason for silence.

"Well you certainly don't want to wake up your Mama."

"I'm already awake as well."

She hadn't even heard the door open, but she did hear the creak of the floorboard as her sister, Yura, emerged from the other bedroom. She walked gingerly, both hands cupping the swollen belly that held her third child.

"You shouldn't be. You need to be resting."

"If only the little one would allow me." She made her way to a chair in the corner and eased her way down into a thick cushion stuffed in goose down. "I swear this one is already more trouble than the other two combined."

"Perhaps that means she will be better behaved once she is out." Kirima turned back to the stove, closed the door, and began to pack herself a meal.

"Hey, we're behaved." Meriwa had emerged further, skinny arms propping her up on the edge, while Hanta had poked his own head up, a mop of messy dark hair growing over his forehead and ears. "We always do what we're told."

"Behaved children would still be in bed."

"We still are." Meriwa turned to look over her shoulder, then turned back. "I'm still touching it with my toe."

"Doesn't count."

"If they're up, then I'm sure they can get a head start on chores," Yura said.

Meriwa's head suddenly ducked behind the edge, blanket covering it. "We're not up. Not yet."

"That's what I thought," Yura said. She turned back as Kirima finished wrapping up her meal, some goat's cheese, thick rye bread, and dried fish meat. "Be safe out there."

"You know I always am."

"Atka always was as well."

Kirima turned away toward the front door. "I know you don't like it, but the family needs it."

"I know. I just wish there was another way."

Kirima sighed. "Many of us do."

She opened the door and stepped into the morning. Somewhere in the east, the sun had already begun its climb into the day, but it was hidden behind the perpetual clouds, a light rain falling like mist. Below her, she could see the roofs of the lowest row of houses of the town of Aliit, and the beach beyond them, wrapping around a small harbor and extending out on either side into high rocky outcroppings, blocking the worst of the winds.

Already she could see the other village fishers as they prepared their boats. Nets were repaired and sails patched, fresh pitch applied to hulls, wood loaded onto the nicer boats to fuel the engines, some of them already being pushed into the water. Few acknowledged her as she made her way past them, most who did giving little more than grunts or side eye glances. She ignored them all, making her way toward the far end, where her own boat rested.

She was almost there as she passed one of the newer boats and heard her name called out. She turned, seeing three men, one older and two around her own age. The older one was tying a net, while the other two had been arranging wood in the space to either side of the engine. One of the younger ones was waving, tall and lanky, dark hair tied back in a bun.

"Hey, Phillip," she said. "Taking her out far today?"

Phillip put a foot up on the edge of the boat and rested his elbow on his knee. "Yeah, there's an island out east of the Company outpost, going to try our luck out there. Innik and Dand had some luck that way, so we figured we'd give it a look."

"Are you allowed out there?" she asked.

He shrugged. "We have as much right to the waters as they do. More, if you ask me."

"Not if they catch you."

Behind him, his brother cleared his throat, but Phillip ignored him. "They won't, those ships are too slow. You sticking to the Narrows?"

Kirima hoisted her pack onto her other shoulder and brushed an errant strand of golden hair from her eye. "As always."

"You should come with us," he said. "We could use the extra hands."

"Phillip," his brother hissed. "Come help."

"In a minute, Calum," he said over his shoulder, turning back and flashing that goofy smile he'd had since they were children. "What do you say?"

"We don't need the help," their father said, coming around the side, using a cloth to wipe his hands. "No help except for what you need to give to your brother." He nodded toward her, acknowledging her by name and turning away before she could respond.

Phillip shook his head. "He's still living in the past. The old superstitions about women on boats, ignoring the fact that half the fishers are women and none of them ever seem to sink."

"You ever tell him that?"

"Of course. Not even sure he believes it, but it seems like second nature at this point. Still, the help would be appreciated."

"Thanks, but I prefer to fish alone anyways. It's the way my father did."

Phillip gave a slight snort. "Guess my old man isn't the only one stuck in the past."

"Guess not," she said, matching his laugh with a smirk.

A small rock flew through the air, striking Phillip in the back. He recoiled and turned, sneering at his brother, who motioned him over. This time, Kirima did laugh.

"Looks like you have work to do. I'll see you when we're back. Good luck, and don't go getting yourselves hurt."

"We won't," he said. "May the Imakut bless your bounty."

"And yours," she said, trudging on the rest of the distance to her boat.

It seemed out of the way, forgotten almost, a lone canoe amongst a fleet of larger ones, a relic amongst those powered by sail or wood burning motor. It had belonged to her father, carved by him and her grandfather long before she or Yura had been born, and it was the same one in which he had taught her to fish using the old ways.

Kirima stashed her meal in a dry spot at the rear, double checked to ensure that the net and paddle were both there, and pushed it into the water, jumping in the moment it was deep enough. She settled into a kneeling position, shifting around until she was comfortable. Once there, she picked up the oar and began to row, smooth, even strokes to either side, propelling her past the gentle waves and into the harbor.

The other boats moved past her, faster regardless of their mode of propulsion, but she ignored them, focusing on her own task. She turned her eyes toward the edge of the harbor, guiding her toward the shrine to the Imakut that sat just at the edge of visibility through the rain.

It came into better focus as she drew nearer, four curving sides coming to a single point to form a roof that rested on four wooden pillars, their bases vanishing into the water below, supported on the sandbar. Each pillar was carved into a different creature, representing the beasts of the deep, the fish, the whale, the seal, and the lobster. In the center was tied the latest offering, as was done every time both moons shone full, a crying sheep standing up to its breast in water, the wool matted as small waves lapped against it.

The last of the boats was pulling away from the shrine, leaving her alone. She eased the canoe alongside the pillar carved like a fish, allowing it to drift until it bumped the column with a wooden thump. She laid the paddle across her lap and pulled the necklace from around her neck, a milky white stone tied by a leather strap, the holy jarak. She held the stone in her fingers, then kissed it and touched it to the column.

"Bless me with your bounty, Imakut," she said in a quiet voice. She held it against the column, silent but for the lapping of water and the bleating of the sacrificial ewe. "Anything you may give would be welcome."

She lingered for a moment more before slipping the necklace back over her head and placing it back beneath her shirt, the stone cold against her skin. She picked up her oar, dipped it into the water once more, and paddled past the shrine and into the open sea, the bleating of the ewe following her like a ghost through the still, wet air. It no doubt knew what its fate was, but it was a necessary thing. By the time she returned that evening, the sacrifice would be gone, vanished beneath the waves to sate the Imakut. The Balance must be preserved.

The water grew choppier as she passed the edge of the harbor, the wind picking up once she was no longer protected by the outcroppings, but even outside of the harbor, it was calmer than usual. A fog had descended, thick enough that she could not see the surrounding islands, but she had long ago learned how to navigate the spaces outside the harbor, helped by the shallow draft of her canoe that allowed her to pass over rocky reefs that the larger boats had to avoid.

There was a distinctive quiet to the morning. The grey filled the air in every direction she looked, seeming to grow out of the very water around her like the plants in Yura's garden. The rain continued to fall as well, sticking to her parka, but not accumulating enough to soak through. It did, however, stick to her hair, matting her golden strands to her head and sending a chill that resonated through her entire body.

Not far from the mouth of the harbor, there was a rock called the Spire that she always used as a landmark, one that rose to a steep point like the end of a chisel straight up into the air. She navigated toward it by sense and familiarity, and after a few moments of paddling, it emerged from the fog, jutting high enough from the water that that she had to crane her neck to get a full view. Even then, the point was still lost in the fog above.

This was always a good place to start, especially in weather like this. She pulled up next to it, feeling along the jagged rock until she reached the small rune carved into the side, the spot where someone had long ago chiseled deep into the stone to mark the direction of north. She turned her head slightly west of it, and once more began to paddle.

Each stroke of the oar was slow, patient, propelling the canoe through the water with only the slightest sound. Her lips began to move as she rowed, a soft song joining in with the rhythm of her movements. She sang the tune in a low voice, the words in the old language, most of the meanings lost to time. It didn't matter that she knew what the words meant, though, as her father had always said. What mattered was the intent, the blessing that gave meaning to her labor, that would bring the fish to her net and nourish her family. Even now, the words brought back memories of sitting at the front of this very canoe, singing the song for her father as he rowed, his net dragging behind the boat.

It served as a reminder to drop her own net, allowing it to drape behind the canoe. She continued her slow pace and her low singing, the row passing to either side to keep the boat heading in a straight line.

Somewhere in the distance, she heard a long, low sound, almost like a moan, no doubt the call of a whale as it surfaced for a breath of air. She closed her eyes, focusing on her song, on the fish that swam below. She could feel the added weight in each stroke, the drag of the net behind the boat making movement harder. And perhaps whatever had found its way into the net.

The sound came again, but this time it was louder, closer, and quite obviously not the sound of a whale breaking the surface. Her eyes opened, the song ceasing on her lips, the blade of the oar rising from the water, hovering just above. There was no sight of land around her, only the glass-like water and the fog and the tiny droplets of rain that swirled in the air around her.

She waited, and she listened. After a moment, the sound came again, and she let loose the breath that she had been holding in a deep sigh. A Company ship was close. She couldn't quite gauge the distance, not without the sound of another horn, but it was certainly close enough. She waited for that horn to come, but the silence remained.

After a few moments, her arms had grown tired holding the oar, so she lifted it, laying it across her lap. As she did, her eyes caught sight of a strange viscous substance that clung to the blade, a dark substance that reflected the foggy grey around her while the edges seemed to flash the colors of the rainbow as she turned it. She frowned, glancing over the side to find more of it floating atop the water, a nauseating smell drifting from it.

Kirima turned, her hands reaching out and finding the rope that tied the net to the canoe. She pulled it in, seeing the way the substance coated the netting even as she pulled it from the water. Two fish rested within, neither making any type of movement as she pulled them out, dead eyes gazing out, their scales coated as well.

"Bastards," she said out loud. She gave a cry as she flung the fish back into the water, her hands settling into her lap as she looked at the coated net lying there in her boat.

Time passed, though likely not long; it was always hard to tell when there was no sun. Her mind seemed at a loss. There was no telling how far this spread, how far she'd have to go to get away from it. And even if she did, did its effect go further than what she could see? What was it? Where had it come from? Whatever it was, it was clear it wasn't good.

Something pulled her from her thoughts, a sound that seemed to grow around her. It was so subtle at first that she wasn't certain it wasn't a figment of her imagination, not until it became a steady rumble, one that she could feel in her very bones. Even then, it wasn't until the horn sounded again that she realized just how close it was.

A curse escaped her lips as she snatched up the oar, paddling as quickly as she could. It felt as if the oar was sliding through the water instead of pushing it, as if she were rowing in place, no matter how fast she worked it.

She couldn't see the approaching ship, but she could definitely feel its presence, the rumbling of an engine shaking her body, her boat, the water around her, like the ones on the boats the others used, but larger. The horn blared again, so close that it seemed like it would burst her ears, but she dared not cover them, dared not release the oar.

A behemoth of a shadow appeared to her left, looming just beyond the fog, the air seeming to part before it like a demon stepping from the darkness. She gritted her teeth, a harried sound escaping her throat as she fought to move the boat, rowing in short, frantic strokes.

The Company ship barreled forward, the water passing to either side in waves. The horn blew again, and the thought of jumping over to the side flashed in her mind, her hand almost pulling away from the paddle in an attempt to pull the rest of her body away from the doomed canoe. But she fought the urge, rowing as frantically as she could.

The canoe lifted in the wake of the ship, its side scraping against the hull of the ship with an ear-splitting grating noise. Kirima pulled the oar in, gripping the side of the canoe as it veered to the side, threatening to flip as it rocked in the waves created by the monstrous ship. She closed her eyes, bracing herself for the dip into the icy water that surrounded her.

Except the plunge never came. Some water splashed in, sloshing around the bottom of the canoe and soaking her breeches, but the canoe remained upright, and her within it. She sat there, breathing heavily as the waters slowly calmed around her, the remains of the wake faded as the ship vanished once more into the fog, the rumbling of its engines and the sounding of its horn growing softer until it was no more.

"That was too close," she said to the empty sea around her.

As her heartbeat began to return to normal, she began to look around. She was certain she was still within the Narrows. Wasn't part of the agreement with the Company that they stayed out of this area? That was what the other fishers had said, and she had certainly never seen any of their ships here. She wasn't versed enough in the agreement to know what it meant, but she could say with certainty that it wasn't good news. Something for Gabriel and the Council to hear about when she returned.

Her hand was shaking as she felt around the bottom of the canoe for the oar, her eyes still glancing back toward where the ship had vanished. Panic welled in her chest when she couldn't find it, the thought that it had gone overboard flooding into her mind, but it quickly faded into frustration when she finally looked and saw it right where she had put it, mere inches from where her hand was reaching.

She let loose a loud sigh. "Get a grip on yourself, Kirima."

It was still a good while before she finally dipped the end of the oar back into the water and began to paddle once more. She still sung the song, but the words seemed to come out more stilted, hollow as they left her lips. Her eyes moved between the space before her and the water beside her, watching until that telltale sheen was gone. It never fully left, though, so she settled for a spot where it seemed less prevalent.

The substance seemed to stick to the netting even when she dipped it into the water and swished it around the same way Yura did when washing clothes. A sigh escaped her lips; there was not much else she could do, not if she wanted to bring anything home. Once more she dropped the net and began to pull it through the water.

All told, she ended up with about a dozen fish, all of them small, most of them covered in the slick substance. Hardly ideal for a day's work, but the end of the day was fast approaching, the long summer day coming to a close. And if her father had taught her one thing, it was to never be caught away from the harbor after dark.

The sky was darkening, and the rain had begun to fall a bit harder by the time she reached the Spire. She could hear voices as she drew close, voices she didn't recognize. She lifted the paddle into her lap and allowed the canoe to drift around the rock. As she passed the corner, she gasped, laying eyes on the very same ship that had nearly run her over. It was no longer moving, its anchor vanished beneath the surface to hold it in place.

Kirima sat there, watching the crew work. They were all gathered to one side of the deck, dressed in outfits colored the familiar dark violet of the Company. There were men and women alike, standing before the backdrop of engine stacks, dark smoke rising into the air. One man stood atop a railing, holding onto a cable as he yelled instructions down to the others. The rest pulled on thick ropes, the other ends attached to a large whale that was being pulled from the sea. She could still see the harpoons sticking out of it, blood seeping from the wounds and running down the white skin, mixing with the seawater that dripped from it.

Kirima shook her head as she watched, the beautiful creature now dead, just the latest of many since they had come to this place. She had heard about the hunts, seen scouting parties from the Company, seen their representatives when they had come to visit Gabriel and the Council, but she had never seen the result of one of those hunts.

Watching it now, she wasn't sure she ever wanted to see it again.

"Rest easy, giant of the sea," she said in a quiet voice. "May your body return to the sea as it was meant to." More words passed her lips, an ode to the dead in the old tongue, their meaning lost to her just like the song. On the boat, the whale's body was now close enough that some of the workers were beginning to cut at it with long, curved blades.

As she was speaking, she saw the leader's head turn in her direction. She could see him squint through the rain before his face turned to a scowl. "Hey, you, get out of here. We already talked to your chief about what happens if you get in the way."

Kirima started at the intensity of his words. He wasn't wrong, but that only applied to the waters around their outpost. She thought of saying something back, but quickly thought better of it, especially as some of the other crew members paused in their work and looked in her direction. She picked up the oar from her lap and began to row, taking one last glance back to see the leader still watching her as she glided through the water. Another thing to mention to Gabriel.

The sight of the ship still weighed heavy on her mind as she made her way toward the harbor. She tried to push it from her mind, thinking instead of the warm fire and hot meal she'd have at home. Anything that would be more pleasant than this pounding rain and these winds.

She was so lost in thought that the sound didn't register at first. It seemed to creep in, as if it had been hiding in the back of her mind before growing and growing until it shoved the rest of her thoughts away.

"It can't be," she said.

She was much too far from land, from where the flocks were kept, for it to have been anything else. But that was impossible; nothing like that had ever happened as far as she knew. She had to be certain. Her pace picked up, propelling the boat forward, curving around the western outcropping and through the mouth of the harbor.

The shrine came into view, and she stopped paddling, the blade of the oar resting just above the water. Her mouth was agape, her eyes wide, her heart pounding as she gazed upon the bleating sheep that still stood up to its breast in water.

The sacrifice had been rejected.

2

The door to the stove sat open, allowing some of the heat from the fire to escape directly out of it and into the living room. Kirima held her hands over it, feeling real warmth for the first time that day. Yura sat beside her, eyebrow furrowed in that familiar way, an extra crease seeming to have formed in the olive-colored skin of her forehead in the past year.

"Are you certain it was not a new one?"

The children had been put to bed, though she had no doubt that they were still awake, listening to them speak. She replied in the same hushed tone her sister had used. "You know how it works, Yura."

She shrugged. "I did once. I'm not going to pretend I follow all the customs or remember the ones we did when I was younger or pay any particular attention to those who do."

"Always when the twins show full. Never any other time."

"Maybe they felt an additional one was needed this time. It's not just you who is struggling to bring in catches."

Kirima shook her head. "I don't know if that's even an option. Besides, we would have heard about it."

"Maybe not. Gabriel doesn't share everything that comes from the Council meetings."

"He would if it was something like this." She paused, holding her hands a bit closer to the fire, the burning almost painful now. "Of course, we could give the whole flock and it would not be enough for what the Company takes."

"Is it that bad?"

"It seems to be getting worse. I saw a ship in the Narrows today."

"Maybe they are scaring the fish away. Perhaps the far side of the island may prove to be a better spot?"

"Our family has fished the Narrows for generations, all the way through

Papa and me. This has never been a problem.”

"The Company was never there when our ancestors were fishing."

"But they came when Papa was still alive."

"They were just setting up back then, nothing like they are today."

"They were already hunting the whales then. Perhaps not on the same scale, but it was happening."

"How can you be sure? You weren't there?"

"Papa told me he saw the ships long before they came to speak to Gabriel and the Council."

"They could have been scouting."

Kirima shook her head. "You don't use ships like that for scouting."

A voice belonging to Meriwa called down from the loft. "Are you two fighting?"

"No, pumpkin, go to bed," Yura said.

"It sounds like you are."

"We aren't, I promise." Her eyes turned to Kirima, and she gestured toward the loft with her head.

"Just like your Mama says," Kirima said. "We're only talking."

There was a pause. "Well don't fight. I don't like it when you do."

Kirima suppressed a laugh and turned to find Yura biting her lip to suppress one of her own. Her sister motioned again with her head, then stood, walking toward the door. Kirima hesitated a moment, not sure she wanted to leave the warmth of the fire behind, but she finally followed. It was the only way they were going to get some privacy. Besides, her grandmother had always said that the cold was good for a baby. She wasn't sure whether she actually believed it, but she wasn't about to argue with a ghost as well.

There was a slight wind, and the same raindrops that had plagued her earlier were still falling. The door closed behind her, and both of them kept close to the house, the eave offering the slightest protection from the weather. Kirima had shed her parka inside, and now wrapped her arms around herself, drawing any warmth she could from her body.

"She has your energy," Yura said.

"And your stubbornness," Kirima said.

Yura gave a laugh, which Kirima always took as a sign she wasn't too upset at their sparring. "Oh, to be a child and to not have to think of the things we do."

"She'll have to eventually."

"I know." A deep sigh, but her lips were still stretched into something of a smile. "But I'd hope to keep that kind of thing from her for as long as I can."

"Sooner or later, though, you have to let them."

Yura stood there for a moment, staring out into the night. "Seems you're not the only one concerned."

Kirima turned, first toward her sister, and then in the direction she was looking. There was a fire burning in the center of the beach, just as there was every night, both an offering to the Imakut and as a boon to the night watch. With the light, she could see the figures as they moved around, checking the boats, checking with each other, and a few breaking off to check in with each home in the village, one coming right toward them. Even with his face obscured by shadow, she recognized Phillip, his lanky build and long gait unmistakable.

"What's happening?" she asked as he approached.

He was out of breath as he spoke. "We're asking around to see if Aiden and Anik made it back. Did you see them? Either of you?"

She caught Yura looking toward her, could almost see that worried face in the corner of her eye, but she was already speaking. "We haven't seen either of them. Their boat wasn't in when I returned."

Phillip frowned and shook his head. "I was afraid of that."

"They haven't returned?" Yura asked.

"Not that anyone could tell. I have a few more houses to check before I meet back with the others. If none of us have found him, the plan is to go out and look."

"That's suicide," Kirima said before Yura could respond. "The Narrows are treacherous enough in the daytime."

"And any part of these seas is treacherous if someone is left overnight," he said. "We can't let them just sit out there."

"Nor can we sacrifice the rest of our fishermen to the Imakut in trying to save them."

"Maybe they'd accept this one," Yura said.

Kirima shot her a glare, but Phillip was already speaking again. "You can speak to Gabriel about it. He's down there making the plans."

"Don't think I won't."

"I know you will."

He headed to the next house as Kirima reached inside to snatch her parka from where it lay drying by the fire. She was still pulling it over her head as she made her way down to the beach. Gabriel was where Phillip had said, giving out orders to fishermen next to the fire, several already prepping their boats to depart. He turned his ample frame toward her as she approached, his skin pale in the flames, his emerald-colored eyes reflecting the light.

"You're planning to send people out in the dark?" she asked. "Are you mad?"

"You know, your father always said hello first before berating me."

"This is suicide, you know? The Narrows are hard enough to navigate in the daytime."

A hand went to his head, running through thick, white hair. "You don't think I know that? What would you have me do?"

"Keep a watch. Keep the fire lit. Even take a boat out to the harbor's edge. But going out there can't happen, not until morning."

"You're welcome to stop them if you want," he said, motioning a meaty hand to the men prepping the boats. "You know how our people are when someone is lost. You've seen it firsthand."

"Papa wouldn't have approved of this either," she said. "Even if his own sinking had come at night."

"Except he had never been the one in charge." His eyes turned, and she followed them to see Phillip running up, his feet thumping in the sand. "Nothing?"

Phillip shook his head. Like the mayor, the fire made him appear paler than he did in daylight, as if the flames drew out the Eilenan blood that ran through his veins. "Nothing. No one has seen them."

Gabriel turned back to her. "The ships are casting off soon. Either help us or get out of the way."

Kirima grunted through clenched teeth. "Fine, but just to make sure you idiots don't get yourself killed out there."

"Many of us have survived much worse," Gabriel said.

"Come on," Phillip said, already moving. "You can come with Calum and I on our boat."

Kirima followed after him. "Your father not going to be around to call me bad luck?"

"He is nursing a chill he caught on the water yesterday. He's back at the house resting."

"Not too serious, I hope?"

"He certainly doesn't think so."

"Not that he'd ever say."

The boat was parked in the same spot from that morning, not far from where her own canoe lay. She could see Calum working on the deck, turning up to look as they approached and scowling when he saw her.

"What's she doing here?" Calum asked.

"Helping," Kirima said. "You need someone to keep you safe."

"We're more than capable of doing this ourselves."

"She's coming," Phillip said. "End of story."

Calum rolled his eyes and returned to his work. Phillip motioned her toward the rear of the boat. "Here, help me push it in."

Kirima stepped up to help. "Do we know which direction they went?"

Phillip's voice strained in the effort. "They usually go east, toward the Triplets."

"In Company waters," she said, grunting against the weight of the boat. "Did you not see them when you were out there?"

"No, they left way before us and were out of sight by the time we passed out of the Narrows."

"Maybe they got too close to the Company and were picked up."

"Aiden knows the lines better than anyone. And I don't think the Company would just pick them up like that."

The boat was far enough into the water that it was floating. He leaped up with practiced deftness, then turned and helped her up. It was certainly a change from the ease with which she slid into her canoe, even with the assistance, but she quickly found herself up on the deck of the boat. Calum was now feeding the fire, powering the engine as Phillip took a hold of the wheel to guide them out of the harbor.

"Go keep watch," Phillip told her. "You know where the reefs are, right?"

"I do," she said. "But I usually go right over them."

"I don't need to tell you that we can't do that with this boat, right?"

"Right."

"Go then. Watch closely."

"Do you not navigate these every day?"

"Father does. He knows the reefs. I don't, not as well as him. Now go."

Kirima turned and made her way to the front of the boat, edging past Calum and maneuvering in the narrow space along the boat's engine to the bow. They were already picking up speed, the engine fueled by the heat to power the boat through the water. She took a glance back, seeing the fire burning on the beach, the buildings of the town lit up by the flickering flames as they climbed the hill that rose from the harbor, all of it fading into the distance of the cold, wet night.

When she turned back, she could already see the approaching shrine. The waters were choppier, the wind swirling a bit more, but she could still see the dark shape, hear the bleating sounds as they passed the sheep.

"It's still there," Phillip said.

"I noticed that as well," she said.

"Hard not to," Calum said.

"What do you think it means?" she asked.

"Maybe the gods have left us as well," Phillip said.

"Or perhaps they have decided to cease giving us their favor."

Kirima watched as the shrine passed. At this rate, the sheep seemed likely to freeze to death in the water long before anything came to take it. Its cries followed them as they continued out of the harbor.

"Eyes front, Kirima," Calum said. "Pay attention."

"Right, sorry."

She turned back, her eyes passing over the water before them. The lantern cast a scant light, ripples spreading out from every drop of rain that struck the surface, a surface that reflected the dark sky above.

"I'm not sure I can see anything."

"There's nothing to see right here," Phillip said. "But watch. You'll be able to."

She squinted her eyes, trying to see past the surface but seeing nothing. She glanced to the side, seeing the outcroppings pass, mere shadows behind the rain. Her eyes turned back, and she saw the reef beginning to appear to the right.

"This way," she said, gesturing away from it.

The boat turned, easily clearing the reef and moving harmlessly past it. They continued through the water, her motioning and Phillip steering where she said, Calum working to make sure the engine continued working. The three of them worked in silence, guided by the pattering of the rain and the rumbling of the engine.

As she kept watch, the water began to change beneath them. At first, it seemed like an illusion, like the drops were distorting the surface in a strange way. Kirima grabbed one of the lanterns and held it closer, watching the way the sheen seemed to blur the reflection of the light.

"Oh no," she said.

"What?" Phillip asked.

She turned back. "That weird liquid. On the water. I saw it earlier today. It's here too."

"The what?" He released the wheel, sliding easily around the engine and leaning over next to her to where she was holding the lantern. "Oh," he said. "That's oil."

Kirima looked up at him. "Oil?"

Phillip nodded. "It's what the company is after. Apparently they get it from the whales somehow." He gave a shrug. "Can't say I've ever seen any of it cutting one open myself, though."

"Do you always see it on the water?"

"When you get this close to their headquarters." He gestured with his head, and she followed his gaze to the dark shape of land just visible in the distance, the rocky landscape dotted with lights that shone brightly against the dark background. "I think some of it escapes when they're barreling."

"I'd never seen any before today."

He frowned and looked back at her. "Were you over this way?"

"No, I went west from the Spire, like I always do. It's where Papa always went."

"West. There shouldn't be any there, not even from a current."

"I saw a ship."

His eyes widened. "A Company ship? Are you sure?"

"Sure as I can be, but I was trying to avoid getting run over by it. I saw it later, pulling in a whale."

He sighed, standing up straight and looking out over the sea. "Did you tell Gabriel about it?"

"No. I was going to, but first the goat and now this have distracted me from it."

"He needs to hear about this, as soon as we're back. They're not supposed to go into the Narrows."

"I know. I'll tell him when we get back."

"Good. For now, we need to keep searching." He made his way back to the rear, slipping back behind the wheel.

"We should move away from the Company area," Colum said.

"You don't have to tell me twice," Phillip said. He gestured off to the right, then turned the wheel in that same direction. "We'll go southeast, toward Bear Island. You don't need to watch the water here, Kirima, it's deep enough. Keep your eyes on the horizon, look for anything that might be a boat."

Kirima relaxed a bit, rubbing her arms. Even with the parka, the night was cold, and the rain refused to let up, seeping through in places. She watched the horizon, her eyes moving left and right and back as she watched for any sign of other boats. Every once in a while, her gaze would drift far enough around to catch sight of the Company's outpost, sparkling like stars that had fallen to the ground. It gave her a strange feeling, remembering the way the leader of that ship had looked at her, the way he had threatened her. It lingered in a mind, sending an extra shiver down her spine.

She wasn't sure if the land was Bear Island like Phillip had said, but it was the place where she finally spotted the boat. At first, it seemed like just another boulder, a piece of the island that rose from the sand, and her tired mind convinced her as much. But as they kept moving, it caught the scant light in just the right way, allowing her to see it for what it was.

"Wait, stop, turn around," she said, leaning out as far as she could and shouting to be heard over the rumble of the engine.

"What?" Phillip called back.

"A boat. Right there."

Calum came over to the side his brother was on, both of them looking out in the direction she was pointing. "Where?" he asked.

"Back there. Come on, either turn around or put us on the beach so I can walk."

Calum looked over at Phillip. "Perhaps we should tell someone else? Signal one of the other boats."

"We can signal them when we're sure it's the boat," Phillip said. "Besides, if they're there, they might need help right away."

He turned the wheel, navigating the boat away from the shore to come back around. Kirima kept her eyes on the spot where she had seen the boat, pointing in its direction so that he knew where to go. She knew where she had seen it, but even so, when it finally appeared in the halo of the ship's lanterns, she was still surprised to see it that close.

"That's their boat," Calum said. "I'm certain of it."

Phillip was already out of the boat, wading through the shallows, Kirima not far behind, lantern in her hand. "Put the signal out," he said to his brother. "There's no way we can get both boats back with just the three of us."

She could hear Calum get to work behind her as they approached the boat. It was all the way up on the beach, as if it had been brought in for the night, the bottom of the hull visible, pointed out toward the sea, hiding most of the deck from view. She could see no structural damage, no visible holes or damage in the hull.

"Seems fine," she said. "Do you think they beached it themselves?"

"Can't say," he said, motioning down to drag marks in the sand. "Someone definitely pulled it here."

Kirima was closer now, circling around the end of it. She held the lantern up, the light cast over the boat, and gasped at what she saw.

There was no sign of either of the lost men, but there was no mistake that something had happened. The mast was cracked, its weight supported by a rock wedged between some trees a bit further up the shore, and the sail was torn to shreds. The nets were there, dead fish strewn about, covered in oil just like hers had been. And there, on the ship's deck, were splotches of blood, fresh blood, bright red in the light of her lamp.

Phillip came barreling around the corner at the sound of her gasp. "What is it?" He looked upon the boat, where she held the light, and just stood there for a moment, taking it all in.

"What do you think happened here?" she finally said.

"I don't know," he said. "Nothing good."

Kirima stepped forward, shining the light into the spaces that still lay in darkness. "Maybe there's a body?"

"I don't know, but something tells me we won't find one."

She turned back, seeing him looking down at an imprint in the sand, that of a footprint. The way it had sunk, and the way the water had filled in, she couldn't tell if it had come from a foot that was bare or booted, but it was there, and it was leading away from the boat, into the sea. Phillip was already walking, and she followed behind, holding the lantern up.

"Kirima, do you remember those stories?" His words came slowly, the words picked carefully. "The ones about the Imakut coming onto land?"

"Yeah."

He turned to the side, and she looked down at the print he stood over, this one well defined in the harder sand left by low tide. It was a print from a bare foot, one that looked like a human print, except not. The toes were sharper and shorter, marked by skin that connected them and sharp points at the end, and the heel came to a point as well.

"I think we need to tell the others."

3

The sun was beginning to rise by the time they pulled back into the harbor, towing the crippled boat with the help of one of the other boats. An attempt was made to search the island some more, but the sighting of one of the massive white bears that gives the island its name quickly put that thought to rest.

Kirima was exhausted, but she resisted the urge to go right to bed, especially when the others began gathering right there on the beach. She found herself in the center with the brothers, the crowd forming around them as Gabriel greeted them.

"Was this all you found?" he asked.

"It was," Phillip said. "Kirima is the one who found it."

The mayor looked between them. "And there were no signs of the bodies?"

"Nothing," Kirima said. "We saw footprints going into the water, though."

Gabriel frowned. "Footprints? Into the water?"

Phillip nodded. "They were...they weren't human."

There were some murmurs around them as Gabriel raised an eyebrow, snow white against his tanned skin. "What do you mean? Like, they were bear prints?"

"No, they were something else," Kirima said. "Like human prints but different."

That drew more murmurs from the crowd. Gabriel's frown only deepened, drawing out the lines in his face. "And you two saw this as well?"

"I did," Phillip said. "Calum was still on the boat, trying to signal others."

"So you saw nothing, Calum?"

"I wasn't close enough to see," he said. "But I wouldn't call either of them liars. And I certainly saw the state the boat was in."

"I see," Gabriel said. He turned to the thin, aged woman who stood behind him, sharp eyes gazing out from a wrinkled, stoic face. "Thoughts, Lusa?"

Lusa closed her eyes and breathed in deeply. "It's as if everything has gone quiet. I cannot sense the presence, not here."

"What does that mean?" someone called out.

"It means nothing," Gabriel said. He looked right at Lusa. "Right?"

"This is like nothing I've ever felt. I must pray on the matter."

A voice sounded from somewhere in the group that surrounded them. "Why are we standing around debating this? We all know what happened here."

"Do we?" someone else asked. "Please, enlighten us, if you're so much smarter than our simuq."

Kirima turned and saw that it was Toklo speaking, one of the older men of the village, a kelp gatherer with a wiry frame and a sharp chin. "There is only one possibility if our sacrifice was rejected. These waters are too far gone; the Balance has been disrupted and the Imakut no longer grant us their blessing."

"You're mad, old man," another voice said, this one belonging to Ishbel, a fisherwoman, middle aged and ragged from a life of working the waters. "There's only one threat to us in these waters, and it's that Company that pollutes the sea, kills the whales, and scares off the fish. I have no doubt that they killed Aiden and Anik, and probably for nothing of their own doing."

There were murmurs, both of agreement and dissent, but most quieted when Gabriel held up a hand. "We have an agreement with the Company, and part of that agreement is that any territory disputes would be brought to the other. If Aiden and Anik were in Company territory, they would have been picked up and brought back here. It has happened before, and there was never a problem."

"The agreement includes them not being in the Narrows, right?" Phillip said. "Because Kirima saw them there yesterday."

This time, the murmurs turned into gasps as Gabriel furrowed his brow, turning in her direction. Kirima suddenly felt dozens of eyes trained on her and found herself wishing she could sink into her parka.

"You saw them in the Narrows?"

She managed a nod, feeling her face flush a bit.

"You're certain it was them and not one of ours?"

"Without a doubt," she said. "It almost ran me over, and when I was returning, they were pulling a whale up. One of them told me to go away in a threatening voice."

Gabriel allowed her statement to linger, long enough that Ishbel spoke up. "Well now there's no doubt in my mind that the Company is responsible for this and not some kind of children's tale. I told you not to trust them…"

"Children's tale!" Kirima couldn't tell who interrupted, but the voice was loud and deep. "These are our people's beliefs you speak of."

Ishbel responded in kind, raising her voice even louder. "Children's tales, that's all they are."

"How about we put you out there and let you see if they're just tales."

"Gladly, if I wouldn't freeze to death in these waters."

"Sounds like you're awfully scared for just children's tales."

Gabriel tried to silence them, but the arguing was spreading faster than even he could silence. He looked back to Kirima, and she only gave him the same look back, the look of concern. All around them, a dozen and more voices seemed to speak at once, blurring into a mess of sound, the occasional one standing above the rest.

"Seems to me people like you are the reason our fishers are bringing in a fraction of the catch we used to. The reason our sacrifices are being rejected now."

"Just wait, if you leave it there for long enough, something will eat it."

"The fault lies in letting the Company hunt here in the first place."

"And who was going to stop them? They brought armed men with those firesticks and enchanters. Are you going to row up to them and poke them with a spear?"

"Lusa is our simuq, surely she can stand against their powers."

"Our simuqs have not held that kind of power in generations."

A long, loud whistle pierced the air from right beside her, loud enough that Kirima threw her hands up and covered her ears. As it finally faded, her eyes drifted over to Phillip, who was lowering his fingers from his mouth, the twitching on his lips giving away the smile he was fighting to hide, the smile of someone surprised at their own capabilities. It was followed by Gabriel's booming voice, a tone she had rarely heard from him.

"That's enough. You all should be ashamed of yourselves, fighting like this, setting this kind of example for the children. Arguing isn't going to get us anywhere, and neither will anyone theorizing on what's happening. Now, it's been a very long night following a long day, and most of us have been awake the entire time. We all need to get some sleep and approach this with clear minds, myself included."

The sound of the crowd was more subdued this time, voices sounding in agreement, others grumbling in a lower volume. The mayor continued.

"After I get a bit of rest, I'm going to take a ride over to the Company outpost and get to the bottom of this. It may not solve both mysteries, but at the very least, it will give us answers to why they are in our waters. Even if we don't find out what happened to Aiden and Anik, perhaps it will set us on the right path."

There seemed to be a bit of resistance, but in the end, the crowd began to disperse, meandering back to their respective homes. A few of the fishers seemed to linger, a few standing around the rescued boat, while a few decided to take their boats out anyway. The wind blew in from the harbor, carrying with it the tired bleating of the sacrificial ewe.

"I want you to come with me," Gabriel said to her, pulling her attention back to him. The brothers were already heading back, leaving the two of them alone. "You and Phillip both."

"What can I possibly bring?"

"You can point out the man who threatened you."

"Will that be safe?"

"We have a truce with them. They will honor it."

"And if they really did kill Aiden and Anik?"

"I don't think they did."

"Then what do you think did?"

Gabriel stared out over the harbor, toward the shrine, listening to the distant sounds for a moment. She wondered how much longer it would live until it succumbed to exposure. Or starvation. "I think they got off course, perhaps hit with a rogue wave that drove them into the beach. From there, they were waiting on help and got dragged off by a bear."

A guffaw escaped her lips. "So you think it's neither."

"I think the only way the Company might have been involved was perhaps one of their ships causing them to go off course. They're likely guilty of no crime worse than carelessness or apathy."

"And the Imakut?"

Gabriel was still staring out into the harbor, silent for a moment. His name was at the tip of her tongue when he finally responded, cutting her off. "I have seen many strange things on these islands, in these seas. I have faithfully seen that the sacrifice was put out each time the Twins shine brightly in the night sky, as was done by every single one of my predecessors. I have spoken the words and led the prayers and been a model citizen in our worship of the Imakut."

Kirima raised her eyebrows at him. "But…"

Gabriel sighed. "Far be it from me to doubt that the Imakut are real, that our sacrifices have been for naught, but the stories of creatures coming from the waves to take for the Balance are generations old at this point. Time has a way of contorting the truth."

"Papa always said that even the most outrageous stories are often rooted in some degree of fact."

There was a sigh that almost came out as a laugh. "Your father and I sparred incessantly, but he was the one I trusted the most. Despite our differences, I always carried a great amount of respect for him. I like to think he did the same."

Buffoon had been his favorite word, at least the one he would use in polite company. She had certainly heard him use much worse. "He always understood the pressure you faced in your job."

"Tell me, Kirima, what do you think? Do you think some manifestation of the Imakut took Aiden and Anik?"

"Papa would say..."

His pale eyes drilled into her own. "I know what Tak would have said if he was here. I want to know what you think."

Kirima worked her mouth for a moment, her mind both running and threatening to crash at the same time. She saw the boat on its side, the blood, the broken mast, that footprint. The mayor was watching her intently, waiting for a response.

"I'm not sure what to believe, but I know what I saw. And I trust my own eyes."

"A chip off your father's block, indeed. Your mother always hated how much you gravitated to him."

"I know." Or so she'd heard. She hardly remembered her mother, most of her memories derived from stories told by her father and Yura.

"Get some rest," he said. "I'll come for you when it's time to leave."

He left her standing there, near the remnants of the fire, the day brightening behind the grey of the sky. The rain started up again as she made her way toward the house.

4

Gabriel appeared at their house early that afternoon. The sound of his knocking seemed like it would have been loud enough to wake anyone in a three-house radius, but she was already wide awake. Sleep had come easily when she had collapsed into her bed, but it was not easily held, not in a house with a pregnant woman and two children with seemingly endless amounts of energy. Even when Yura had chased them out, they did not venture far, and once outside the house, they had abandoned all semblance of moderating the volume of their shrill voices. After a few hours of drifting in and out, she gave up, climbing out of bed to help Yura around the house.

When he arrived, she was standing atop a stool, arranging some jars on a shelf that Yura could not reach. She nearly dropped one at the sound of the knocking, but managed to catch it, placing it on the shelf somewhat askew and stepping down to answer.

"Not sleeping?" he asked.

"Tried," she said. "I take it you're ready to go?"

"As ready as I can be."

She nodded. "Lead the way then."

"How long will you be?" Yura asked, leaning on the thick wooden table they sat around for dinner. "Not another all-nighter, I hope?"

"We should be back by sundown," Gabriel said. "Just after at the latest."

"I hope whatever you're getting yourselves into isn't dangerous."

"Not at all," Kirima said, pulling her parka over her shirt and tightening her bun. "I'll be back soon."

"Be safe."

"Didn't tell her, did you?" Gabriel said once the door was closed behind them and they were walking between the buildings down to the beach.

"No reason to add extra stress," Kirima said. "I didn't even tell her

24

about last night."

"She didn't ask?"

"Of course she did. I told her we found nothing."

"She'll find out eventually. You know how word travels in this town."

"I'd recommend not until after the child is born."

"She won't hear it from me."

"Good."

Phillip was waiting at the main path, the dirt road that divided the town in two, running up the rocky hill past the rows of houses, all the way up to where Gabriel's house stood, looking over all the rest. Down on the beach, most of the boats were out, her own and Phillip's family boat two of four remaining, even after the long night. She was about to step toward the beach, but stopped, nearly stumbling when Gabriel went up the path instead of down.

"Where are you going?" she asked.

"Just follow me," he said.

She and Phillip exchanged a look, but they followed. He led them up past a couple of rows of houses, turning down the path in front of one of the last rows. They walked past them, nearly all identical to the one she shared with Yura, the same stone and wood and earthen builds that held in the warmth of the iron stoves. In between, children played in the dirt or ran around, watched by men and women who did not venture out, those who tended to gardens or made repairs or hung up freshly cleaned laundry. Some glanced in their direction, while others waved, calling out to Gabriel, who always managed a smile and a calm word, even with his current demeanor.

They passed the edge of the town, hiking in silence across the rocky terrain, beneath towering pine trees, water from the night's rain still dripping from their branches. She could hear the calling of birds above, adults and hatchlings alike, hidden in their nests high above them.

"It's been so long since I've walked this path," Phillip said. His voice was quiet, awed.

"Papa used to take walks with us," Kirima said. "When we were little. He knew the name of every plant, every bird call, everything about these woods."

"We never did anything like that," he said. "Calum and I were helping on the boat pretty much from the time we were able."

"I wish I could remember everything he taught me," Kirima said. "It was so long ago. Another lifetime, it seems like."

"Maybe you should start coming out here again. I'm sure seeing things will help your memory."

"Maybe so," she said.

Gabriel led them off onto a smaller path, one that was narrower, the ground not quite as tread, the vegetation growing thicker around it. It wound down a slope, between a pair of massive boulders, and onto a small beach that curved around a nearly completely hidden harbor. In the center was a boat, larger than any of the ones owned by the village. The hull was painted a pristine white, with designs painted in black atop it, and an engine rose from the middle. Barrels were tied to the side, and even from that distance, she could smell the strange aroma of the oil in the water.

"Whose boat is this?" Kirima asked.

"It's mine," Gabriel said.

She looked back at him, her mouth agape, while Phillip managed to maintain a much more even gaze. "I've never seen this before. Where did it come from?"

"And why is it hiding back here?" Phillip said.

"It was a gift from the Company, for the town," Gabriel said. "It's here because I can't risk it not being operational should we need it."

"Need it for what?" Kirima said.

"This is the only boat here that is a sure thing to navigate the deeper waters toward the southern islands of Eilena, or to Adhan."

"Would we ever have a reason to go that way?" Kirima asked as Gabriel climbed onto the boat using a ladder at the rear. "Does anyone here ever have a reason?"

"Occasionally," he said. "Come on, we're wasting daylight. I meant it when I said I want to get back by sundown."

Kirima glanced at Phillip, whose face communicated exactly how she felt. "Do you know something that we don't, Gabriel?"

Gabriel said nothing, hitting a button to start the engine. "Are you coming?"

Another glance exchanged with Phillip, then she stepped toward the boat, climbing on, Phillip right behind her. The engine was loud, but not quite as loud as the others used by the fishers. Kirima glanced around, finding a large tank at the base of the engine, and a doorway going down into what looked like a homely space beneath the front deck.

"This uses that oil?" Kirima asked.

Gabriel nodded, working the wheel as he maneuvered the boat out of the small lagoon. "One barrel is supposed to last for days. The Company representative said it could get you almost all the way to Adhan and back."

"Are they trying to tell us we should leave?" Phillip asked.

"It was part of the agreement," Gabriel said. "They wanted to provide us with a way to raise concerns with the headquarters in Adhan if it were to come to that."

"This seems more like a bribe to me," Phillip said, crossing his arms. "What else did they give you?"

Gabriel didn't look at either of them, his eyes focused on the water before them. "Nothing, I swear. This is a boat for the village, not just me."

"Then why do you keep it hidden?" Kirima asked.

"Because others would act just as you do now. Perhaps worse." He turned toward Kirima. "Ask yourself how your father would react."

He might have killed Gabriel where he stood. "He would have seen it as a bribe to sell away the waters our people have subsisted on for generations."

"He wouldn't be wrong," Phillip said. The way his face had turned, she wasn't certain he wasn't going to kill Gabriel himself.

Gabriel let out a long sigh. "I wish I had a choice in the matter. Your father, may he rest peacefully, was an idealist. He always felt that we could continue the old ways for as long as our town survived. He saw the old influx of Eilenans, my ancestors, and their integration in the ways as proof of that. But the world outside doesn't sit still. Our land and waters came under Eilenan rule peacefully, but it is under their rule. We could accept the terms, the generous terms, that the company provided and allowed them to work these waters peacefully, or we could have resisted, and they would have taken it anyway."

"How can they do that?" Kirima asked, her voice coming out softer than she intended, almost inaudible to her own ears over the drone of the engine and the splashing of the water beneath them.

"Because they have the power."

"We could have fought them," Phillip said.

"And our town would have been wiped away. I told you before, they have their own guards, their own enchanters, and what do we have? Spears? Maybe a bow and some crooked arrows? Some kitchen knives? Lusa's meager powers? Don't think I make these kinds of decisions lightly."

They were all quiet for a moment, the boat motor running as it took them out into the sea, much faster than any boat she had ever been on. The Company outpost was visible in the distance, buildings running up the side of the rocky island slopes, trees cleared to make way, a fleet of ships parked at the docks, smoke wafting from massive chimneys. Even in summer, snow still clung to the highest parts of the island, white against the grey of the stone.

"You make it sound like we are helpless against them," Kirima said. "What if they refuse to stop entering the Narrows? Can we do anything?"

"No."

The word lingered in the air, and she exchanged a glance with Phillip. Had it always been this way? Had Papa known about it? Did anyone else in town know?

"Maybe Oki or one of the others can help us," Phillip said.

"I wouldn't put faith in anyone who left to work for them," Gabriel said. "No more than I'd put faith in the old stories."

"Oki?" Kirima asked.

"You never know," Phillip said. "You can always ask."

"They left us for a reason and have not returned, not even for the feasts. That should tell you all you need to know."

"Who?" Kirima asked.

"My uncle," Phillip said. "He and others went when the Company offered work that wasn't fishing. When we were little."

"I didn't know you had an uncle."

"Father doesn't speak of him."

"None of us do," Gabriel said. "Or of anyone else who turned away from our town. They may as well all be dead."

The island was growing nearer. Kirima could see more details in the outpost, something that much more closely resembled a large town, or perhaps a city, for all her knowledge of what one was. The chimneys belonged to two mammoth buildings, each seeming large enough to fit their entire town within. The ships were all huge, just like the one that had almost run her over the day before, attacked to wooden platforms that extended out over the water. In the rear, she saw more large buildings, nearly as tall as the ones with the smoke, these built from bricks, their surfaces covered in windows, and scattered around were numerous smaller, wooden buildings, not unlike the houses back home. Wires ran between them all, and she could see lit lanterns atop poles.

"I've never been this close before," Kirima said. "Is this what it's always looked like?"

"It's gotten bigger over the years," Gabriel said. "No doubt the reason they were in the Narrows. Might be that they're starting to run out of whales to harvest."

"No sacrifice," Phillip said. "Not even a shrine."

"Would they?" Kirima asked.

"They have our people working for them. Surely they would ask for one."

"They left us," Gabriel said. "No doubt they left the ways behind as well."

A man in the Company uniform appeared at the end of one of the wooden platforms, waving to them, accompanied by several others, many of them holding what looked like sticks of wood and metal in their hands, the ends pointed toward the ground. Kirima was unsure whether he was directing them in or telling them to go away, but Gabriel steered toward him regardless. A moment later, the boat was parked right next to the dock, the engine cut, the man looking down at them as one of his men held the mooring line.

"What are you doing here?" the man asked. "These waters are restricted to Mhara Electric Company boats only."

"I'm here to speak to Eoghan," Gabriel said. "You can tell him that Gabriel from Aliit is here to see him."

The man was chewing on something and turned to spit before speaking. "Concerning what?"

"A few different matters. I'd prefer our discussion be in private."

The man considered them for a moment, first Gabriel, then herself and Phillip. He had thick hair cut short and combed to the side, a bushy moustache, and eyes that seemed perpetually squinting, even as he examined each of them.

Finally, he turned to one of the men standing with him. "Go deliver the message to Eoghan. Bring his response back promptly."

The man turned back, and they all stood there for a moment in silence. It was Phillip who vocalized what Kirima was thinking. "So are we just going to wait here?"

"No one without authorization comes on without Eoghan's approval," he said. "Should that approval be granted, you'll be accompanied everywhere to ensure you don't get into trouble."

"Trouble?" Kirima said. "Do we look like we'd cause trouble?"

"Vagu people have posed a particular problem for many of our outposts. While this one has not yet seen issues, most have. Company policy is to always err on the side of caution."

Kirima glanced over at Phillip and mouthed the word, "Vagu?"

Phillip met her eyes, tapped his chest, and mouthed, "Us."

"I assure you, we're not here to cause trouble," Gabriel said. "We do not even bring weapons with us. Eoghan will know."

"We shall see," the man said.

They all stood there in silence. Kirima made her way over to the edge of the boat opposite the wooden platform and gazed over the edge into the water. That sheen was here as well, but unlike how it had been in the Narrows, there were no spots of clear water, no places that the oil didn't cover. Her eyes followed it to where the water met the sand, the waves lapping at the beach, each time leaving a trail of dark coloration behind.

As she watched the waves, she caught sight of the same man running back from the building. She raised her eyes, watching him as he ran through the sand, the loud sound as his feet struck the wood of the platform. By the time he reached the boat, she could hear his breathing, growing even louder as he pattered to a stop.

"Eoghan said to bring them without delay," the messenger said. "He seemed upset at being asked."

The man grunted, turning to them. "Come on then, be quick."

The one holding the rope tied it down to one of the posts, while another stepped forward, holding his stick to the side as he extended his other hand to help each of them onto the platform. The man was already moving, heading toward a windowed building that blended in with one of the massive ones with the chimneys.

Two of the accompanying men ran ahead, grabbing the handles of the twin doors and pulling them open. Where the outside was a dreary color to match the terrain, plain and simple bricks, the inside was clearly built to appeal to the senses. The space was wide, lights in the ceiling burning like the sun, the walls brightly painted, the room filled with expertly crafted furniture. To the left sat a massive stone fireplace, a large blaze burning within, and to the right was a large desk, a young woman in the same Company uniform seated behind it. The woman's eyes moved, but she gave no other sign of recognition toward them as they moved toward the staircase in the rear.

The stairs were soft beneath her feet, softer than powdery snow or even her goose down mattress. Even through her boots, she could feel herself sinking in with each step, each time briefly wondering if she would just continue to sink. Their path wrapped around, coming to a landing above the room they had entered.

Through another pair of doors was a large room, this one occupied by a lone man, also clad in a Company uniform, though the coloring was a bit different, with bits of gold in several places. He was tall, broad, with thick limbs and a shaved head and chin, his earthen colored skin shining in the bright lanterns that shone above, lanterns that seemed to shine without a flame.

"Leave us." The man's voice was deep, like it belonged to one of the drums played during Kiaq. The men obeyed immediately, the doors closing behind them. The man, Eoghan, she assumed, motioned toward the chairs, his voice somewhat softened, but still with more than a hint of power behind it. "Sit, please."

Three hardback wooden chairs rested in front of his desk, and each of them took one, Gabriel sitting in the one in the middle.

"Can I get you something?" Eoghan asked. "A drink? Some food?"

Kirima felt her stomach rumble at the suggestion, but Gabriel said, "No thank you, we only hope to be here for a short time."

"I'll have Kenna bring something anyways, in case you change your mind." He rang a small bell on his desk, then set it down, easing into his thickly cushioned chair and leaning back. "My apologies for the way you were treated, Gabriel. There have been troubles at other outposts that keeps our security force on edge, even though they know that your people here have been nothing but respectful. I assure you it will not happen again."

"It was nothing," Gabriel said. Kirima wondered if Eoghan heard the same twitch in his voice that she did. She wasn't sure she had ever heard Gabriel speak like this to anyone, certainly no one in the town.

The doors behind them opened, and Kirima turned back to watch as the woman from downstairs emerged, a tray in her hands. Now that the woman was closer and standing, she could see that she was tall, slender, perhaps half Eilenan. Her skin was on the paler side, similar to Gabriel's, and she had hair that was a rich brown and eyes to match. As she drew closer, Kirima caught a scent that she seemed to wear, something not unlike the blooms that came along with early summer.

Kirima watched as she brought it around to the desk, placing down several cups that were steaming, along with a tray of meats and cheeses, though they were like none she had ever seen before, the meat cut thin and the cheeses of different shapes, sizes, and colors. There were little fruits as well, dried ones that she couldn't place, not like the wild berries that grew in the woods on their island.

The conversation continued as she watched the food being delivered. "What brings you here, Gabriel and…"

Gabriel looked between the two of them. "Kirima and Phillip."

Eoghan repeated their names. "Youth, the future of any successful settlement. You always need someone to take the reins and guide the future."

"I'm afraid our reason for being here is not cordial," Gabriel said.

An amiable grin had been on Eoghan's face, though Kirima had found something off in it, as if it was a fake, his size and presentation betraying his intentions. Now, though, the grin faded into a frown that sent a shiver down her spine. "I'm sorry to hear that, Gabriel. What's the problem?"

Gabriel shifted in his seat before leaning onto the armrest to his left. "Kirima here was out fishing the Narrows, and she says she was nearly run over by one of your Company ships. Said she saw them later pulling a whale from the waters there."

"By the Spire," Kirima said. All eyes turned briefly on her, and she suddenly felt incredibly small. It was no wonder Gabriel looked so uncomfortable.

Eoghan's dark brows furrowed further, his gaze turning back to Gabriel. "That is very upsetting to hear. Our captains are well aware that the Narrows are off limits to their whaling."

Gabriel visibly relaxed in his chair, breathing out deeply. "Yes, that was always the agreement. It was very concerning to see a ship in our waters."

"It's very concerning to hear of it." He turned back to her. "Kirima, do you think you could identify the ship for me? I would like to have a word with the captain."

"I think I can."

Eoghan stood and made his way around the desk. "Then come along. The last of the ships should be coming in for the night."

Eoghan led them down the stairs through the waiting room, where Kenna had returned to her desk, focused on her work as they passed through. Kirima had known it was warm in the building, but she had not realized just how warm until she stepped back out into the cold. She felt it on her cheeks and even through her parka, sending a shiver down her spine. She glanced around at the others, but none of the others seemed affected in the same way, Eoghan least of all.

They walked along the beach, the buildings looming to her left, impossibly tall, as if they were mountains themselves. To the right, she could see the boats, a line of identical vessels, just like the one she had seen in the Narrows, though looking at them all together, she could see that they had different designs painted on their sides. She saw fishes, whales, wolves, bears, even mountains and stormy skies.

Near the end of the row, she paused, her eyes focusing on the designs of the ship. This was the first time she was able to really look at it up close, seeing that the designs were not like waves as she had initially thought, but some kind of legless serpent, its jaws stretched wide to reveal razor sharp fangs.

"That's the one," she said, pointing toward it.

"The Boreal," Eoghan said, narrowing his eyes. "Lenox is the captain."

It seemed the Boreal had just arrived back for the day. Several crewmembers were moving around the deck, cleaning and putting away equipment while another group was lowering their catch of the day down onto the platform to be taken to one of the large buildings. And there on the deck, giving orders to the crew, was the man who had told her to go away

"Captain Lenox," Eoghan called out. The man looked up as Eoghan motioned. "Come down here."

The look on the captain's face was one of annoyance as he removed his gloves and tossed them down before making his way to the edge of the ship and climbing down to the platform. He went around the whale carcasses, jogging the rest of the way to them.

"You wanted to see me, Governor?" His eyes darted toward her and back, and she thought she saw a glimpse of recognition, so quick that it seemed an illusion.

"This girl here said she saw you in the Narrows yesterday. Were you there?"

Once more his eyes went to her, lingering for longer than before. He ran a hand over his mouth. "She must be seeing things, because we were over in the western straits yesterday. Everyone knows the Narrows are off-limits."

Eoghan considered him for a moment. "I see." He turned to Kirima. "Do you by chance have any proof, Kirima?"

"Proof?" She looked over at Gabriel, who could only manage a shrug. "No, but I saw what I saw."

"I'm sorry, girl, but it's your word against his." He held out two large hands. "Without proof, there's nothing I can do."

Kirima felt her hands ball into a fist, her teeth clench, but a hand on her shoulder pulled her back from her anger. "I am sure it is just a misunderstanding," Gabriel said.

"Might be we drifted further than we meant," Lenox said. "It can be easy to get lost when you're chasing down a whale."

"Of course, an honest mistake," Eoghan said. "We do apologize. I know Captain Lenox will be much more careful in the future, won't you, Captain?"

"Absolutely," the man said. Kirima watched him, but he did not look back in her direction. She scowled at him nonetheless, if only so that others may see.

"Very good, dismissed, Captain."

The captain scurried off, back toward his boat. Kirima was still watching him when Gabriel spoke. "There is one other thing I'd like to bring up."

"What is it?" Eoghan asked.

Gabriel's eyes seemed to dart around, and he stepped a bit closer, his voice lower. "We recently had two fishermen vanish, their boat found abandoned on Bear Island."

Eoghan rubbed at his chin. "I know your people call it that for a reason. Would that be the cause for their disappearance?"

"It seems the most likely answer in my mind, but of course, my people have different ideas."

"I can assure you, if any of your fishermen ran afoul of us, I would have brought it to you. None of my ships encountered them."

Kirima exchanged a look with Phillip as Gabriel said, "That is comforting to hear. There is, however, another theory aside from the Company doing the deed."

"What is it?"

"Are you familiar with the Imakut?"

"Your people's gods, are they not?"

"In a way. The Imakut is the name we give to the spirit that lives within all wildlife around us, all the fish in the sea and creatures on the islands and in the air. When the Twins are both full, we give sacrifice to them from our flock. It's a way to maintain the balance for what we take."

"I see," Eoghan said slowly.

"There are concerns that with the Company hunting the whales in addition to our subsistence, the Imakut are no longer satisfied, and are taking a sacrifice of their own."

Eoghan raised a thick eyebrow. "I'm not sure I understand. Are you asking me to stop our operations because your people think it's causing some mystical creature to attack?"

Gabriel shifted in place, rubbing at the back of his head, not looking directly at the Company governor. "No, I'm not asking that. But I do think it would put a lot of my people at ease if you would start putting out a sacrifice as well."

There was a silence, broken only by a loud guffaw from the governor. It grew into a hearty chuckle that seemed to last for several moments before he finally spoke again. "I suppose that's a better option, but if I didn't know you, I'd say that was an attempt at a joke."

Kirima saw Gabriel's chest heave. "It would be a good gesture. Any of our people working for you could help with the process."

"I have no doubt," Eoghan said, still struggling to keep his laughter down. "But I need you to understand something, Gabriel. I respect you, and I understand you're just trying to do what's best for your village. I'm willing to work with you on reasonable requests, but I don't consider putting livestock out to get eaten to be a reasonable one. No matter what your people may believe."

"I understand your hesitancy, but I ask because it's very important to my people."

Eoghan considered him for a moment. "Alright, Gabriel. I'll do it on one condition."

Gabriel seemed to visibly relax. "What condition?"

"If you can stand here and tell me, in all seriousness, that you believe that my putting a sacrifice out will prevent some kind of attack from your...whatever you call them, then I will do it."

Gabriel said nothing at first, standing there silent for long enough that she nudged him with her elbow to get him going. He didn't seem to acknowledge the nudge, but he did speak. "I..."

"Just say it," Phillip said in a very slight whisper. Kirima nodded in agreement.

There was a deep sigh. "I can't say it."

"Why not?" Phillip said, his voice louder.

Eoghan only smirked. "I thought as much. I won't do something based on a religion that you yourself don't even seem to follow."

Gabriel said nothing, his face drooping in a melancholy look. He turned away from the governor. "That will be all. Come along Phillip, Kirima."

"Give your people my regards," Eoghan called after them. "The Narrows will be clear, you have my promise on that."

Kirima wasn't even sure they were out of earshot when Phillip began talking. "What is wrong with you? Why didn't you say you believe?"

"Because it wouldn't be true."

"Why not?" Kirima asked, but her words seemed lost as Phillip talked over her.

"Does it matter if you believe or not when just pretending you do would get us what we need? You may not believe it, but many of us in the town you preside over do."

"Lying about that is not something I felt I could do."

"But you could lie about the boat?"

Gabriel said nothing. Phillip made a sound and turned away from him, walking ahead toward the boat.

As they drew nearer, their path forward was blocked by a group of workers making their way from their ship. Some dragged their catch across the sand, while others simply walked beside. None of them looked at the visitors, but she watched them, each and every one of them. It was unmistakable, the light hair to go with the bronzed skin, made more so by the days spent out on the ships.

"These are our people," she said.

"They are," Gabriel said.

She turned to them. "From our town?"

"Oki!" Phillip took off, jogging toward one of the men, a tall, lanky one, his hair falling wet and stringy down to his shoulders.

Neither of them moved, Kirima from shock, Gabriel from restraint, she assumed. "His uncle," she said.

"You knew he was here."

"I didn't expect to see him."

Oki didn't acknowledge Phillip, so he ran up behind him, tugging on his sleeve.

"Why don't you believe?"

"That's a personal matter."

Oki finally turned, his eyes lighting up briefly. She could almost see the goofy grin on Phillip's face at that moment.

"Is it because of your ancestry? Because many others believe."

"The only similarity we have remaining with the Eilena of our ancestors' time is our appearance. We have worked hard over the years to make ourselves a part of the community."

As quickly as the excitement had been visible, it faded into a deep frown. Oki held up his hand and shook his head.

"Yet you don't share our beliefs and you speak against them when doing so would harm us."

"We will speak about it on the boat."

Oki had turned away, walking quickly to get back into his spot in the line. Phillip stood there, watching after him, even as the last one passed by. Kirima frowned, running up to him, finding a gaze on his face that was half sullen and half shocked.

"What happened?" she asked. "What did he say?"

"He said not to talk to him," Phillip said. "I haven't seen him in years and that's all he has to say to me?"

Gabriel placed a hand on each of their shoulders. "We should get going. It's going to be dark soon."

"Yeah," Kirima said softly. "We should go."

Phillip said nothing, but he went with them willingly. They made their way back to the boat, the guards still standing there. They boarded the boat, the guards untied the rope, and Gabriel started it up. He turned away from the outpost, and none of them looked back as they left it behind.

They were scarcely away from the dock when she approached Gabriel at the wheel. "Alright, tell me."

"What did you think of Eoghan?"

She folded her arms over her chest. "He seemed ready to brush us aside, especially when his captain lied."

"Would you trust him?"

"No. I don't think he'd do anything for us unless it benefitted the Company."

"Good, you shouldn't."

"Why did you lie to him, then? Why not push harder?"

"I couldn't lie to him. He would have known."

"How? He doesn't know you that well, does he?"

"He has a way, like he can just look at you and know. I saw it in practice years ago, when the Company first came."

"Do you think it would have gone any worse if you had lied and he had called you on it?"

"When they first came, I got stories about the Company, about what they did to people like us who didn't work with them. And stories of bad things that happen even to those who do. I wasn't kidding when I said they were dangerous. Entire towns have been destroyed because people making whatever Company governor or whoever angry."

"And we let them control us," Phillip said.

"How did they get so much power?" Kirima asked. "How can they do this?"

"Things work differently in Adhan, and that's where the power lies," Gabriel said.

"We're not in Adhan, though," Phillip said.

"But what happens in Adhan determines what happens to us."

"Do we not have a say in it?" Kirima said.

"Not directly."

Kirima shook her head, while Phillip threw his hands up in the air. "We're in no better shape than our people who went over to the Company. Maybe worse."

"Working for them is far worse than our situation," Gabriel said.

"Is it?" Phillip asked. He let loose a deep sigh. "He wouldn't even talk to me. Why not?"

"Because they control them. They don't want to lose the labor, so they cut them off from their home in all ways they can."

"And people willingly go to them," Kirima said.

"They offer a better life," Gabriel said. "Or so they tell you."

The boat pulled through the Narrows as night descended. They came around the back of the harbor, guided by a focused light that shone from above the steering wheel. The boat slid into the hidden alcove, and Gabriel dropped the anchor over the side.

"Not a word about the boat, okay?" Gabriel said as he cut power to the engine.

"Alright," Kirima said. Phillip nodded, the same sullen look on his face as he dropped from the boat. Kirima followed, then Gabriel, and they began making their way back toward the town. Kirima expected to see Yura outside with the children, but the space in front of the house was empty. There were the sounds of speaking near the fire on the beach, and as they stepped out, she saw a crowd gathered on the beach..

"What's happening?" she asked.

"Nothing good, I'd expect," Gabriel said.

They reached the edge of the beach, and people began to notice them. It was Calum who came running, the crowd parting to let him through.

"What is it?" Phillip asked.

"It's Father, they've taken him," Calum said between breaths.

Phillip's eyes widened. "Who took him?"

"The Imakut."

"That's impossible," Gabriel said.

Kirima was already moving past them, to the spot that the people were gathered around. There, she could see where the sand had been kicked up, the puddle of blood, and surrounding it all, those same footprints she had seen that night. There were more this time, going both to and from the sea, without a doubt belonging to something not human.

5

It was a few days before Phillip and Calum returned to the water, and in that time, three more were taken. After their father was taken, Gabriel had put out several decrees — watches at all hours, the fire maintained throughout day and night, no boat venturing out with fewer than three aboard, bringing weapons — but it seemed to do nothing to prevent it. Nor did the new sacrifice that replaced the dead ewe in the shrine seem to help, once more resulting in a cold wet sheep standing in the water. The idea to suspend fishing entirely was floated, but quickly shot down from the outcry that came from almost the entire town.

Since her canoe would only fit a single person, Kirima took to going out with Ishbel and her daughters. As soon as Phillip and Calum were ready to return, though, she jumped at the chance to join their boat instead.

She had almost expected to be the first out there, with how the two of them had dragged in the days since their father's taking, but she found them both at the boat, tending to their usual chores as they prepared to go out.

Kirima approached, standing a short distance from the boat, not saying anything at first. They continued their work, Phillip stacking wood and Calum applying pitch, somehow with a few streaks on his cheek. Neither looked at her, but after a moment, it was Calum that finally spoke.

"Are you going to come help or just stare?"

"Wasn't sure if you still wanted me to."

Calum wiped a combination of rain and sweat from his brow with his sleeve and looked her way. "Gabriel says we need a third. Don't think we'd rather have anyone else."

Kirima offered a smile as she tossed her sack onto the deck and climbed aboard. "What can I do?"

"You know how to check nets?"

"You know I do."

He nodded toward the pile in the back corner, the boat's nets gathered together in a tangle. "Go ahead, will get us out faster."

Kirima went over to the pile, picking up the nearest end and stretching it out, checking for any tears. She was only at it for a moment when Phillip spoke.

"That was always Father's job."

She looked up, but saw that he was not looking at her, instead focused on the wood he was loading into the shelf.

"Well, he's not around to do it," Calum said, a tone of annoyance seeming to creep into his voice.

"I know," Phillip said with a chuckle. "I'm just thinking of what he'd say if he knew that we were not only letting Kirima come with us, but actually giving her his job."

At first, Kirima only looked between them, unsure of how to react. Phillip's serious gaze had turned into a smirk, as if he was trying to hold in laughter. Her eyes settled back on Calum, still holding a glare of his own until it suddenly faded into a wide grin.

"You know women are bad luck on a boat," Calum said, imitating his father's voice.

"Your mother never had a thought of coming on a boat, not once," Phillip said, his imitation not quite as good as his brother's.

They were both laughing now, and Kirima found a grin of her own, glancing between the brothers and the net that she still ran through her hands. Phillip placed the last few pieces of wood into the shelf, then stepped toward them, brushing off his hands.

"What do you say we get off this beach, spend some time fishing?"

"Best idea you've ever had," Calum said.

"Normally, I'd argue, but I think I can let it slide today."

Both the boys hopped out and began to push. Kirima continued her work as the boat moved beneath her, sliding in spurts with that familiar grinding sound of a hull scraping against wet sand. She felt the front tip a bit as it came to a float, then the rest of the boat rock as the rear joined it. Calum was up first, turning and offering a hand to pull his brother up.

"Do you need me to keep a watch again?" she asked as Phillip moved to the steering wheel.

"We can navigate them fine in the daylight," Calum said, tossing wood into the fire as the engine roared to life. "Focus on the net, we need that to be whole."

She found a spot where a hole had formed and tied it up. "Which direction today?"

"I think to honor Father, we should go to his favorite spot," Calum said. "His secret spot."

"You're reading my mind," Phillip said.

"Where's that?" Kirima asked.

The brothers exchanged a glance. "Promise to not tell anyone?" Phillip said.

She stared at them for a moment, then shook her head. "I promise."

"Good, because we'd have to give you to the Imakut if you did."

"Calum…" Phillip said.

"Oh, right. Bad taste, I guess, given our current events."

"That reminds me, do you have weapons?" Kirima asked.

Phillip motioned off to the side of the engine with his foot. "Brought some spears. And you have your knife, don't you?"

"Always," she said, patting where it rested at her waist.

"Might want to keep it handy," Calum said.

"You think we'll actually see anything?" she asked. "We never did when I went out with Ishbel, not once."

"Doesn't mean it won't happen today," Phillip said.

He cut the engine, allowing the boat to drift. From where she was seated, Kirima could see the pointed roof of the shrine, and now that the engine had been reduced to a mere rumble, she could hear the bleating of the sheep, the most recent attempt to placate the Imakut. She climbed to her feet, staring at the sheep just as the two brothers were, the three of them standing there in silence.

Finally, it was Phillip who spoke. "Is it even worth asking for a blessing? Seems they're not giving them anymore."

"Could it hurt at this point?" Kirima asked. "Might be we need as much good grace as we can find."

Calum hawked and spat in the water beneath the shrine. "They can take it all for what I care."

"Calum…" Phillip said.

"No, don't start." His voice was quiet, but forceful. "I don't want to talk about it, not now, maybe not ever. And I sure as shit don't want to worship any gods that turn their back on their own people like this."

They were all silent as Calum turned away, moving to the far side of the boat. Kirima felt her hand go up to the necklace, gripping the jarak that was tied to the end, feeling the cool of the smooth white stone against her palm. She said nothing though, the words not even spoken in her mind. How could she? Nothing felt more right at that moment than what Calum had said.

"We should go," she said to Phillip. He nodded and started up the engine again, maneuvering them away from the shrine and toward the Narrows.

Calum had taken a seat at the bow of the boat, so Phillip had gestured her over to help with the engine. She fed it wood, making sure the fire stayed lit, taking what opportunity there was to watch the area around her.

They were headed west, passing the Spire and slipping through the Narrows toward where it met the sea on the far end.

It seemed so much smaller driving through in a larger boat. In her tiny canoe, the land to either side seemed impossibly far, the effort to row between seeming to take hours. Now, though, it felt as if she could reach out and touch it, like the boat they were in could cross in mere minutes. She watched as they passed the spot where she had nearly been run over by the ship, splotches of oil still present, but mostly dissipated by wind and waves.

Phillip took them past the western boundary of the Narrows, marked by a stone arch that had mostly collapsed into the sea. He slowed briefly as they passed beneath the remnants, watching over the side as he navigated in the space between massive rocks, the water turned white as it crashed against them and rushed between.

"Hang onto something," he said.

She gripped a rope tightly as the boat rose and suddenly propelled downward, passing between two exposed rocks. The boat tipped back upward, and as it did, a wave crashed over it, spilling water over them. Kirima felt her breath taken away by the chill and wetness, and as she regained her senses, heard the sound of laughter from Phillip, accompanied by a more subdued cackle from Calum. Her shock turned into a glare.

"You could have warned me."

Phillip allowed his laughter to die, though he still wore a huge grin. "Father did it to both of us the first time we passed through here. Consider it the price of admission."

Kirima wiped the water from her face, then shook what she could from her parka. "Any other surprises in mind?"

"That's the only one," Phillip said, still grinning. "And it's much better on the way back. Hardly a splash."

She wrung out a loose end from her undershirt. "I'll throw you over if you're lying to me."

"I'm not, I swear," he said, holding up his hands briefly before grabbing the wheel again. He stared ahead for a moment. "Father would have laughed at that. Might have even made him forget why he didn't want you aboard."

"I don't know that I ever saw him laugh," she said.

"He did it all the time. Just not when you would have seen it. Mostly when we were out here. I don't think there was anything he ever loved more."

They were silent for a moment. Beyond the mild swells of the sea, she could see an island, a few jagged peaks that sloped down into rocky beaches, curving around to circle a harbor not unlike the one their own town sat upon. The peaks were higher than most of the ones that bordered the Narrows, the beaches shorter, the waves on this side seeming to crash against them with a fury.

"I've never seen this place before," she said.

"There are many islands like this," Phillip said. "All around here. Father had an old map somewhere that showed many of them."

"Do they all have names?"

"Most of them. This one is called Quitaq."

The name sounded familiar, but she couldn't remember why. It drifted at the edge of her mind like a leaf in the autumn wind. "Maybe one day we'll name them all."

"Maybe so."

Phillip went the opposite direction of the harbor, wrapping around the northern end of the island and around to the other side. On this side, there was no beach, the mountains coming to an abrupt end in the form of towering cliffs, as if a chunk of land had been sliced away by a giant knife. Waves crashed at the bottom, and a stiff breeze blew across from the northwest, carrying crying birds up to nests high upon the cliff wall. When she looked the other way, she could see more islands, some near, some far, more like the mountains of Quitaq, as if they had once been a part of a single range that had fallen into the sea.

The boat drew nearer, close enough that she could see the rocks that the waves crashed against, but not so close that they were drawn into the swirling tempest. Phillip cut the engine and allowed the boat to drift, rocking in the swells.

"This is the spot?" she said.

Phillip nodded. "This is the spot."

Calum came around from the front, leaning against the railing. "Father always said the currents that run between these islands pull the fish from all around to this one spot."

Kirima glanced between them. "Is that true?"

Phillip shrugged. "Sounds believable enough to be true. And whenever we went out this way, which wasn't often, we'd always get a good catch."

"Mother says it's because she prays extra," Calum said. "Gives a little extra to the Balance when the fish aren't so plentiful."

"Haven't been here recently, though," Phillip said. "Not since everyone started having trouble bringing in fish. I think he was waiting for things to be really dire."

"Might be he thought it was suffering the same fate as the rest of our waters," Calum said, gazing over his shoulder at the cliffs.

"It never failed him before," Phillip said. "I don't think it'll fail us now."

"Only one way to find out." Calum was already moving toward the nets at the rear of the boat. "Did you finish, Kirima?"

"I think so. As best I could tell."

"Good enough for me." He began to toss the nets over the end, draping them behind the boat.

"Come on," Phillip said, returning to the wheel. "I need you to keep the fire like you were."

Phillip checked once more over his shoulder, then started the engine back up and began to ease it forward. Kirima watched Calum as she fed the fire, the way he untangled the net, directing it in the direction he wanted, his eyes ever on the churning water behind them as his hands worked.

The boat wound back and forth along the island's cliffs, dragging the net behind it. She lost count of the number of times they went back and forth, but when Phillip cut the engine and drifted to a stop, they had been out long enough that the sun had climbed high above them, peeking through the clouds, the light shining on the drizzle that filled the air. He looked back at Calum as he gathered the net in.

Kirima stood, wiping her hands on the front of her pants. "How did we do?"

Calum pulled the net up, reaching in and tossing a single fish onto the deck. They all watched as it flopped around in its dying throes. "A single fish," he said. "All that for a single fish."

They were silent for a moment, watching as the fish twitched, finally giving out. Finally, Phillip said, "Maybe we'll have more luck in the afternoon."

Calum walked up to the fish and gave it a kick, sending it sliding across the deck. "What's the point? It's getting worse by the day."

"Calum…" Phillip said.

"No, Phillip. It's not getting any better. People are vanishing, and who knows who will be next? It could be us." He shook his head, leaning on the railing. "The only thing to be grateful for Father dying is that he won't live to see our people die out like this."

"Don't talk like that," Phillip said, though his voice lacked the force his brother's did. He glanced over toward Kirima, a bit of helplessness in his gaze.

Kirima cleared her throat. "Phillip's right. There have always been lean times, and our people have always survived. We'll get past this too."

"You haven't seen the village on Quitaq, have you?"

Kirima frowned, looking over at Phillip. "Village? What village?"

"Show her, Phillip. She should see. Everyone in Aliit should see."

"What's he talking about, Phillip?"

Phillip let loose a deep sigh, turning toward the wheel and starting the engine back up. "You'll see."

They wrapped around the island, coming into the harbor she had noticed earlier. From this angle, she could see it all, the snow-capped mountains sloping down toward the water, the way it grew gentler, allowing for trees to grow, though still much steeper than their own village. And she could see the ruins.

At first, it had almost seemed lost in the trees, the growth around it clearly newer, but not so young that any still had the appearance of saplings. In between, she could make out the stone foundations and the skeletons of wooden structures, support beams and roofs that had collapsed in on themselves. It was a town that had been destroyed quickly and left forgotten for many years.

"I…I never knew this place was here," she said as they drew nearer, the ruined town climbing up the slope far above their heads. They passed into shadow, the midday summer sun lost behind the peaks, and she felt a chill, though it was accompanied by a stillness, where no wind blew, where no waves crashed, where not even a bird sang.

"Few do," Phillip said. "I think those old enough to remember have chosen to let it fall from the collective memory."

"What happened here?" she asked.

"Father said it was the work of the Imakut," Calum said. "The result of a people who did not keep the Balance. It's where he taught us the importance of our gift."

They were nearing the shallows now, the rocky shoreline visible beneath the water. Phillip cut the engine, and they came to a drift, rising and falling with the slight movements of the harbor's tide.

"I never knew your father was so devout," she said, her voice quiet, her hand reaching up and closing around her jarak . It seemed the proper thing, as if the very presence of the ruins commanded it.

"More than most people knew," Phillip said. "Even with his Eilenan blood. Perhaps because of it."

"The opposite of Gabriel," Kirima said.

"Perhaps if Father had been more vocal about it, he could have gotten through to the Council," Calum said. "But he always felt it was not his place. Now, I fear, it's too late."

"Let's get away from this place," Phillip said. "It gives me little comfort to sit in the shadow of this place. It feels cursed."

"Just a bit longer," Calum said. "I think it would do us all some good to be reminded of it."

They sat there for a few more moments in the silent presence of the destroyed village. Kirima wasn't sure what to do, so she sat down, leaning against the side of the boat and staring up at it. She wanted to look away, but it felt like that would be wrong, like it would upset the Balance just as much as the Company taking a whale. So she watched, never taking her eyes from it even as Phillip started up the engine and drove them from the harbor, her eyes only breaking from it when it was finally gone from her view.

They rode on in silence, the position of the sun telling her that Phillip was taking them eastward, back toward home. It wasn't much longer before she began to see the islands and slender channels that made up the Narrows.

"We're not fishing anymore?" Calum asked.

"I don't think it's going to be any better this afternoon," Phillip said.

"Father wouldn't give up."

"Father isn't here."

"If we don't consider his lessons, what good were they?"

"Is there another area we can try?" Kirima said, raising her voice to match the intensity that was growing between the two.

The brothers were silent, neither looking at the other. Finally, Phillip said, his voice quiet, "Maybe some of the lesser run channels."

"We can give it a shot." Calum's voice was restrained as well.

"Then let's do it," Kirima said. "But after lunch."

Her stomach was rumbling at that point, a hunger setting in that she hadn't even noticed. Phillip pulled into one of the channels, bringing the boat to a halt in a secluded alcove, nestled between two small bluffs.

Kirima grabbed her satchel and took it to the front of the boat, sitting cross-legged at the bow as she pulled her lunch from her sack. It wasn't long before Phillip came and joined her, a bowl of kelp and cold fish in his hand.

"Is this how it's been since he was taken?" she asked after they sat there eating for a few moments.

"No," he said. "There isn't as much to argue about at home. And I don't think he wants to do it in front of Mother. I know I don't."

"I'm sorry you're having to go through this."

"Yeah." He stared off, looking toward the top of the bluff across from them. "I guess you know how it feels on a certain level."

"Yeah, I guess I do," she said.

He looked over at her. "I'm sorry, I didn't mean to…"

"No, it's fine. He is always close in my mind and in my heart."

"He taught you that song? The one you sang while we dragged the nets?"

"I…" She felt her face flush. "I didn't even realize I had been singing."

"I wish you did it more. I liked it."

She gave a slight chuckle. "I never thought it sounded good coming from my lips, never as good as when Papa sang it."

"Your ears never hear your voice the way others do."

She gazed at him from the corner of her eye, a sly smile on her lips. "Are you saying I can't trust my ears?"

It was his turn to laugh. "Not as much as you should be able to."

She beamed at him, and he returned the gaze. They settled in, eating in silence for a time, feeling the slight mist, broken by the warmth of the sun as it shone through the clouds above. She could hear some birds calling, red swallows, if she remembered her father's lessons correctly.

"Do you think it's real?"

Kirima turned at the sound of his voice, finding him once more staring out, this time toward the end of the strait, toward the open sea. "Do I think what's real?"

"The Imakut. Quitaq. The Balance. All of it."

"It's never really crossed my mind to not. Is there reason to believe otherwise?"

"I don't know. Maybe? None of this seems real, like there should be a reason for everything that's happened."

"That reason is the Imakut," she said. Her mind was working now. He was wrong, wasn't he? Papa would have known, he always seemed to have the right answer.

"But if it is, then why now? And why us? Why not attack the Company when they are the ones taking the whales from the sea and not giving to the Balance in return? What did our people ever do to deserve this?"

Kirima was silent for a moment. "I don't know," she finally said, her voice quiet. "I feel like my father would know, like your father would know, but we don't have those kinds of answers."

She heard him sniff and turned to see him lowering his arm from where he had wiped his face on his sleeve. "I feel so lost right now."

Her hand reached out, resting on his shoulder. She said nothing. There was nothing she could think to say.

"I don't know, is this normal? Is this what my own father felt when Grandpa died? I never saw him shed a tear, but we were so young at the time. Maybe I just didn't notice."

"Our fathers were people too," she said. "I know Papa cried when Mama died. I'm sure your father grieved as well."

"Maybe he did." Phillip sniffed again, once more wiping away his nose. "I just wish he was here to talk one more time."

"Me too," she said.

There was a cry from the far end of the boat, a yelp emerging from the mouth of Phillip's brother, followed by a splash. Both of them were on their feet immediately, and Kirima quickly saw that the back of the boat was empty.

"Calum?" Phillip called out.

"Did he fall in?" she asked, following him as he moved toward the rear of the boat.

"Surely not, he's not careless. Calum!"

There was the sound of more splashing before they reached the end of the boat, of struggling, of gasping for air. The sound of drowning. They both moved faster, reaching the rear just to see him disappear beneath the surface, the dark water stirred up into a froth from struggle.

"Can you see him?" Phillip said. "Can you see anything?"

"Nothing," Kirima said, her eyes scanning the roiling water. The bubbles seemed to permeate the surface, making it impossible to see through the already murky sea. "Wait, there!"

She pointed as she saw the hand emerge, barely visible yet unmistakable. Both of them lunged, leaning over to grab for it, both of them only grabbing at water, Calum's hand too far away. As they stood up, Phillip began removing his parka.

"I'm going in."

Kirima watched him struggle to dress down, her mind working, wondering how long Calum had been down there, how long he could hold his breath. It didn't seem like long, but she remembered falling out of the boat as a child, how the cold could shock the breath right out of you when you weren't expecting it. There was no time to lose.

Phillip didn't even have his parka fully over his head when she dove in. She thought she heard him shout after her, but it was lost in the sound of the water splashing around her ears. The salt stung her eyes, but she forced them to stay open, kicking her legs as she dove deeper.

It wasn't long before she saw him, his hand drifting over a hanging head, reaching up toward the surface, and seeming to draw further away. She reached out and grabbed his hand, straining as she tried to pull him back up. Something held him down, something much stronger than her, but she persisted, even as her lungs began to burn.

She almost let go when she felt something grab at her own leg, gripping her by the boot. She kicked, again and again, but it continued to hold onto her, dragging her and Calum further down. She could see the light fading above as darkness and cold enveloped her, threatening to crush her lungs as she fought for breath.

Her hand fumbled at her belt, wrapping around the handle of her knife. She tore it from its sheath and began to slash through the water. At first there was nothing, the blade slicing through cold, dark water. She leaned forward, searching blindly for whatever held onto her ankle. She slashed and she slashed, and without warning, the blade struck something. Something that was not her own leg.

The grip around her ankle seemed to tighten and turn, but she didn't let up, striking again and again, the blade cleaving into whatever was grasping her leg. She still couldn't see what it was, or just how much damage the blade was doing, but she was not going to give up, not while she was still conscious.

The blade came up and descended, and it suddenly seemed to give. She could still feel the grip on her leg, but it seemed lighter, and the blade struck nothing. She pulled on Calum and found that he was no longer being held down. She kicked as hard as she could, fighting against her burning lungs and her aching muscles as she drove up toward the surface. She could see it lightening around her, but it felt impossibly far, like there was still a shadow over everything. Her lungs felt like they were going to burst, her heart pounding against her ribs like a drum.

It didn't seem real when she broke through the surface, even as she drew in a deep breath of cool air that felt warm after all that time underwater. It was only when she heard Phillip calling out her name, his voice coming louder and louder as the water cleared from her ears, that she truly realized that she was above, and that she was alive.

She felt hands grab her from above, and she had to fight the urge to throw them off. She could feel him start to pull her up, but she waved her free hand at him. "No, Calum first."

Phillip released her, and she did her best to lift his limp brother up. Phillip grabbed hold, pulling him over the railing with a loud grunt, the two of them both thumping onto the deck. Kirima didn't wait for him to reappear, using what strength she had remaining to pull herself up. Her arms almost failed her, but Phillip was there to pull her the rest of the way into the boat.

"Is..." She had to take several deep breaths to get more than that out. "Is he alright?"

Phillip was down on his hands and knees, his ear hovering just over Calum's mouth. "He's breathing."

He turned his brother onto his side, slapping him several times on the back. After a moment, Calum began to cough, spitting up water onto the deck. Kirima could feel the relief wash over her as she watched Calum slowly come to life, first putting a hand down, then slowly turning over so that he was propping himself up, still coughing, sucking in air the same way she had been. Phillip had come to a crouch, hovering over him with a hand on his back.

It was several moments before everything seemed to settle down. Kirima was sitting with her back to the railing, her breathing still heavy, but not quite as bad as it had been. Calum had managed a seated position, occasionally taking sips from the waterskin in his hand while Phillip remained crouched before him, a worried look on his face.

"That's something I never want to do again," Calum said. His head was turned slightly toward her. "I suppose I have you to thank for my life."

"It was nothing," she said. "I'd like to think you'd have done the same for me."

"I doubt I could have beaten Phillip to it," he said.

"I managed that. He took too long getting his parka off."

Calum shook his head. "Willing to let me drown to keep your clothes dry."

"Next time, I'll make sure she lets you drown as well," Phillip said. "Did you get a look at what it was?"

"No," Calum said. "It all happened so quickly. I was just sitting on the edge over there, eating, and suddenly I was in the water. Did you Kirima?"

This time, he turned his head fully toward her, Phillip as well. Before she could say anything, she saw both of them give the same look, their eyes widening.

"What?" she said with a frown. "Is something wrong?"

"I think that might be our answer," Phillip said, gesturing toward her leg.

Kirima's eyes followed his gesture down to her ankle, the same ankle that had been grabbed when she had been pulled downward. There, still attached with a firm grip, was a hand and part of a wrist, severed roughly and still bleeding a thick, dark blood. Or at least, it looked like a hand. The color was off, a greenish blue, the skin scaled, the fingers connected by thin skin, each one ending in a sharp claw, claws that had cut through her pants and drawn a bit of blood.

They were all silent for a moment as they stared at it. Finally, it was Phillip who spoke. "What should we do?"

"Throw it back," Calum said, turning and spitting. "Let them feast on that."

"No, wait," Kirima said. She reached down and pulled it off, not without some difficulty. "We should get back. We can show Gabriel, everyone. This is the proof we need."

"You're right," Phillip said. He was already standing, making his way to the wheel. "Maybe this can even convince the Company."

"We can only hope," Kirima said as the engine roared to life. She stood as the boat began to move, watching the spot they had just been as it vanished   into   the   distance.

6

Both Yura and the boys' mother, Suluk, were there to greet them when the boat returned, and Kirima could already see the concern melt into relief on her sister's face as both women came forward. Suluk was on her boys in a moment, wrapping them both in a huge embrace, while Yura approached much more slowly, holding her belly as she walked down the beach, refusing help from Phillip when he tried to step away from his mother to offer.

"What's wrong?" Kirima asked, not giving Yura a chance to refuse her as she grabbed her sister by the arm to support her.

"Three more came back missing people," she said. "Several are still out, but people are already fearing the worst." She trailed off, looking down as Kirima's still dripping clothing. "What happened?"

"I'll tell you about it later," she said. "We need to speak to Gabriel. Immediately."

The frown that crossed Yura's face was one normally reserved for the children, but her tone remained the same. "He's by the fire, I think, trying to keep things calm. I don't think our esteemed simuq is helping things."

"Be nice to her, she's responsible for delivering your child."

Kirima broke away from her, making her way toward the fire, where she could already see Gabriel standing, partially surrounded by townsfolk, his hands held up before them as if he was trying to calm them. She pushed her way through, shouldering her way to the front and ignoring their protests. Gabriel turned toward her, his eyes widening slightly before narrowing.

"Kirima," he said. "Glad to see you're safe." He paused. "Are Calum and Phillip okay as well?"

"They're fine," she said. "But we have something you have to see."

"Gabriel," Lusa said from beside him. "Whatever she has to show you can wait. These people need you."

"No, this can't wait." Kirima grabbed him by the arm, pushing back through the same people, dragging him with her, chased by Lusa's scowl as it drilled into their backs.

Once they were free of the crowd, he fell into stride with her, no longer requiring her to pull him, though she maintained her grip on his arm. "I hope this is as important as you make it sound," he said in a quiet voice, taking a glance back. "Lusa is in a mood."

"Trust me," she said.

Suluk was leading Calum away, a blanket draped over his shoulders, but Phillip stood by the boat, Yura standing a bit further away, now joined by both her children. Meriwa gave a small wave that Kirima returned, but her focus immediately shifted to the boat.

"Right there, on the deck," Kirima said. "Have a look."

She stepped back, watching as Gabriel climbed up, standing on the lip as he gazed down at the hand, laying right where they had left it. It seemed like he stared at it for a long time, though that may have just been in her mind. Either way, his face seemed to have paled by a full shade when he stepped down.

The crowd had made its way over, and Lusa stood at the front of it, hands resting on her cane. "What is it, Gabriel? What was so important that it couldn't wait."

Gabriel ignored her, turning toward Kirima and Phillip. "Where did that come from?"

"Something pulled Calum into the water," Phillip said. "Kirima jumped in after him."

"Something grabbed me while I was down there," Kirima said. "I hacked at it with my knife."

"Gabriel," Lusa said, her voice more forceful. "What is it?"

Gabriel said nothing, his eyes shifting around, looking everywhere by at them or at the crowd behind him.

"Show them," Kirima said. "They have a right to see what's taking our people."

He didn't move at first. It was only when Phillip took a step toward the boat that he cut him off, reaching over and grabbing the hand. There was a collective gasp when he held it up so that everyone could see. A silence fell over them, and then it seemed that everyone began to speak at once.

"This can't be real."

"No, it's real. They're real."

"Did they manage to kill one?"

"What can we do now?"

"Well, we know they can be hurt."

As the conversations continued around her, Lusa remained quiet, her eyes narrow, her lips drawn into a thin line. She took a few steps toward them, drawing nearer and speaking so that only they could hear her.

"It seems we have our proof," she said. "Now we must take action."

"I need to take this to the Company," Gabriel said. "Maybe if they see that it's real…"

Lusa shook her head. "We must speak to the Council first."

"The day draws late," Gabriel said. "There will be time to talk when I'm back."

The line of her mouth slowly turned downward. "The Council will not be pleased with this."

"They can tell me as much as they want when I'm back." He turned toward her and Phillip. "You two should come as well."

"I need to check on Calum," Phillip said. "Make sure Mother doesn't need help."

Gabriel's eyes focused on her. "And you, Kirima?"

Kirima was about to open her mouth when Yura stepped forward. "Oh no, not after the day she's had. She needs rest, not to have the stress of going to the Company."

Gabriel looked at Kirima, but Yura stepped in between them. "I mean it."

He let loose a heavy sigh. "Very well. I'll be back soon. Until this is figured out, no one goes back out." There were some grumbles from the crowd, but he raised his voice to be heard over them. "I want the fire burning all night, with double watches."

"Perhaps another sacrifice?" Lusa said.

Gabriel seemed to stammer silently before getting the words out. "Do what you will. The others haven't worked. I fear the only way we regain the balance is with the Company's help. I'll be back by nightfall. Hopefully I can speak some sense into Eoghan."

He turned away, making his way back toward the village, no doubt heading toward his boat in the hidden cove. Lusa remained there for a moment, leaning on her cane, then turned away with a grunt, leaving her and Phillip and Yura standing there.

"What now?" Phillip said.

"I guess we wait," Kirima said.

"Well while you wait, we need to get you into something dry," Yura said, taking Kirima by the arm. "And feed your something warm." She snapped her fingers toward her children. "Go put the broth on the stove. Quickly."

The kids ran ahead as Yura led her up toward their house. "I'll meet you later," Kirima said over her shoulder to Phillip, allowing herself to be led along without resistance.

When she finally did return to the beach, dried, fed, and warmed, Phillip and Calum were already there, sitting in the sand. Phillip was leaning back, supporting himself on his long arms, while Calum sat with his legs crossed, hunched over as he used a shell to carve meaningless shapes into the dense sand.

"Still waiting?" she said, taking a seat across from them.

"Still waiting," Calum said.

"Do you think Eoghan will listen to him?" Phillip asked.

"Who?" Calum asked.

"The governor," Kirima said. "And no, not based on what Gabriel said last time."

"But he has the hand," Calum said. "Surely that will help, right?"

Phillip shifted in place, shaking his head. "I don't think so. I mean, you don't think they're only attacking us, do you?"

Kirima frowned. "I mean…" She paused. Truth be told, she hadn't thought of it before. "I don't think you're wrong, but if that's the case, what reason would they have to lie to us? Better yet, what reason would they have for not wanting to make it stop?"

"They have their own soldiers, and those firesticks," Phillip said. "Maybe they can fend them off."

"Or maybe they don't care if they do lose men," Calum said.

"No, I don't think that is the case," Kirima said. "No one else from the village will join, so they'd have to bring people in from far away. People who don't know these waters."

"Maybe they plan to bring us on to help whether we want it or not," Calum said.

"Oki was scared to talk to me," Phillip said. "He wouldn't even say more than a couple of words before leaving me standing there. Maybe he was scared of something else?"

"I don't think that's it," Kirima said. "Those guards seemed scary enough as it is." She paused. "But if he knew what was happening, surely he'd want to tell us, right?"

"He was scared of slipping up," Phillip said.

"It certainly seems like they're hiding something," Calum said. "But even if we know that they are, does it do us any good? I don't think they plan on helping with the Balance regardless of what is said."

They sat there in silence for a moment, leaving the sound to the waves lapping gently at the coast and the fire crackling off to the side. In the distance, she could hear the sound of a motor, the unmistakable sound of the mayor's whale oil-powered boat. "Gabriel knows, doesn't he?" Kirima said.

"He has to," Calum said. "Surely."

"Somehow, I think he's known the entire time," Phillip said.

Kirima stood, taking a moment to brush sand from her pants. "I don't want to wait around and risk Lusa intercepting him before we get a chance to talk to him. I'm going to go see him at the boat."

The brothers stood with her, following after as she made her way to the alcove where Gabriel hid his boat. By the time they arrived, the boat was already in place, the motor cut. Gabriel was on shore, tying the mooring line to a tree. As he turned toward them, she could already see the answer in his face, but she decided to ask the question anyways.

"How did it go?"

The words seemed to come out in a long sigh. "About what you could have expected."

"Even with the hand?" Phillip said.

Gabriel seemed to pull the hand from nowhere, tossing it toward them. Phillip managed to catch it, nearly fumbling it into the water. "He would hardly look at it. 'Stop wasting my time with these ridiculous superstitions, Gabriel.' That's what he told me. He doesn't think I've changed my mind from what I said last time."

Phillip was holding the arm out, making a face as he looked it over. "What do we do now?"

"I'm going to call the Council," he said, trudging past them. "We'll be meeting at my house within the hour to discuss things. I want you there."

Kirima frowned. "We're not allowed at the Council meetings. You know that." She had tried to get her father to take her once. He had laughed and said that even if she was allowed, he wouldn't let her just to spare her the boredom.

"You'll be my guests for this one. You're the only ones who have fought one off, so that makes you more experienced than anyone else in the village."

"Hardly comforting," Calum said.

"We think Eoghan knows," Kirima said. She hadn't intended to be the one speaking it, certainly not then, but the words just came flying out of her mouth.

Gabriel stopped, his pale eyes running over the three of them as another sigh escaped his lips. "He does, and he probably did when we went there. I was too blinded to see at the time."

"Blinded by fear?" Phillip said. "Like Oki?"

"Perhaps. Or perhaps I simply did not wish it to be true."

"That he would choose to ignore it?"

"That the Imakut were really responsible." A silence fell between them. "Come, the Council."

Gabriel's house sat above most of the rest of the town, propped against the rocky crag that sloped down to the beach, looking down upon the rows of houses and buildings that made up the rest of the town. The path turned into wooden steps climbing up to a wooden foundation supported by thick beams of wood and stone. Light streamed through the glass windows, and as they approached, Kirima could already hear the sounds of conversation coming from within.

The inside was warm, heated by a large stove like the one in her own home, but it was not so warm as other places, certainly not as much so as the Company building. The air smelled of mint, and lit lanterns hung in every corner, bathing the room in a bright light. Seated in chairs and on benches were a half dozen others, the most respected of the village called when the problems went beyond the capacity of Gabriel to deal with.

Lusa was there, of course, sitting quietly in a thickly cushioned chair, her hands resting on the head of her cane. Next to her was Miki, his mouth still open from whatever conversation he had been having with Sawney, the latter leaning his bulky frame on his knee, his grin revealing several wide gaps in his teeth. The other three sat on the same bench, Seona, Alpin, and Sesi, each looking and smelling as if they had just come from the boats.

Kirima couldn't quite get a read on how the room had been before they had entered, but it was certainly more silent as all eyes turned toward them. Gabriel said nothing, fetching more chairs and gesturing for her and the brothers to take a seat before making his way to his own cushioned seat.

The silence seemed to hang for another moment or two before Miki broke it. "Well? What happened?"

"Eoghan was much less cordial than my last visit," Gabriel said. "He refused to even acknowledge the hand and had me escorted back to my boat by his guards. I was told in no uncertain terms that I should not bring up the matter again."

That brought about mutterings from the council, Alpin's high-pitched voice sounding out the loudest. "What can we do about it now? It's already been shown that the Company will not listen to us."

"Doesn't seem to me like there's anything we can do," Sesi said, stroking the long, stringy beard that grew from his chin. "It has been passed down that the Imakut have come for our people before, but it always ended eventually."

"In the stories we were told as children," Sawney said. "Who's to say any of that is real?"

"Are you mad?" Miki said. "How can you possibly deny this?"

"People vanish all the time, there's no saying it's the Imakut."

"How can you say that?"

"Have you seen one yourself?"

Miki gestured toward Kirima and the brothers. "They have. Is that not enough for you?"

"That arm could have come from a decaying corpse for all we know," Sawney said.

"Are you calling us liars?" Calum said.

"I'm saying you don't know for sure."

Calum was standing now. "I almost drowned from one of those things. Our father was taken by one, he and several others now."

"Enough." Kirima wasn't sure she'd ever heard Gabriel's voice be so forceful, but the look on his face told her that this wasn't the first time an argument like this had broken out. He continued. "The Company made it clear that they will not contribute toward the Balance, whether they believe that the Imakut are responsible or not. So we need to find a solution that does not rely on their help."

Alpin scoffed. "We'll all be dead before we find a solution."

"What else is there to do?" Seona asked, taking a pause to hawk and spit off to the side. "We give to the balance, and they do not accept it."

"Perhaps we're not giving the right kind of sacrifice," Lusa said.

All eyes turned toward her, the simuq remaining stoic, hardly moving. "I'm afraid to ask what you're going to say," Gabriel said.

"We all know of the fate of Quitaq," she said. "We know how its people were taken and the village destroyed, but few seem to know of Tuqaq, a village even further west, beyond where any of our fishers venture in normal times."

There were murmurings around the room, seeming to confirm what Lusa had said. Kirima watched the woman, her narrow face, her grey hair tied back in a tight bun, her voice projecting with a power that betrayed her meek frame as she continued.

"This was many years ago, just like what happened Quitaq, long before anyone in this room was born, before any of these islands were a part of Eilena, even before the wayward ones came and joined our town. Like with Quitaq, the villagers of Tuqaq found themselves in the bad graces of the Imakut."

"No one can say for certain what caused it, the reasons lost in the years that the tale was passed down. If you were to go to Tuqaq today, you would probably hear a dozen different reasons. Overfishing, failure to put out the right sacrifice, fishing in the wrong spot, even the idea that it was a trial put forth by the Imakut to test their faith. Whatever the case, people began to vanish, just as they have here."

"It started from their boats, their canoes found floating, empty, with the nets still dropped. Then, people began to be taken from the town itself, with nothing left but footprints. They tried everything once they realized what had happened; praying, doubling the sacrifice, placing guards, even coming to other towns, our own included, but nothing worked. Finally, they did the last thing anyone could think of, the thing they thought was never possible."

A silence fell over the room, a silence only broken by Kirima's voice, the sound drawing all the eyes of the room. "What did they do?"

"They gave one of their own to the Balance, girl," Seona said, spitting again. "May the Imakut curse them forever for such an act."

Lusa nodded. "A sacrifice they made, but cursed they weren't. The Imakut accepted the gift, and the Balance was restored. They made the decision that Quitaq did not, and so they were spared. They did what needed to be done."

"I will not have this conversation again," Gabriel said.

Kirima looked over at him, her mouth agape, though no one else in the room seemed surprised by his words. Had this really been spoken about in this room? Was this truly something they had seriously considered?

"Will you not do what must be done, Gabriel?" Lusa asked. "Are you truly such a weak person?"

"If I am weak for protecting my people, then so be it."

The words brought murmurings from the others as Lusa spoke. "You are weak. It was said that the screams of the people of Quitaq were carried on the wind down the Narrows for days after the town was destroyed."

"I come here for practical solutions, not for stories."

"Your stubbornness will doom us all."

"Enough."

Lusa's voice was raised, almost shouting, drowning out the rest. "You refuse to sacrifice the one to save the many, and thus doom us all."

"I said enough." Gabriel tried to raise his voice, but it was lost beneath that of the simuq.

"You are weak, Gabriel, and the Imakut can sense it. It is a weakness that permeates through this town. If the Imakut do not claim us, then the land will. Wind, rain, floods, and drought, it will take back what belongs to it. Only the strong can survive in a place like this, and there is no longer strength..."

"Enough!"

The roar that came from Gabriel was accompanied by his hand slamming down on the table beside him, and the room was immediately silenced. Kirima felt herself jump, turning to exchange glances with both Phillip and Calum. Was this how the meetings always went? Was the rift in the Council really so deep that it would result in this kind of yelling and insults?

Gabriel was standing now, his bulk seeming to command the room as he stood over the others. "We are not sacrificing anyone. That is the end of it."

Lusa seemed ready to argue, but her lips remained tightly sealed, her eyes saying all that her voice could not. Gabriel continued.

"Our options are limited, and none of them attractive, but that does not mean that we will give up easily. First things first, we need to stop this bickering. There's something out there trying to kill us, something we don't know much about, and the last thing we need is to argue amongst ourselves. What we do know is that these attacks will not stop, and we need to do something about it, something that doesn't involve sending a sacrifice to the depths. So first thing tomorrow morning, I'm setting out for Adhan."

Alpin stood. "Adhan? That's days away. What can you possibly hope to accomplish there when the danger is here?"

"You can't just leave," Seona said. "Not when our people need you."

Sawney sat there with his arms crossed, leaning over to Miki. "Sounds to me like he's getting out while he still can."

"Saving his own skin," Miki said with a scowl.

Kirima looked at Gabriel just as the others did. She said nothing, but she did not disagree. She didn't know how far Adhan was, but even in that boat, it was not a short trip. How many people might die in that time? What could possibly there that could help them?

"I am not fleeing," Gabriel said. "I'm going to Adhan because I think we can get help there. We have a representative in the Assembly, there are scholars of the Imakut, and the Company headquarters is there. Perhaps I can get through to one of them about our plight, perhaps I can get some kind of assistance."

"And if you can't?" Lusa asked.

"Then I will find someone who will," Gabriel said. "The Company paid us money, something they find valuable, but that we have never had a use for. This may be the use we've been looking for. Whatever the case, I will not return without some kind of help."

Kirima glanced over at Phillip. "Money?" she mouthed. He only shrugged.

"Alright, so you go on this voyage," Sawney said. "Fool's errand, it seems, the one thing we all seem to agree on. What are we to do? Wait around to die?"

"This isn't something I can do without your support," Gabriel said. "I can go for a day unnoticed, but people will start asking questions after the second or the third, and I need you to be around to answer them. They'll ask why I went, just like you did here, and they'll come up with more, perhaps adding their own theories to it. I need you here to allay those fears, to keep the peace until I can return."

The council members mumbled as Gabriel turned toward her and the boys. "I want the three of you to come with me."

"Us?" Kirima said. "Why us?"

"You are the only ones here who have encountered the Imakut and survived, and you can help me convince them that the hand is real, that this isn't a hoax. I need you to tell your story."

Phillip made a face. "Will that really be a problem?"

Gabriel sighed. "If some of our own still refuse to believe it, how do you think someone leagues away will react?"

"I see."

"I can't go," Calum said. His eyes shifted when the others looked his way. "Mother would absolutely kill me if I tried. It was enough of a struggle to leave the house."

"Are we not old enough to make that decision ourselves?" Phillip said.

"She's already been through enough with Father being taken. What if something happens on the way?"

"Calum, you do not have to come," Gabriel said. "Kirima and Phillip will be more than enough. And we will be perfectly safe, I can assure you." He focused on the two of them. "Go home, get some rest. I'll be by early."

"Should we bring anything?" Kirima asked.

Gabriel shook his head. "I'll have the provisions we need." He motioned with his hands. "Go now. I have other matters to discuss with the Council."

The three of them left out the front door, making their way down the steps back toward their homes. The day was gone, another starless summer night fallen on the town, dark but for the fire that burned on the beach, the early night's watch taken their place in its glow. A cold wind blew from the north, as if winter threatened to make an early appearance.

"Adhan," Phillip said. "I never thought I'd ever see it. It doesn't even seem like a real place, just something you hear about."

"I don't know anything about it," Kirima said. "Other than it's a city."

"Said to be the greatest city in Eilena," Phillip said.

"Father always said the greatest in the world," Calum said.

"If only he could be joining us," Phillip said. "He always wanted to see the place his ancestors left."

"I hope it's everything he ever hoped it was," Calum said.

"You can still come," Phillip said.

"Mother will tie me to the bed if that's what it takes. Besides, someone needs to look after her as well. She's been taking it hard, you know."

"I know," Phillip said. "We all have."

They were all silent for a moment. Kirima searched her mind for something to say, tried to remember what people had said to her when her father had died that had helped at the time, but nothing came. Perhaps that was because nothing felt like it helped during that time.

Phillip turned to her. "I'll see you in the morning."

"I probably won't," Calum said. "So be safe on your journey. Make sure you watch out for my brother."

"I will," she said.

Yura was still awake, seated before the stove, tending to the fire. She turned her head slightly as Kirima walked in. "Tell me what happened."

"Are the children asleep?" Kirima asked.

"Probably not, but I don't think it matters."

Kirima removed her parka, hanging it from its familiar hook. "Gabriel wants to go to Adhan. He's taking Phillip and me."

The fire enhanced the creases in her face as she frowned. "Adhan? Why?"

"He thinks he can find help there. One way or another."

"It's so far away."

"It's also the biggest city in Eilena. If help exists, it probably exists there."

Yura turned away from the fire, pulling her robe in closer over her belly. "Can anyone help us at this point? I mean, the Imakut have always seemed to be such a powerful force to me. Is it possible for us to stop this?"

"I don't know," Kirima said. "But we have to try. If only for the children."

Yura's hand went to her belly. "Is this a world we want them to live in? A world where they have to work themselves to the bone to survive? A world where the Imakut can decide they haven't received enough from us and come to take them?"

"I mean, there's still plenty to enjoy," Kirima said.

"Like what?"

"Like the sunny days spent out on the water. Like the joy of catching the biggest fish of the day. Like the celebrations, where lambs are slaughtered and roasted, and everyone sings and dances deep into the night. Like the joy of falling in love. Do you not remember that, when you and Katjuk were wed?"

Yura shook her head. "Maybe it's better elsewhere. Maybe that's the solution, we all just leave this place."

"And go where?"

"I don't know. Some place where the sun shines. Some place where it doesn't snow. Some place where the Imakut aren't a thing."

"Does a place like that exist?"

"I don't know. Maybe. I'd like to think it does."

"Maybe that's what we'll end up doing, if we can't find any help." Kirima shrugged. "Either way, so long as we're all safe."

"I hope that will be the case."

"Me too."

Yura shifted in the chair, adjusting her belly. "How's the baby?" Kirima asked as she watched her sister.

"Ready to come out," she said. "She kicks like crazy at night, hardly lets me get any sleep. It feels like it could be any day now, but Lusa thinks it'll be another moon."

"Have you picked a name yet?"

"Not yet," she said. She gave a little laugh. "Katjuk had names picked out for Meriwa and Hanta before they were even conceived, it felt like.

Now, I don't know."

"You could name her after Mama," Kirima said. "Or maybe Katjuk's mother."

"Definitely not her. That woman was a devil. A shame she's not here, she would have scared the Imakut right back beneath the waves."

Kirima gave a laugh at that. "Papa wasn't fond of her either. He used to complain about her when we went fishing. Mostly that he feared that Katjuk would end up being no different."

Yura smiled, shaking her head. "Papa was good at a lot of things, but I don't think he was that good at reading people. Katjuk was nothing like his mother. He knew it, and she certainly knew it. I think that's why she was so mean toward me; she thought I was stealing him from her."

"Reminds me of how Lusa speaks," Kirima said. "I think she worries that she has lost her power over the town, that being simuq doesn't hold the respect it once did."

"Time once was that the simuq could command the weather and speak to the Imakut. Perhaps if Lusa could do either, she would command more respect."

"Do you think they could really do that in the past?" Kirima asked.

"Until recently, I questioned whether the Imakut were real," Yura said. "I suppose now, anything could be true."

"Papa always believed."

"And Mama never did. I suppose we know who took after who."

Kirima found herself looking down at her hands, resting in her lap. "I wish I had known her better."

"I wish you had too. For what it's worth, she loved you more than anything in the world."

"I know. At least, I feel like I know."

"Papa too. It was enough to make a girl jealous sometimes."

"You always could have come."

Yura shook her head. "Fishing never interested me, just as finding a family never seemed to interest you."

"It doesn't not interest me. I may want to settle down one day."

"You're lying to yourself as much as you're lying to me." Before Kirima could speak, Yura cut her off. "That's alright, though. Not everyone is cut out to make a family."

"You mean like crazy old Uki?"

That drew another laugh from her sister. "I called her that one day, and Mama gave me a smack. She said, 'That woman is not crazy. She is strong enough to live by herself and bring in her own food and suffer the insults of children and adults alike without a second thought. If anything, she's the strongest person in the village.'"

"So I'll be the one living by myself and ignoring the insults of everyone else?"

"Of course not." Yura leaned forward and kissed her on the forehead. "As long as I live, you have a place to live. And the children and I certainly won't allow anyone to speak ill of you."

"We sure won't," Meriwa called from above.

"Well, I guess that's our cue to go to bed so the little ones will," Yura said. She started to rise, and when Kirima moved to help, she slapped at her. "No, I can do this on my own. Need to be able to when you're not around."

"Or you could take advantage of the time when I am here."

"Nonsense." She did not object, however, when Kirima took her arm, helping her the rest of the way up and leading her to the bedroom.

"I suppose I don't have to tell you to take care of yourself," Yura said once they were in the tiny, windowless room. Kirima helped her ease down onto the bed that she and her husband used to share.

"Of course not. And I won't be alone."

"Phillip and Gabriel." Yura shook her head. "Would either of them be helpful if worst came to worst?"

"Yes. I think so."

Yura shook her head. "As I thought. I'd say I pray for you, but I'm not sure that's the best course of action given what's going on right now."

"No, probably not."

"I might do so anyways. I suppose it couldn't hurt. Maybe on some level, the Imakut still hear us."

"Maybe so." The words didn't sound convincing to even her own ears, but if Yura found them so, she said nothing on the matter. "I hope I can make it back for the birth."

"If I had my way, the child would already be out. Go on, Kirima, get some rest. I'll be up to see you off in the morning."

"Good night."

Kirima left her there, making her way to her own bedroom. She plopped down onto her bed and fell asleep almost immediately. In her dreams, she saw herself being pulled under the water, the surface growing further and further. Except unlike that day, nothing could break the creature's grip. Through the surface, she could see the town and all the people, her sister and her niece and nephew, Gabriel, Lusa, Phillip and Calum, but none seemed to know what to do. So she lingered there, helpless, until the surface faded, and everything slipped into darkness.

7

Kirima wasn't sure what she had expected the voyage to Adhan to be like, but she certainly hadn't expected to be so bored.

Sure, there were sights along the way, sights unlike anything she'd ever seen before. There were mountains that grew so high they were lost in the clouds. There were islands that stretched further than the eye could see. There were ruins that seemed as if they had once housed giants. There were trees and plants and animals she had never dreamed could exist. But mostly, she found herself watching water pass by, miles and miles of water that seemed to have no end.

At night, they would make camp on a beach if one was available, or anchor and sleep on the deck if there wasn't one, though half of each night was split between her and Phillip keeping watch to allow Gabriel to sleep. They had tried the space beneath the deck, but they had all found it cramped and stuffy, especially as the air warmed. Food was plentiful, both caught from lines dropped over the side or taken from the dried stores that Gabriel had packed, but amusement was not. She could feel her body itching to move, to do something besides pace the small deck, even as her mind knew that she could not.

The first three days had felt like a full cycle of the moon by the time they were over, but it was on the morning of the fourth that a large island rose on the horizon, the land climbing toward the clouds in the form of mountains. It stretched in either direction, as far as the eye could see, yet there was not a city in sight.

"Is this Adhan?" Kirima asked. She had lost track of the number of times she had asked that same question, but Gabriel had kept his patience in each response. This response, however, was different.

"This is part of it, yes."

Finally. Her eyes scanned the land that was visible, either end seeming to vanish behind the morning haze. She could see a few other boats in the distance, but there were no houses, no buildings on the mountain slopes, no signs of inhabitation.

"I don't see a city."

"Just wait."

Gabriel began to steer the boat to the left, piloting it along the shoreline in an easterly direction. She watched the land pass by as the boat moved along, seeming to glide over the water, bouncing occasionally as it passed over small swells. The mountains seemed to grow out of the distant haze before vanishing once more behind them in the same way. And then suddenly, the mountains and shore beside them were gone completely.

The boat angled to the right, entering the gap where the mountains should have stood. At the far end, she could see them rising from the sea once again, continuing where the previous ones had left off, forming a partial ring of land instead of what had seemed almost like a continent. And it was then that she saw the city.

It was as if the haze had parted before the sun just to give the city a grand reveal, and grand it was. Kirima found her breath completely taken away.

The city rose from what looked like a single island at first glance, but when she focused harder, she could see the bridges that spanned two pieces of land just ahead of them. There were buildings of all shapes and sizes, all of them seeming to dwarf even the huge ones with the chimneys at the Company outpost. Some of them seemed to shine as if only made from glass, while others seemed to be topped by massive needles. As they drew nearer, she could see cylinders made of a dull, reddish metal running along and between the buildings. Surrounding the city were boats and ships of all shapes and sizes, navigating the waters between the buildings and in the waters surrounding the city, protected by the mountainous barrier islands, which she could now see bordered on all sides.

"This is Adhan," Phillip said beside her, his words almost a gasp.

"This is Adhan," Gabriel said. He seemed no less in awe than either of them, one hand remaining on the wheel while the other ran through his thick hair, shining a brilliant white in the sudden brightness of the sun.

"It's so big," Kirima said. She looked at Gabriel, then back at the city. "Where do we even go? How do we know where to begin?"

"The map said the important buildings are in the center of the islands," he said. "And I'm sure someone will tell us if we ask them directions."

A horn blew as a massive ship passed by them going the other direction, causing her to jump, so loud that it seemed to reverberate through her very bones. Kirima stepped back from that side of the boat, craning her neck as she gazed toward the top of it. It seemed like it could house the entire town just on its deck, and perhaps much of the Company outpost as well.

"This place is like a dream," Kirima said, turning her head away from the ship and back toward the rapidly approaching city. "None of it seems real."

"It's very real," Gabriel said. "I had always heard that it was a wonder to behold, but this was beyond my wildest imagination."

"Calum is going to be so mad when I tell him about this," Phillip said.

If he's still alive. The words almost slipped past her lips, but she held them back. A morbid thought, and one that drove some of the luster from the city as she remembered the reason they were there in the first place.

Gabriel navigated them between the islands, passing beneath the towering bridge that was supported up by round columns, each one seemingly crafted from a single white stone, and held from above by what looked like ropes braided from metal. Up ahead, she could see that there was a third island, further from the other two, but joined by other bridges. It was to this third island that they headed, the buildings here seeming shorter, more spread out, but no less impressive.

"Do you know these places?" she asked.

"By reputation," he said. "This island ahead is where the temples are, and where the richest live."

"Richest?"

"Those with the most money."

"Money. You mentioned that before, at the Council meeting. What does that mean?"

A chuckle escaped his lips. "It's easy to forget that most of the folks in our village have never learned about this. Money are little pieces of metal that people use to barter with."

"Pieces of metal? So if I find some pieces of metal on the beach, I can trade it for something?"

"Well, no, these pieces have writing and pictures carved into them."

Kirima frowned over at Phillip. "I don't understand," he said. "Why don't they just trade one thing for another?"

"Well, trading money makes it easier."

"Sounds harder to me," Phillip said.

"Me too," Kirima said.

"I'll try to explain it later," Gabriel said. "Just let me do the talking if we buy anything."

The boat was approaching a long wooden platform, just like the one at the Company outpost, except this one was much larger, and there were many more like it jutting out from the island. Most of the available space was filled with other boats, both large and small, though here she saw no sign of the massive ships like the one that had passed them. Was that the only one, or was there another place where ones like that gathered?

They were not met by guards like they were when they went to the

Company outpost, but she spotted them quickly. These guards carried the same sticks that the Company men had, but they wore different uniforms, these a mixture of red and gold with traces of black, the material seeming thinner. As she watched, they moved about the space, their eyes watching with unbreaking sharpness.

She watched as Gabriel stepped onto the platform and made his way toward a man flanked by a pair of guards, a man who seemed to project authority. Gabriel said some words, then took something from his pocket and handed it to the man. The man nodded, then motioned to a pair of boys who were standing off to the side, boys in loose, dirty clothing instead of the pristine uniforms the guards wore. The boys jumped at the motion, running over and tying the boat's mooring line to a wooden post. One of the boys removed a small white stick and made a marking on the post before running off to the next task.

"What just happened?" she asked as Gabriel helped her onto the platform.

"Was that money?" Phillip asked.

"No more questions about money," Gabriel said. "Speak as little as possible. There are strange customs in Eilenan cities about what to say and what not to say."

Kirima frowned, but said, "As you say. We'll be quiet."

Gabriel motioned with his head. "Come on."

They reached the end of the platform, and Kirima realized that she was looking at more people than she had ever seen at one time in her life. They seemed to be in constant movement, like ants after their mound had been disturbed, their voices filling the air with a dull roar like the buzzing of a beehive. She watched them pass as Gabriel consulted a piece of paper he held in his hand. She reminded herself of Gabriel's words, the thought stopping her from asking what he was doing.

"We're heading through this market," he said, folding the paper and putting it away. "Stay close, it's very easy to get lost in these crowds."

Gabriel seemed to plunge right into the crowd, not worrying at all about who he ran into or shoved aside. Neither did anyone else seem to worry about it. Kirima felt herself battered around, almost like being in a boat when a gale blows in and the waves knock it every which way. As she passed, she caught all manner of scents, from flowery extracts to sweat to that of salt and fish, the scent that she knew so well from back home.

They emerged on the other side and into a wide, flat area. To either side and the far end, she could see buildings rising high above them, but in between was more people, filtering through wooden stands, all filled with different types of things for trade. Closest to where the ships were, she could see different kinds of fish, some familiar, but many more different, all kinds of shapes and sizes and colors. She saw crabs and what looked like crabs with larger claws and longer bodies, turtles, urchins, squid, even a dolphin that was being carved up right there. All being traded not for other goods but for those pieces of metal that Gabriel had spoken of.

They moved deeper in, and she began to see other things. Skinned rabbits and birds and different cuts of meat, both dark and light, some pieces so large that she couldn't begin to imagine what kind of creature they had come from. Piles of what looked like dust in many different colors, the display bringing on an array of fragrances so strong that she had to fight the urge to sneeze. Tiny trinkets that the vendors tried to pass of as holy or magical. Fruits and vegetables of all colors, in shapes unlike anything she had ever seen. Drinks that gave off scents both bitter and sweet, some hot and some cold.

What also caught her off guard was just how warm the weather was. The air had certainly grown warmer as they had moved further south, until they had reached a point where they had all shed their parkas in favor of the thinner undershirts all three wore. Now, though, amongst all those people, it was nearly suffocating, as if the very air and any semblance of a breeze was sucked completely out. A heat not like the kind that radiated from a fire, but like that which rose from a pot of boiling water, the kind that seemed to cling to the skin and draw the sweat out. Kirima found herself pulling her hair up, tying her braid into a bun as best she could, but it was little help; she could still feel the sweat dripping down her neck, soaking her shirt.

"Excuse me, young lady."

Even with all those around her, the voice seemed to be directed right at her. She turned and looked and found a man standing in one of the stalls, beckoning her over. She pointed at herself, and he nodded, his motioning continuing as she found herself drawn in his direction.

"Do you have the time?"

"The what?"

"What time is it? The time of day."

Kirima glanced up at the sun, partially hidden behind a few thick clouds that threatened rain, spaces of blue sky between. "Around midday, I'd say. Perhaps a bit before."

"But you don't know the exact time?"

"Exact what?"

The man held up a small device made of metal and glass, a rhythmic sound coming from it. "Seems to me you need one of these."

Kirima examined it for a moment, reaching out her hand. "What's that?"

He pulled it back, just beyond her reach. "Why only the finest watch this side of Adhan."

"But what does it do?"

"Why, it tells time. Have you never seen a watch before?"

She shook her head. "A watch? What does it watch?"

"It doesn't watch anything. It just tells you the time."

"Why would I need to tell time?"

The man paused, his mouth hanging slightly open. "To tell when you need to be somewhere, to know how long something takes, to know how much light is in the day. A thousand reasons."

"Well can't the sun tell you that?" she asked. "That's how I always tell."

He gestured, pointing at her before drawing his hand back. "Of course, but staring at the sun is not nearly as accurate as this watch. Crafted by the most skilled watchmaker in the entire city. He has made pieces like this for the most elite of the elite in this country. Members of the Assembly, high ranking bureaucrats, the richest merchants, famous actors, and more, and none have ever returned unsatisfied. And you can have this at only a fraction of the cost that they paid for it."

Kirima felt a hand on her arm, pulling her gently away. "Sorry, she's not interested," Gabriel said.

The man's voice followed them, though it seemed almost like a spell had been broken, his voice now lost in the sea of people of around her. "What a strange object," she said.

"You have to be careful," Gabriel said. "Enchanting is supposed to be illegal for selling, but the city guard can't see everything."

She thought back to the stories her father had told her, of the powers the simuq had in the old days, the way they could use the songs to draw in the fish to fill the nets. Was that the same thing? "Was he enchanting?"

"It certainly seemed like it," Gabriel said, glancing over his shoulder.

"Must have to for something so useless," Phillip said.

Kirima followed Gabriel's gaze, but she could no longer see the stand, as if it had vanished into thin air. "I didn't know something like that was possible, certainly not on a person."

"It's more than possible, and very much dangerous. The laws that bind our own people always prevented it from being used that way. Some in other places don't follow such laws."

"A watch," she said. "What a strange trinket."

"You'll see lots of things like that, the deeper you look. Like I said, things work differently here."

They reached the edge of the market, the outer boundary marked by a path of stones that veered off between two buildings. There was another stream of people here, but the smells of the market were replaced by something much worse. She saw what looked like elegantly carved carts pass by, drawn by massive beasts that walked on hooves not unlike the sheep back home, clopping loudly on the stones with each step, their long-snouted heads bobbing as they walked.

"Watch out, they don't stop," Gabriel said.

They waited until there was a gap in the traffic, then made their way across in quick steps. The ground felt weird beneath her boots, the unevenness and hard surface of the stones seeming to reverberate right through her bones. Her eyes wandered, up to the sides of the buildings, built from wood and stone and windows of glass, clearer and shinier than any back hope. Metal pipes ran along the sides and even across the street over their heads, some frosted like a window on a winter's morn and some letting off steam like a boiling pot.

They turned the corner, and there was another wide-open space, this one filled with trees and grass instead of the wooden stands like the market had. In the middle of the trees rose a tall building, gilded walls holding up a curved, pointed roof just like the shrine that sat at the end of the harbor. Canals had been dug through the land, clear blue water passing over white sand leading right to the shrine.

"This will be the best place to start," Gabriel said. "The scholars here may be able to tell us something."

"Do you think they'll know what to do?" Phillip asked. "I mean, surely they will, right?"

"You know how our own people have reacted," Kirima said. "You shouldn't be surprised if they do not."

"They can at least point us in the right direction for who can get us help," Gabriel said. "Hopefully."

As they drew closer, she could see the carvings in relief on the side of the temple. It was not unlike the ones on the shrine at the end of their harbor, except here there was so much more. She saw a school of fish swimming around the base of the roof. She saw a massive whale so large it stretched over a corner, across two different walls. She saw an ocean floor with crabs and seaweed and many other creatures she didn't recognize.

"How long do you think it took them to build this?" she asked.

"Years," Gabriel said. "Maybe decades. They go to whatever lengths they need to build these monuments."

They walked a path that was made of thousands of tiny rocks, each step bringing about a crunching sound. It led them across the grass and to a short series of stone steps at the base of the temple. The ascended it, reaching a pair of massive wooden doors, a set identical to the one that sat on each of the temple's four walls, all propped open to allow the sea breeze to waft through the massive space to create a pleasant cross breeze. In the center of the temple stood a wide fountain, fed by the canals they had seen outside. The pool it created was deep, deep enough that when Kirima ventured a look into the depths, she only saw a darkness that engulfed the bottom and whatever may lurk below.

The temple seemed empty at first glance, and her eyes wandered, drifting more toward the walls and the paintings that covered them. It was much like the exterior, except instead of carvings in stone, it was painted in vibrant, life-like colors on the wall, as if she were standing at the bottom of the sea right then.

"Welcome, travelers." The voice was sudden, unexpected, drawing her eyes from the paintings to a lone woman now standing before the pool in the center, clad in clothing not much different from her own, though much cleaner and more neatly sewn, as if done by a master seamstress. "I hope this place finds you well."

"Well as can be," Gabriel said. "May your walls stand strong."

"And your heart as well." She bowed deeply. "We find few followers in these parts."

"I fear they follow more than I do." He motioned to her and Phillip. "But we come seeking answers."

"I promise no answers, but I will try my best."

"Which is all we can ask," Gabriel said. "We come seeking help against the Imakut."

"Help against the Imakut?" The woman's eyebrows seemed to raise, dark brown to match the short hair on her head, the woman's skin even more tanned than Kirima's own. "What help could I provide in the favor of those who provide for us?"

"We fear our favor has run out," Kirima said. Gabriel shot her a look, but she continued. "We put out our sacrifices, yet our people vanish at their hands."

A frown crossed the woman's face. "The Imakut? They provide, and we give back. There must be a Balance, as there is in all things. Is there not a Balance in what you give and what you take?"

"The Company built an outpost many years ago and began whaling operations near our village," Gabriel said. "It was only recently that our sacrifice to the Balance was not accepted, and with it, our people began to be taken."

"And you are certain that it is from the Imakut and not from an accident, or perhaps another creature? Perhaps a bear, a shark, crocodile, maybe even a mountain cat?"

Out of those things, Kirima had only heard of bears, but she said nothing. What strange creatures did they have in these parts?

"We found footprints by the spots where they vanished," Gabriel said. "They were taken from land, and the footprints lead into the sea. They were similar to human footprints, but not quite the same."

At some point, another woman had appeared without them noticing, this one slightly darker of skin, her head shaven, her body thin as a reed. "Another instance," she said. Her voice commanded attention, seeming to fill the massive space within the temple. "You may leave us, Kalle, I will take it from here."

Kalle gave a deep bow, and walked away, her footsteps slapping against the hard floor. The woman waited until she vanished through a partially hidden door on the far side, and then turned back to them. She eyed them for a moment. "Northerners, of course. What village?"

"Aliit," Gabriel said.

"Aliit," the woman said. "I cannot say I am familiar with it, but there are many such villages in our islands. Tell me your names."

"I am Gabriel, this is Kirima and Phillip."

"Phillip and Gabriel," she said, her eyes passing between them. "It is odd to see believers take Eilenan names."

"Some came to our village long ago," Gabriel said. "Before we were even part of Eilena. Our cultures became one long before it was necessary."

"I see. Your accent is different as well. It is of no matter, though. You came here for help. I am High Priestess Catriona, Speaker for the Imakut."

"Well met, High Priestess," Gabriel said with a short bow. "You seemed to have overheard the nature of our troubles."

She nodded. "I did. You are not the first to experience something like this and come seeking our aide."

"Does that mean you know how to help us?" Kirima asked.

The woman's bright eyes turned on her, considering her for a moment. "Every town in the north islands seems to have its own way. Some would consider speaking out of turn to be a transgression. I take it that is not your way?"

"I brought them here to speak," Gabriel said. "I will not silence them."

"As you will." The woman straightened up a bit. "You all know the ways, that providing the Balance has allowed us to exist by the will of the Imakut. If the Balance is upset, then retribution is exacted."

"We know," Gabriel said. "We have faithfully maintained the Balance for as long as anyone can remember. It has only been since the Company moved in that we started having problems."

The woman's face seemed to darken. "I see."

"You mentioned this has happened before?" Kirima said.

"Yes, you are not the first to begin seeing problems when the Company moved in, especially in recent years."

"What did the others do?"

She was silent for a moment. "They tried what they tried. We have no record of success or failure."

"So you just didn't hear from any of them?" Phillip asked.

"Correct."

"What did they try?" Gabriel asked.

"Adding to the Balance, both with livestock and humans. Entreating the Company. Fighting back."

"And you heard from none of them," Kirima said.

"Which means they all failed," Phillip said.

"Now now, you don't know that for certain," Gabriel said.

Kirima looked toward the woman, her face remaining still. "You think they did." She slowly nodded. "Then what can we do?"

"You can try the same as those who came before you, but without hearing from them, there is not much you can hope to improve on."

"So that doesn't help us at all," Phillip said.

"I am sorry if you came hoping for definitive answers. The Imakut are as much a mystery to us here as they are to you. We go based on the information handed down to us from our forefathers, and we hope that the steps we take are enough to see us through this life."

"Perhaps there is something else you could help us with, then," Gabriel said.

"I can try," the woman said. "But I offer no guarantees."

"We think that the Company not contributing to the Balance is the reason for the Imakut's attacks, but they have refused to contribute toward the balance. Perhaps you know someone there?"

"I fear speaking to the Company would do you no good. They keep their offices under strict control and defer to any decisions their local governors make unless proof of corruption is brought forth to their board. Even if you are successful in that, it will only serve in a new governor being appointed, likely one who will still ignore your requests."

"What about the Assembly?" Gabriel asked.

"I can point you toward the representative for the northern district, but I'm afraid getting direct access will be a significant challenge. Especially without proof."

"We have proof," Kirima said. She turned to Gabriel. "The arm?"

"Yes," Gabriel said, as if he had forgotten it. He reached into the satchel he carried, pulling out the long object wrapped in oilcloth. As he unwrapped it, the stench of rotten fish filled the air. Kirima wrinkled her nose, and Phillip actually turned away, while Gabriel only shifted his face as he fought to avoid breathing it in.

The priestess looked over the now rotting flesh, the scales, the claws. Whether she was surprised or disgusted or even curious, she gave no indication in her face. Finally, she looked back up at them. "Put that away, the flies will circle quickly in this heat. We must get you in front of someone quickly."

Gabriel carefully rewrapped the arm as the priestess snapped her fingers, and another priestess appeared as if from nowhere, handing her a sheet of paper that was folded in two. "This letter will at least get you into the office of your Assembler. From there, it is mere luck as to whether you can gain an audience, but that thing might help you. Bria here will guide you to the trolley and give you directions."

"With any luck, it will," Gabriel said. He motioned with his head, and turned, Phillip and Kirima falling into line as he followed the priestess.

"If you succeed, please let us know." They turned to look back at Catriona. "You are not the first, and it seems you will certainly not be the last."

"But can we be the first to succeed?" Kirima asked quietly.

"For the sake of our people, we can only hope," Gabriel said.

8

The Assembler's office sat on a different island, part of a group of massive towers that rose around a domed building that seemed to shine like a diamond in the sun.

The priestess had led them to a cart, one lined with padded seats and windows facing all directions. A man sat at a control panel in the front, sitting by a motor not unlike the one in the boat. Kirima found herself jumping when it started, the wheels rumbling over the metal rails that lined the street, and as she grew used to the movement, found herself watching as everything passed by, her mouth agape as the city zipped past them. The cart passed up a slope to cross one of the massive bridges, and came down the other end, carrying them to the next island and depositing them out when it reached the end of the railing.

Every part of this new island seemed completely different from the last one. The buildings were taller, the streets cleaner, and the crowds, though still as thick, were filled with people in what looked like fine clothing, colorful coats, high boots, elaborate hats, and gold tipped canes. Kirima found herself staring and found the people staring back at the three of them just as much. She had never felt as out of place as she did while walking those stone streets.

The building that held the office seemed as if it had been carved right from a mountain, impossibly high and covered in windows, a wide painting spanning the space over the entrance. It was of a mountainous island, covered in pine trees and surrounded by water with chunks of ice floating in it. It was a vision that seemed so close to home she could almost feel the cold, salty breeze coming off the water.

The inside of the building was cool, cooler than it should have been with the way the sun beat down outside. Lights hung from the ceiling, lanterns that seemed to be lit without a flame. Metal pipes ran along the sides, and she noticed an opening where wind seemed to be coming from, the source of the cool air. People moved to and fro within, all of them seeming to be in a hurry, while a few others sat on cushioned benches, waiting with marked impatience.

Gabriel led them through to a wide desk, where multiple people sat. He picked out a young, handsome man, his dark hair styled upward to a point, the beginnings of a beard creating a shadow on his face, wearing a dark blue coat that closed at the front and a thin wrapping around his neck. He flashed a smile as they approached.

"How can I help you?"

"We're here to speak to our Assembler," Gabriel said.

"I'm afraid His Honor is booked solid for months. He is, of course, a very busy man. I would be more than willing to take a message that I will personally deliver to one of his aides."

Kirima stepped up beside Gabriel. "We've come a really long way to speak to him."

The smile did not falter as he turned his head slightly to face her, but she could see that the eyes did not hold the smile like the lips did. "I understand, I assure you. Anyone who His Honor represents would have to come a long way to reach Adhan. Unfortunately, as I mentioned, he is a very busy man."

"Isn't there anything we can do?" Gabriel asked. "Anyone we can speak to?"

The man pulled out a piece of paper and a pen, which he dipped into a well of ink. "As I mentioned, a message is the surest way to communicate with him. His people are very diligent in reviewing messages from constituents and acting on them."

Phillip caused her to jump when he slapped the top of the desk next to her. "That's not good enough. Our people are dying, and we came all this way to stop it. Delivering a message isn't good enough."

The sound had caused the facade on the man's face to drop just the slightest as he turned to Phillip. "I am sorry for your troubles, but there is nothing I can do for you. If you are going to let your emotions get the best of you, then I can forgo the message and have you escorted out."

"Show him the arm," Kirima said.

"I'm sorry, the what?" the man said as Gabriel once more unwrapped the severed arm and laid it out on the desk. The stench was not quite as bad, perhaps because of the cooler air, but it was certainly present. In this light, she could see the maggots that had formed, eating away at the skin, and she felt her own stomach turn.

The man gaped at it for a moment, his mouth moving as he stood from his chair, backing away from the arm. Finally, words emerged, coming out in stammered speech. "What is this? Why did you bring this?"

More eyes were turning toward them as the others behind the desk stopped their work, the commotion growing even louder as a hush fell over the space. Kirima fought to ignore the rest as she spoke. "This is the arm of the creatures that are attacking our village. We've come to ask the Assembler for help."

The man looked down at the arm and then back up at them. "You people are sick. Beyond sick. Bringing a severed arm into an official building? What kind of savages are you?"

It was only Gabriel grabbing onto him that prevented Phillip from going right over the desk and attacking the man. They struggled for a moment before two guards appeared, both of them grabbing Phillip and pulling him back with relative ease. Kirima could feel her heart beating as she watched, seeing Phillip struggling against the guards, seeing Gabriel try to calm things, seeing all eyes on them, both from those behind the desk and those in the lobby, many of them stopping to watch. The man they had been speaking to was standing and pointing now, his voice growing to be heard over the commotion.

"Have them escorted off the premises and call the authorities. If they continue to trespass, they can see how they like prison." He motioned toward the arm that still lay there. "And dispose of this…thing."

A commanding voice spoke from behind them. "That won't be necessary."

Phillip had stopped struggling, and Kirima followed his gaze to the woman who had appeared behind them. She was short, shorter even than Kirima, but composed herself in a way that made her seem much larger. Her light-colored hair was tied back in a tight braid, revealing the smooth skin of her face, tanned from the sun. She wore a red jacket and a long black skirt over heeled leather boots, and a golden pin in the shape of a fish over her heart.

The man at the desk cleared his throat and lowered his eyes. "Yes, of course, Madam Iona. The arm as well?"

Iona looked over at it, wrinkling her nose. "They seem to think it's important. Wrap it up and give it back to them. I recommended disposing of it soon, however."

The guards released Phillip, and he quickly stepped over to where Kirima stood. Iona motioned the guards away, then turned to the three of them. "Come with me, I will see if I can help you."

Her steps sounded loudly on the floor, so loudly that Kirima was shocked she had not heard the woman approach. She led them to a hallway behind the desk where the walls to either side were occupied with doors without handles, each with a series of numbers above it. Iona pressed a button, a bell sounded, and one of the doors slid open without her touching it, revealing a small room. She stepped into it, but the three of them hesitated, standing outside the doors, looking at it with suspicion.

"It's an elevator," she said.

"A what?" Kirima asked.

"It will take us to the higher levels."

"It is...is it magic?"

"It's science. Everything here is powered by the oil brought in from whales."

Kirima looked at the others, then back to the elevator. "Is it safe?"

"Perfectly."

She hesitated, licking her lips as she looked at every corner of the small space, then stepped onto the elevator. She felt it shift a little as she put her weight on it, but when she stepped back, she only bumped into Gabriel, who was not backing away. She swallowed the lump in her throat and continued forward, settling into the back corner.

Once they were all inside, Iona pushed a button from many that lined the wall, and the doors slid closed. The room shifted again, and Kirima reached out and grabbed a railing on the wall, holding it so tightly that her knuckles turned white.

All this time, Iona stood with her hands folded at her waist, watching them with an expressionless gaze that almost seemed curious. "It will be over soon," she said.

She turned out to be correct as the sound of the motor soon came to a stop, and the elevator slowing and coming to a jerking stop before the doors slid open once more. Phillip was the first out, and Kirima pushed past Gabriel to be next. Her heart was pounding, her breaths coming in heaves as she glanced back into the tiny room as the mayor followed after her, his face composed, but sweat clinging to his brow. Iona was the last out, walking past them as if nothing had happened.

"I apologize for putting you through that, but this building is far too tall to climb the stairs. Come, my office is this way."

The hallway that the elevator had opened onto was thickly carpeted, the walls covered with red paper decorated with golden designs. Iona led them to another hallway and through a door at the end into a large room. As soon as they entered, Kirima's eyes went not to the desk covered in neat stacks of papers or the shelves that lined the walls or even the paintings of northern islands and creatures. No, her eyes went to the windows that went from floor to ceiling to form the back two walls, giving her a clear view over the Assembly Hall and streets far below them. In using the elevator, they were suddenly far off the ground, as if they had just scaled a mountain, and her stomach immediately turned at the thought, even as her eyes were unable to look away.

"Kirima?" Phillip shaking her arm finally drew her back to the present with a deep gasp. "Are you alright?"

"Have you never climbed a crag back home, girl?" Iona asked. "This is no higher than the cliffs in the place I grew up."

"Much of our time is spent on the water, not on our lands," Gabriel said. "Our island is not so high."

"You are safe here," Iona said. "Even the summer cyclones cannot topple these buildings."

"Cyclones?" Kirima said.

"Anything can fall," Phillip said.

"Cyclones?" Kirima said again. "Like, storms?"

"We're at the end of the season," Iona said, taking a seat in her chair and gesturing toward those across the desk. "And this building is perfectly safe. Please, sit."

Gabriel was the first to take her offer. "Thank you for having us here. I did not expect such a reception. My father always told me that he had never been turned away on his visits to Adhan."

"Your father lived in different times, I'm afraid, times that we may never see again. Assembly members are accessible by those with the means, not by those who truly need their help."

"So what are you?" Kirima could feel her stomach settling a bit now that she was seated, the angle through the window now showing only the sky and the tops of the distant mountains. "And why help us?"

"My name is Iona, and I am an aide to Assembler Blair. I stepped in when I saw you because not all of us are so cutthroat that we forget the reasons we came to Adhan in the first place. I witnessed three people seeking help, clearly out of their element, and I stepped in to help."

"We appreciate your help," Gabriel said.

"You can thank me once we see if I can do anything. So tell me, why did you come seeking an audience? And why is there a decaying arm in your possession?"

"A delicate matter, really…" Gabriel began.

"Not a human arm, I presume?"

"No, of course not," Gabriel said.

"It's from the Imakut," Kirima said. She was getting too tired of dancing around the subject, and this did not seem like a woman who liked to waste time. "We think, no, we know that they've been taking our people, and we think that it's because the Company has upset the Balance."

She wasn't sure how she expected Iona to react. Perhaps bemusement, laughter, any degree of skepticism. After all, she had always heard how the Eilenans looked down at their religion, had seen it firsthand from those in their own village. But the woman gave none of those, only folded her hands in front of her, resting her index fingers on her chin.

"The Imakut," she finally said.

Kirima nodded. "We've had half a dozen disappearances, maybe more since we left."

"I'm sorry, but this may be beyond my capabilities. Have you spoken with the temple? Surely this is something they can better help with."

"They sent us here." Kirima felt her stomach drop out, the words barely coming past her lips. "We asked, but the people there had no definitive answers for our problems."

"Strange," Iona said.

"They also said it was not the first time something like this had been brought to them," Phillip said. "Yet they still had no solution."

"I see. I'm afraid I'm not sure what the priestesses thought we could do."

"Well, like I said, we think the Company upset the balance," Kirima said. "We spoke to their governor at the outpost, thinking he might be willing to contribute, but he dismissed us completely."

Iona stood, turning toward the windows, her hands clasped behind her back. "If it's the Company you're dealing with, you may be out of luck getting them to budge on any such matter."

It was Phillip who spoke, his voice quiet. "Even from our representative?"

Iona nodded slowly, then gestured out the window. "This island is the smallest of the three on Adhan, and it has held the seat of the Eilenan government since the decision was made to move the capital to this place. King Calum III built himself a new palace on this island, and it was from that palace's base that the Assembly Hall was later built after the People's Pledge was ratified and the new government was formed. All these buildings you see around us were built up and added to over the years, each serving as a place for each district's Assembler to hold their office and their staff. Of course, as things grew more complex and more layers were added, each one grew as well. Since the original charter, only one building on this island has not been built for the government."

Kirima followed her gesture to a building that stood out over all the others, taller, wider, sleeker, shining even brighter than the Assembly Hall that now stood in its shadow.

"That building is where the Mhara Electric Company makes its headquarters."

They all stared out the window in silence, looking at the massive building, a building that seemed like it shouldn't be able to exist at all. Except it did, no matter what Kirima's mind tried to tell her.

"The Company was formed not terribly long ago when you consider the history of our country. But when they showed what was possible with the use of whale oil, they sparked a hunger that even they with their reach can scarcely match. All this, everything around us, is made possible by their works, and through it, the people have demanded more. So their operations continue to expand, covering nearly the entire northern district, and already they are looking for ways to extend to the waters beyond our borders."

"I'm not sure if you have a concept of addiction in your village, but it's very much prevalent in the cities, in the dens where people go to smoke their cares away or the bars where they go to drown themselves in drink, anything to take them from this life for a short time. The Company provides a drug of another kind, one that is even more potent, its use even more widespread. It is the drug of comfort, of convenience, and once someone experiences it, it's hard to convince them that they must sacrifice it for any reason."

"But we're not asking for people to sacrifice their comfort, or even for the Company to stop hunting the whales," Gabriel said.

"I'd like to see them stop," Kirima said.

Phillip shot her a wide grin while Gabriel only ignored her. "All we ask of them is to help with the Balance."

"To you, it is a simple ask," Iona said. "Something given for something taken. Assembler Blair grew up in the northern islands, not in the same environment you did, but in enough of a proximity that he understands your culture. But the Company does not. Should this issue be broached, the Company would say that such a requirement would limit their ability to hunt, to provide that which the public wants, that sacrifices of another kind may be required. It is an argument they have used before, and when this quality of life is threatened, people jump in to protect it. No matter what Assembler Blair says or how he votes, he cannot win."

Kirima just watched her for a moment. She wasn't sure she had ever felt so helpless. "Then what can we do?"

There was a silence in the room. Finally, Gabriel spoke. "Can you offer us help in fighting them?"

"From the military, no. But I can point you in the direction of some people who might be willing to fight with you. For the right price, of course."

Gabriel looked at the other two, seated to either side. "It seems that's our   only   remaining   option."

9

The place Iona had pointed them to was not far from the market they had entered at, nestled within a small alley between a pair of buildings. Here, everything seemed closed in, the street in shadow both from the buildings and from the pipes and wires that ran so close to each other that they almost formed a roof of their own. There were tables set up along the walls, about half occupied, the sounds of loud talking filling the air as people dressed in identical outfits brought out food and drinks.
"Which one do you think it is?" Phillip asked as they walked between the tables, picking their way over spilled drinks, broken glass, and even a man lying on his side, snoring loudly.
"She said we'd know," Gabriel said.
There was a loud smashing sound, a glass shattering to pieces as it struck a brick wall, followed by some shouting. "I think that might be it," Kirima said.
The building that the sound had come from, a tavern Iona had called it, had a short awning built of wood, extending over the small tables that lined the front. There was a door that was propped open and a large window that had a jagged hole in it. Through the gap, she could see a pair of men in the midst of a fistfight while others watched from the wings through a haze of smoke, cheering and shouting and drinking. Every single person in the room looked like they were ready to join the fight right then and there.
"This is definitely the place," she said.
"Come on, let's see if we can find someone," Gabriel said. "Split up once we're inside and get someone who we can talk to."
The notion was easier said than done. The sound of the cheering grew to a near deafening roar as soon as they stepped inside, so loud she wasn't even sure she could hear her own thoughts. The air was filled with an oppressive heat, any breeze blocked by the massive, sweating bodies around her, the

stench of smoke and sweat seeming to make it impossible to breathe. She hardly made it a few steps before fighting off a coughing fit, her eyes watering and her throat burning as her body seemed to fight against going inside.

Phillip and Gabriel had already vanished by the time she recovered enough to move any further. It felt like she was inside the chimney they used to smoke fish, as if her insides were drying out just like the filets. She fought it off, wetting her mouth and swallowing as she moved deeper into the room.

The tavern went much deeper than it had seemed from the outside. There was a point where she squeezed past the crowd and found herself no longer pressed in, still in a crowd, but able to move and breathe a bit better. The room had the same electric lights, but they seemed to do little good, most of the light streaming in through the broken window up front, sunrays visible through the smoky air. Against one wall, she could see tables and chairs and benches, and against the other a long counter with shelves behind it filled with all manner of bottles and glasses.

Here, she spotted Gabriel, speaking to someone on the far end of the room. She certainly couldn't hear what he was saying, not from that distance with the shouts from the fight, but it at least told her she wasn't alone. She turned toward those on the side closest to her, by the long counter, and spoke to the first person she saw.

"Hello," she said. "I was hoping to…"

"Piss off," the man said, gesturing with his head.

Kirima physically recoiled, her mouth agape, but the man didn't even look at her. So she moved on. Three more people gave similar responses, though more did not even give her a chance to say what she wanted to say.

She continued until she reached the end of the counter, where a tall, muscled man sat, an empty plate and half-drunk glass on the counter before him.

"Hello," she said. "I was hoping to speak to you about some work."

At first he didn't acknowledge her. She thought perhaps he hadn't heard her, and prepared to repeat herself, but the man interrupted her in a rumbling voice. "What kind of work?"

Kirima felt her heart flutter. Here was someone who might actually be interested. She swallowed the lump in her throat, trying not to stutter as she spoke. "We're in need of someone to help us fight. You are a fighter, aren't you?"

"I am," he said. "And I never turn down a good fight."

The fluttering grew in her chest. "That's great. Let me find my friends and we can make a deal."

"Wait." She felt a strong hand on her wrist, the man using his other hand to finish his beer. "Tell me about the job now."

"Can we at least go somewhere quieter?" she said.

The man grunted. "Tell me here. Don't want to leave unless I know it's worth my while. Where is this? Who will I be fighting? What's the pay?"

"It's in Aliit…"

"Aliit? Never heard of it."

"It's up north."

Another grunt. "Forget it."

The fluttering in her heart dropped away, as if falling through a hole in her gut. "But…why?"

"I don't want anything to have to do with whatever's up there. It's a bear, isn't it? One of them big white ones."

"No, it's…"

A voice came from the other side of her, the words seeming to drag across the man's tongue as he spoke. "Spoken like a true coward."

The man's fist slammed down onto the counter, and it was as if all the noise around her ceased, even as the fight continued at the front of the tavern. "What did you say?"

The one on her other side laughed and drank from his own glass. "You heard me."

The man was up in a flash, and Kirima gave a yelp as she was shoved backwards. Someone caught her, keeping her from falling, but her eyes remained on the two men who had been speaking. The one she had been talking to was larger, towering over the other now that he stood at his full height, his breadth at least twice that of the other. For his part, the man who had been to her right hadn't even stood, or even looked at the other for that matter.

"Care to say it again?" the larger man growled.

The seated man sucked on what looked like a tube with fire at the end and blew it toward the larger man's face. "You heard me."

The large man's fist moved so quick that she almost didn't see it. The other man's head snapped to the side, and he held it there, perhaps considering his options or perhaps simply recovering from the blow. She heard a gasp and realized that it had come from her own lips, audible in the sudden quiet of the tavern. The entire crowd seemed to be holding their breath, waiting for the next move. The large man drew his fist back, but he was interrupted when the other smashed a glass across his face.

A voice called out, "Fight!" and all attention turned toward the two. Kirima felt herself pushed aside, shoved roughly as people fled from the first fight, which seemed to have wound down, and crowded in to watch this one. Beneath the cheering, she heard another glass break, but any sense of what was going on was lost as she found herself staring at sweat-stained backs.

A hand gripped her arm and pulled her away from the crowd, and this time, she did look back, finding Gabriel with a concerned look on his face. "Are you alright?" he yelled above the noise.

"I'm fine," she said.

"Come on, let's get out of here."

It was much easier getting out than it had been getting in, the space in front emptied except for a man who lay there, blood leaking into a puddle from his nose and mouth. She paused to look. "Is he…"

Gabriel urged her onward. "Best not to ask."

They burst out into the fading day, the air that had seemed stifling before now almost pleasant after the stuffiness of the tavern. Kirima breathed in deeply, still catching whiffs of smoke, but relishing in the relatively clean air.

"Let's not do that again," Phillip said from behind her, leaning on a table.

"Neither of you found anyone, did you?" Gabriel said.

"I thought that one was going to join," Kirima said. "Before the fight broke out."

"Maybe when they're done?" Phillip said.

She shook her head. "He refused. The other called him a coward, that was what started it."

There were more sounds of breaking glass, and a series of cries went up from within, drawing their attention. "Wonder who's winning," Phillip said.

"Not sure it's worth it to find out." Gabriel shook his head. "Should have known this wouldn't go well."

"There's no way you could have known," Kirima said. "Iona seemed certain we could find help here."

"We don't even know if the money is enough."

"Maybe we can use it to buy weapons," Phillip said. "Like those sticks the guards at the Company carry."

"Guns," Gabriel said. "They're called guns."

"Guns," Kirima said. "I like firesticks better."

Gabriel grunted. "Call them what you want. They don't do us much good if no one knows how to use them."

"So what, we just go home emptyhanded?" Phillip said.

"We can't do that," Kirima said. "We need to be able to protect the village."

"I'm not sure," Gabriel said quietly.

"Maybe we can go back to the temple, talk to the priestess again?" Phillip said.

"I don't know…"

Gabriel was cut off as a man stumbled out the door, coming out with enough momentum that he knocked over several tables and chairs with a clatter. He managed to keep his feet, though very unsteadily, swaying on uneasy legs before finally coming to a standing position, turning around as he did. As he did, she caught a look at his face, seeing it for the first time in the light, but unmistakable as the man who had instigated the fight. His nose was crooked, and blood ran from his bottom lip down a sharp chin.

Short, wispy hair clung to his scalp, and a leather vest, loose shirt, and ragged pants hung from his wiry body. What most struck her, however, was his skin, so pale that it seemed like freshly fallen snow.

The man ran the back of his hand across his chin, smearing the blood across his skin. He looked down at the back of his hand, then looked back toward the tavern as he shouted. "You're going to have to hit harder than that."

There was no response but the constant buzz that came from within. Kirima glanced toward the door, expecting the large man to step out, but it was a different man who emerged, tall and dressed in clean, well-crafted clothing, long hair tied back in a bun to reveal a face that seemed ageless. The other tried to put his hand down on a table and mostly missed, stumbling once more.

"You sure have a way of making friends, don't you?"

The first one regained his feet, steadying himself with a hand on the table, managing to motion toward the door with his other hand. "He started it."

"Did he?" The second had removed a pouch and a piece of paper, and he was now working the paper into a tube between fingers stained a shade of black. He nodded toward Kirima. "You were there, weren't you?"

"I…he called the man a coward," Kirima said.

The man nodded. "If you didn't start it, you certainly escalated."

"Whatever." Kirima could hear the slur in the man's voice. "Let's just find the Giant and get out of here."

"Wait," Kirima said, stepping forward.

Neither of them so much as looked at her, the second man still working at the paper in his hands, the first still turned away from them, hand shading his eyes as he seemed to squint toward the sun. Finally, it was the second who spoke. "Well?"

"Are you, you know, soldiers?"

"Depends on who you are." He placed one end of the paper tube in his mouth and conjured a flame over his open palm. He used it to light the other end, blowing smoke as he closed his palm around the flame. "And what you're looking for."

Kirima felt herself gasp. "You're an enchanter."

"Something like that. Get on with it. My friend here will wander if he gets bored."

"Piss off," the man said over his shoulder.

"We're from a town called Aliit," Kirima said. "We came here looking for help."

"You certainly weren't from around here. Didn't peg you as coming from that far away."

"You've heard of Aliit?" Gabriel asked.

"One of my trainees was sent there when I was with the Company. I assumed it was far away because they only sent the worst performers there.”

“I know the place,” the first man said, his voice turning into something of a mumble. He turned back to them. “Can’t say I recognize your faces, but you’re certainly northern. It’s been decades since I was last there, but you never forget the look. Fish out of water.”

“What’s wrong with him? Do we need to get him to a healer?” Kirima found herself thinking of when Toklo had suffered a burst vessel in his head, the way he had lost his balance and stammered a bunch of words before falling.

“Siluk?” The man shrugged as he puffed on the paper tube, the smoke giving off a strange, almost sweet smell. “He’s just had a bit too much to drink.”

“Like water?” Phillip asked.

“Firewater.” Siluk began to cackle as if it was the funniest thing in the world.

“Do you not have spirits where you live?”

Kirima frowned. “Like spirits of our ancestors?”

The man stared at her for a moment, then shook his head. “Never mind. My name is Griogair, but you may call me Grier. If you have business to discuss, then by all means.”

“Business,” Siluk said. He was leaning on the table now, almost lying across it. “You don’t know business, Grier.”

Grier ignored him. “What do you want to hire us for? Pirates? Bandits? Wildlife?”

Kirima looked over at Gabriel, who nodded. “Are you familiar with the Imakut?”

“Can’t say I am,” Grier said.

“You what?” Siluk said, raising his head. “How can you not know of the Imakut?”

“I didn’t grow up in the north.”

“There’s a temple back there.” He waved his hand blindly over his head. “Somewhere. Big island, I think. Trolley could take you there.”

“We’re not going to the temple,” Grier said.

Phillip leaned in close to her and Gabriel. “Is this someone we actually think can help us? He can’t even seem to walk straight.”

“This will wear off,” Gabriel said. “But it certainly doesn’t inspire confidence.”

“He seemed capable in a fight,” Kirima said. “And his friend is an enchanter. And didn’t they say something about a giant?”

“I haven’t seen a giant since we’ve been here,” Phillip said.

“Doesn’t mean one doesn’t exist.”

“Feel like it would be hard to miss.”

"You seem uncertain," Grier said. "If you would rather not hire us, it is not a problem. But I would like to get my friend here somewhere he can rest."

Kirima turned toward him. "Wait, no, we do. Or at least I think we do. How much?"

"Thirty geads apiece," Grier said. "Plus transportation both ways and accommodations once we're there."

"Geads? Is that money?" Phillip asked.

"It is," Gabriel said.

"Do we have enough?" Kirima asked.

"Barely." She noticed that Gabriel was palming the bag that hung from his belt. "Almost all the money we have."

"Is it worth it?" Phillip asked.

"It will be if we win," Kirima said.

"Which you have no way to know," Phillip said.

"But I don't think we're going to find any better options than former Company men."

"My ears are burning," Grier called out. "Do we have a deal?"

"You have a deal," Kirima said before either of the boys could say anything.

"You, him, and that giant of yours." She paused. "Is that all there is?"

Grier flipped away the paper tube, burned down to a tiny size. She could smell the acrid smoke that had poured from it, lingering in the air around them, so potent she could almost taste it herself. "That's all. I trust you have a boat? Because we don't."

"We do," Kirima said. "By the market."

"We'll be there," he said. "Thirty minutes or so."

She looked over at the boys, neither of them seeming to understand either. "We'll see you then," she said, the words coming out slowly, emerging in spurts.

He nodded, stepping over to Siluk and taking him by the arm. "Come on, we've got a job to do."

They all waited until the men were out of earshot before any of them spoke, and it was Phillip who did so. "I think we made a mistake. I don't think these men can be trusted."

"Do you have a better solution?" Kirima asked.

"There has to be something better," he said.

"I'm afraid Kirima is right," Gabriel said. "We've already been gone for too long from the village. I almost fear we may return to nothing but burnt remains. We have to hope that they are the answer to our prayers."

"And if they aren't?" Phillip asked.

Gabriel sighed. "Let's not think about that right now."

"That one that could barely stand, what was wrong with him?" Kirima said. "I mean, we saw him fight inside, but it didn't look like he could out here."

"He's been drinking," Gabriel said.

"That's what the other guy said," Phillip said.

"Grier," Kirima said.

"Whatever. What does that mean?"

"It's alcohol," Gabriel said. "It changes a person's mind until it wears off. There's a reason we don't have any in the village."

"Are you certain?" Phillip asked.

"Certain," Gabriel said. "I've seen it plenty in other places."

"I hope you're right."

"Let's get back to the boat," Gabriel said, stepping toward the end of the alley. "Don't want them to be waiting for us."

He led them through the market, stopping to buy some supplies at a few booths. They were still packing things away in the boat when the trio arrived.

Siluk led the way, standing a bit straighter, but still with a sway to his walk. He wore a wide brimmed hat and what looked like circular stones over his eyes, jet black, no doubt dark enough to block out the light of the sun. Grier seemed no less amused than he had back in the alleyway, walking closely behind, as if ready to catch him should he fall. Behind them trailed a short woman, the size of a child, but clearly an adult in her features. She wore long pants and a hat similar to Siluk's, a long braid that dropped down her back and a scowl on her face.

Siluk's arms were held out to either side. "We're here! I hope this boat has enough alcohol for wherever we're going. Which is where, again?"

"Aliit," Grier said. "In the north." He stopped next to the boat, frowning down at it. "Which, is this boat powerful enough to get us there?"

"It got us here," Gabriel said.

"Even with the added weight?"

"Doesn't matter," Siluk said, tossing a sack onto the boat, then slapping Grier on the shoulder. "If the motor burns out, you can always whip us up a current to take us the rest of the way."

Kirima felt her eyes widen. "You can do that?"

Grier's eyes tittered about, air passing through pursed lips. "Probably," he said. "I'd rather not have to, though."

She looked away as he climbed onto the boat; the last thing she wanted to do was make him angry and cause them to go back on the deal. Her eyes turned on the small woman.

"Are you the Giant?"

"I am." Her voice was husky, harsh, matching the scowl on her face. "You got a problem?"

"You're short."

"And you have eyes." She shoved her own satchel into Kirima's gut, the weight and force surprising her, driving a gasp as whatever air she had in her lungs was driven from them. "I bet you impress all the boys with them."

"I…"

"A mouth too, a lovely one, I'm sure, if you ever find your way to shutting it."

Kirima did shut it, hard enough that her teeth clicked together painfully. She rubbed at her jaw as the Giant climbed over the side. From the end of the boat, Siluk was laughing, a hearty guffaw from the base of his gut. Grier had the slightest smirk, but she could see the laugh in his eyes.

"Our dear Effie," Siluk said as the laughter calmed. "So full of life and joy."

"Fuck off, Siluk," she said as she wedged herself between two of the barrels. "If you didn't drink away our savings, then we wouldn't have to drag ourselves to the frozen north."

"It's not quite frozen this time of year. You'll grow to love her, just as we have." Siluk turned to Kirima, nudging her with his elbow. He had managed to get a bottle from somewhere and took a drink from it. "When do we leave?"

"Is that everything?" Gabriel asked as he emerged from beneath the deck.

"Is there more that's needed?" Siluk said, motioning with his hand. "Go on. If we are all you were waiting for, then by all means. The sooner we get to this place, the sooner we can be back here and significantly richer."

Gabriel looked toward Grier, who only nodded. "He speaks the truth."

Kirima felt Gabriel's eyes turn briefly to her as he turned to the ship's controls. "I hope we are right about this."

"I suppose we'll find out quickly," she said.

10

For the first day or so on the water, the trio kept mostly to themselves. Siluk ran out of drink by the time the sun set that first evening and spent the rest of the night complaining about it, followed by the next day complaining about how miserable he was. Grier seemed somewhere between annoyed and amused, while Effie mostly ignored it, save for the occasional vulgar insult tossed in his direction.

On the second night, they made camp on a rocky beach, the boat pulled onto the sand, and a fire made to keep them warm. Dinner was from the last of the provisions brought from their home, not yet dipped into the strange southern food that Gabriel had picked up at the market, which Kirima was thankful for. The food smelled strange, and her insides seemed to turn at just the sight and aroma of it, with no telling how her stomach would react to actually eating it. She much preferred the dried salmon, seaweed, and cranberry preserves they had eaten since leaving Aliit.

After dinner, she returned to work on shaping a blade from a nice, sturdy stone she had found on their first night camping. She used a smaller rock, striking at it over and over again, honing it down to the shape she needed, singing one of the songs her father used to while working on his tools. She was working on one of the edges when a shadow moved between her and the fire. Her eyes traced up, the song lingering on her lips as she found Grier standing before her.

"What are you making there?" he asked.

She held up the stone, turning it over so that the right angles were caught by the light. "A knife," she said. "My old one was lost to the sea."

"A knife, eh?" He crouched down, tilting his head to get a better look. "Stone. No steel?"

"We use what we have available to us." Her eyes went to the knife at his side. "Your knife is steel?"

90

He pulled it out, holding it up, the side of the blade glinting in the light. "One of the better ones I've ever had." He held it out to her. "Take a look."

She took the knife in her hands, feeling the weight, or lack thereof. "It's light." She touched the edge. "Sharp."

"Why don't you hang onto that one," he said. "It'll last a lot longer than any stone knife."

"Are you sure?" she looked up at him. "I mean, don't you need it yourself?"

He shrugged. "I've got another two, and plenty of other means. You seem like you need it more than I do."

"Thank you," she said. "I don't know what to say."

"You don't have to say anything." He flicked at the skin right beneath his low lip with his thumb, his eyes gazing out over the moonlit water. "Was talking to Gabriel. He said you're responsible for that severed arm he's carrying around."

"I cut it off, yes, that was when I lost my knife. I did it to save Phillip's brother."

"Noble of you."

"Either of them would have done the same for me."

"You must be close."

"We are. Me and Phillip more so."

"Lovers?"

She felt her eyes widen and her cheeks flush. "Oh, no, not at all. Nothing like that."

He gave her a sly smile. "Nothing to be ashamed of girl." He let it linger for a moment, then allowed the smile to fade. "I'll let you off the hook. Tell me about these things we're going to be fighting."

"The Imakut," she said.

"Yes, that name was mentioned back in Adhan." He pulled out his pouch and a paper, and began to roll it in bitterweed, as he had told her on the first day. The scent from this close gave the name credence. "It still doesn't tell me what they are, what we're up against."

"We...don't really know," she said. "Other than the arm, no one has ever seen one. Before people began to be taken, there were many in our town who doubted they are even real."

"So, what?" He paused to lick the edge of the paper and roll it over. "They some kind of gods or something?"

"Something like that," she said. "Some call them gods. My father always say it was more nature, all plant and animal life in the seas around us." She watched as he conjured a flame to light the paper. "How do you do that?"

"Do what?"

"Make the fire just appear like that?"

The flame had vanished, but he brought it back with the flick of a finger. "This is the result of years of training."

"Just to make a small flame?"

A slight smile crossed his lips. "For more than this, of course, but this was the first step, and it was the hardest of them all."

She watched as he moved the flame over his fingers, as if in a trance. "So it's something you just learn?"

"Like any skill, some are inclined to more aptitude, but yes, anyone can learn it to some degree."

"Do you think you could teach me?"

"Someone your age, perhaps, but probably not. They started us young for a reason. Always thought your people had enchanters, though."

"We have a woman who claims to be, our simuq, but most say the power has long ago left our village."

"We'll see when we get there." He puffed out a large cloud of smoke, then used his hand to fan it away. "Back to this Imakut, though. What else can you tell me about them?"

Kirima thought for a moment, staring at the sand that gave way beneath her feet. "We saw footprints. That first night, and again when Phillip's father was taken." She lifted her foot from the sand and placed the tip of the knife into it, tracing out the features from her own print. "It's a bit like this. There's something coming out from the heel." She smudged the lines between each toe. "The toes are connected, almost like a flipper." She drew lines out from the tips of the toes. "And claw marks, like a bear print."

"How many, do you think there were from the prints?"

Kirima scrunched up her nose and mouth as she thought back to the prints in the sand, the ones she had seen at each vanishing. "I never learned to track on land. Two, perhaps? Maybe three."

"And you think more will come?"

"Gabriel certainly thinks so. There are other towns that have been attacked by them. But no one alive has ever seen one, no one knows how to fight one. And the Company has been no help."

The smile remained, but his face seemed to drop, sadness seeping in. "No, they wouldn't. The Company is not going to help unless it benefits them."

"You said back in Adhan that you worked for them at one point?"

"I did. We all did."

Siluk appeared suddenly, plopping down into the wet sand next to Grier. "I can't believe that you have no drink. The other young one over there, what's his name, Peter?"

"Phillip," Grier said.

"Phil, right. He didn't even know what alcohol was. Hadn't heard of wine or mead, nothing about whiskey or gin, vodka or rum, not even beer.

Incredible, isn't it? I don't know what kind of place we're going, but it sounds downright miserable."

Kirima frowned. "That's my home you're talking about. And didn't you say you were from the north?"

"I haven't been there in decades, and I can assure you, there was a good reason I left. Regardless, I'm sure you love your home. But it really does sound miserable to me."

"I'd watch my tongue," Grier said. "She's holding a knife."

"A knife, eh?" His eyes drifted down to the steel in her hand. "I've won a few knife fights in my day. Ah, but this." He suddenly reached over, snatching up the unfinished stone. "This brings back memories."

She felt her own frown drop as she watched him examine the blade. He ran his thumb over the edge. "Good craftsmanship here, girl. One of the better blades I've ever seen. Certainly better than anything I ever attempted to make."

"You think so?"

"Sure do."

Grier shook his head as he blew out more smoke. "He's not exactly a good judge of crafts himself."

She watched him, turning the blade over in gloved hands. In the fire light, the pale of his skin seemed to be as white as the crystal of her jarak. She almost didn't realize how intently she had been staring before she saw that he was looking back at her now. She averted her eyes, saying nothing.

"You want to ask about my skin, don't you?"

Kirima nodded. "I've never seen any person who looks like you, certainly not from the north."

He gave a chuckle, and she realized she was staring again. "You won't find many who look like me anywhere. "I've got a condition, makes my skin and hair like this. Makes it so I can't really be out in the sun. They used to call me a vampire back when I worked for the Company."

"Don't think she knows what that is," Grier said.

"Eh? Oh, right, guess not. Always forget how different the north is."

"It doesn't sound like you like the Company," she said. "Either of you."

"Few who work for them do, and if you come for a job, anyone around does their best to warn you away."

"But then why did you work there?"

"Money," Grier said.

Siluk was nodding, waving his hand around. "May not seem like it from where you're from, but for a lot of us, the Company is the best pay we can get. Especially if you want to live in a place like Adhan, if you want to start a family. Few people like doing it, but it's almost always the best choice."

She found herself glancing over to Phillip, who was sitting by the fire, watching them without trying to look like he was. She wondered if he was working up the courage to come over, or if he was just being distrustful. Maybe he was thinking about his uncle. Maybe his father. Maybe none of it at all.

"Some people in our village felt the same way," she said.

"Yes," Siluk said. "No matter where they go, they always draw some in. It's the promises. Promises of a better life, but people quickly find it's not much better."

"And they can't leave?" she asked.

"Not easily."

Kirima watched them for a moment, but neither seemed eager to continue speaking about the Company. "Are you an enchanter as well?" she asked Siluk.

"Only of firearms," he said. He suddenly pulled out what looked like a smaller version of the firesticks that the Company men had been carrying, spinning it around his finger. "You don't need magic when you can shoot someone from a hundred and fifty meters away."

"The distance gets longer every time you say it," Effie shouted from the other side of the camp.

Grier smirked as Siluk turned and shouted, "I can certainly hit you from here."

"And you'd be dead soon after," she said.

"I don't miss."

"You don't have to."

"What's with her?" Kirima asked. "She seems like she doesn't even want to be here."

"She probably doesn't," Grier said. "Effie has never been one for cold weather."

"Are any of us?" Siluk said, still waving the firestick around.

"You're from there," Grier said.

"All the more reason for me to hate it."

"Effie is different, though. She holds an intense hatred for it. I suppose the only reason she's here is that we need the money."

"Why do you call her the Giant? Is it a joke?"

Siluk grinned while Grier only rolled his eyes. "Of sorts," Siluk said. "As I'm sure you can tell, she is hardly fond of it."

"Why call her that, then?"

"In good fun, my dear girl, in good fun. Perhaps you will earn yourself a nickname and see for yourself."

She found herself frowning. "I'm not sure I want that."

"Few do, but they are created all the same." Grier finished smoking and began to roll another. "Especially by folks like Siluk."

Siluk held his hands out to either side. "I call it like I see it."

Kirima found her eyes pulled back to the firestick that he still held in his hand. "Could you teach me to use one of those?"

"What, my pistol?"

"Pistol," she repeated slowly. "Yes, the pistol."

Siluk shot a glance over to Grier. "Seems she prefers my methods over yours."

"She already asked me as well," he said. "The girl is eager to learn."

"Ah, it seems she is." He flipped it in his hand, holding it by the barrel as he offered the handle to her. "Go on, take it."

She reached out, carefully wrapping her hand around the handle, feeling the weight in it as he released his end of it. "It's heavy," she said. "Heavier than I expected."

"Keep your finger on the outside of the trigger guard." He paused. "That metal thing that encircles the lever. Yes, that, good. You never want to put your finger inside unless you actually mean to fire it."

She turned toward him. "Can I?"

Siluk's hands shot up, pushing the barrel off to the side. "Not at us."

"Oh, no, of course not." She felt her cheeks grow hot. "I mean in general."

"Not yet." He climbed to his feet, then held out his hand. She took it with her empty one and he pulled her to her feet. His hands reached up to her shoulders and he turned her to face the sea, away from the boat. "Square your shoulders. And hold it with both hands."

"You were just using one, weren't you?"

"Yes, but this thing packs a kick. Until you're used to it, two hands."

"Okay."

Siluk was silent for a moment as he fussed around with her, using his foot to nudge her left leg forward and easing her arms up so that they were about even with her shoulders. "There," he said, taking a step back. "Now look down the sight and fire when ready."

"Any time?"

"Any time. Make sure you brace yourself, both for the kick and for the sound."

She did, and when she finally pulled the trigger, both still shocked her. The pistol fired, the end of the barrel erupting in fire, sending it and her arms flying back. It was all she could do to keep it from jumping right up and smacking her in the face. As the blast sounded, it was followed by a muffled ring, Siluk's voice coming in a bit quiet, as if she was listening to it through the thick layers of her winter parka's hood.

"Not bad for a first time. Can't imagine you would have hit anything like that, but you certainly didn't hesitate to fire it."

"Do others hesitate?" she asked as she allowed him to gently take the pistol from her hand.

"Some do. If you hesitate at the wrong time, though, you die." He began to load it, ejecting a metal casing, then grabbing another piece of metal from his pocket and sliding it back in.

"I guess I'll be sure to not hesitate then."

He winked at her. "Just make sure you're aiming at the right person." He handed her the pistol back, a new shot loaded into it. "Try again."

"Can I try loading it next time?"

"Let's see if you can figure out aiming and firing before we take it any further." He pointed to the beach. "See that piece of driftwood there?"

She nodded. "I see it."

"I want you to take aim at it, but don't fire yet. Do you have it lined up down the sight?"

"Yes."

"That wood is, what, thirty paces, Grier?"

"I'd say twenty-eight."

Siluk licked the tip of his index finger and held it up to the breeze. "Wind's blowing in. Alright, girl, I want you to bring your gun up slowly, until the sight is lined up with the edge of the water."

"Just like aiming a spear," she said.

"Yes, just like a spear. Kind of." He took a step back, looking down the beach. "Fire when ready."

This time, she gave no hesitation when pulling the trigger. The bang didn't seem as loud, the concussion not as sharp, and her eyes remained fixed on the piece of wood, where she saw a strike as several splinters flew into the air.

Kirima turned to Siluk, her eyes wide. "I hit it!" she said. "I actually hit it."

Both the men began to clap. "Bravo, girl," Siluk said. "Bravo."

"I can't believe it."

"Get some practice in you, and it'll be as easy as anything you've ever done. Second nature." He stepped up and took the pistol from her. "But not tonight. It's already getting late, and we still have a lot of traveling in front of us."

Kirima gave a slight bow. "Thank you for teaching me."

"No need to thank me. There's still plenty to learn."

"I still appreciate it."

"Get some sleep. We'll see you in the morning."

The two men made their way to their corner of the camp, by where the Giant now lay with a hat pulled over her face, snoring loudly. Kirima found her way to her own pad, nestled next to a rock that shielded her from the worst of the wind that blew in from the sea. Her heart was still pounding in her chest as she laid down, the adrenaline pumping through her veins so hard that she thought she might never fall asleep.

Except she did. And when she saw the shadows emerging from the water, as she had so many nights before, this time she saw herself standing with Grier and Siluk, each of them firing guns, killing the shadows where they stood. It seemed so perfect, so right.

But it couldn't be that easy, could it?

11

"I forgot how much it rains up here," Siluk said.

They were growing closer to the village, their arrival coming well before sunset if Gabriel's instincts were to be believed. A sun that she did not think they would see that day. It had already been a bit overcast when they had made camp the night before, but the misty rains had begun falling that night, soaking them where they slept.

Kirima was still dry beneath her parka, but that didn't stop her from being cold and miserable, though no doubt not as cold and miserable as their new companions were. Siluk had his arms wrapped around himself, while Grier calmly smoked, seeming mostly unaffected by the weather change. Effie, however, crouched in a corner in the cabin, wrapped in her blanket, muttering beneath her breath, and practically growling at anyone who ventured close.

"It's better than snow," Grier said.

From down in the cabin, Effie shouted up to them. "We should have taken the job in Omak."

"It rains even more there."

"But it's warm rain."

"Omak?" Kirima asked.

"A large city, in the far south," Siluk said. "Probably further than is worth your trouble to ever bother traveling."

"Is it like Adhan?"

"Not at all. Adhan is a hive of thieves and swindlers and murderers."

"And Omak?"

"The same, but they aren't so proper about it."

"Oh." She wasn't sure she understood, but she didn't say anything more. After the warmth of Adhan, she found herself empathizing with Effie at the moment, especially since shedding the parka had meant water getting into places it normally did not. She found herself thankful it wasn't winter. That sort of carelessness was a death sentence when the temperature dropped and ice floes filled the Narrows. For now, it was discomfort, and she wanted nothing more than to get home and allow herself to dry off in front of the stove.

"There it is," Gabriel said, pointing.

"Eh?" Siluk said, squinting his eyes against the rain. "There what is?"

"Their village," Grier said. "Between those rocks there."

Siluk watched for a moment more before saying, "Oh, I see the shrine. And people. Something going on there?" He squinted as he looked up in the sky. "Twins were just recently out, can't imagine it's time already."

Phillip sat at the front of the boat stood, shielding his eyes against the rain. "Looks like they're granting an offer to the Balance."

"Another one?" Gabriel said. "That would be the fourth in a week if they put one out as I said. Or maybe they waited for some reason?"

Kirima was still trying to see for herself. She could see the outline of the shrine, growing clearer as they approached, and with it, the shadows of a pair of boats and some figures standing in the water. They were struggling with something, something she couldn't quite make out. But there was also something wrong with the scene in general, something that her mind seemed to be blanking on. Finally, it came to her, but it was Phillip who actually vocalized it.

"Gabriel, does it ever take that many men to bring a sheep out?"

He frowned. "No, it's usually just myself and one other, usually Miki. Now that you mention it, it is odd. Maybe they don't know what to do?"

Kirima squinted further, the scene growing ever clearer as they approached. There was a definite struggle happening, several men grappling with something in between them.

"Perhaps a larger sacrifice," Siluk said. "A seal, or perhaps even a bear?"

"No, they wouldn't change…"

The shapes had shifted just enough for her to see, and she felt her stomach turn, almost hard enough to make her vomit. It was just a glimpse, but she could see what was struggling against the people there, what was being chained down to the shrine to be sacrificed to the Imakut. The words spewed from her mouth, cutting Gabriel off mid-sentence.

"That's a person."

All eyes turned toward the shrine, with even Effie climbing out of the cabin to look over the edge. They were silent for a moment as everyone stared.

"No," Gabriel said.

"Surely not," Grier said.

"I'll be damned," Effie said.

Phillip and Siluk were both silent, while Gabriel spoke in a whisper.

"They wouldn't."

Kirima turned toward him, breaking her gaze away as she rapidly tapped Gabriel on the shoulder. "We need to hurry. Can't this go any faster?"

"Hang on."

Gabriel pulled on a lever, and the engine began to run louder, their speed in the water picking up quickly. They struck a wave and came down hard, jostling everyone in the boat. Kirima lunged forward, grabbing onto one of the railings by the wheel, while others scrambled elsewhere. Gabriel gripped the steering mechanism as tightly as he could, gritting his teeth, struggling to keep his eyes open as the ocean spray combined with the rain, whipping around their heads.

Kirima only opened her own eyes when she heard the engine start to slow, then suddenly cut out, the boat turning in place. She stood up, turning to see that some were still struggling while others had turned to look at them, the boats beyond them rocking in the wake of Gabriel's. Immediately, she recognized members of the council, up to their knees in water where they stood beneath the shrine's roof.

"What is happening here?" Gabriel asked, his voice raised in a way she had not heard in many years.

No one standing at the shrine said a word. The sound of a boat motor could be heard, and as she looked, her eyes spotted the one belonging to Phillip and Calum's family drawing closer, except it was not Calum at the helm. Instead, their mother leaned out, her cheeks flushed and damp, her voice crying out hoarsely.

"Gabriel, you must stop them!"

"Stop them for what?" Gabriel said. "What's going on?"

The struggling at the shrine had stopped, and suddenly, the person they had been working to tie down burst through, and she saw Calum there, bruises and blood on his bare skin as he fought against his captors. He shoved one aside, making for one of the boats, but two of the men grabbed the ropes, pulling him back roughly. She watched as he fell, sputtered as he struggled to keep his head above water.

Before anyone could even speak, Phillip was over the side, his knife in his hand. Some of the people around Calum regained their wits, their shouts filling the air as some drew their own blades. Phillip held his out before him, turning it toward each one in turn.

A loud bang sounded behind her, causing Kirima to flinch, covering her ears as she turned to see Siluk with the gun in the air, trails of smoke still rising from the barrel. He slowly lowered it, directing it toward the people in the shrine.

"Stand aside," he said. "Let the boy go."

She could see the surprise that mingled with the fear in their eyes. Calum had managed a sitting position, but they still held him tight. He had a dazed look on his face, blood dripping from his nose, a purple bruise on his cheek. Phillip stepped toward him, but it was Lusa who stepped in front of him, moving with surprising nimbleness.

"This is the sacrifice demanded of the Imakut," she said. "I will not let you or anyone stop this from happening."

"Lady, I don't know who you are, but I have no problem shooting you," Siluk said.

"No," Gabriel said forcefully. "No one is shooting anyone." No one moved, and he waved his hand. "Put the gun down. Now."

Siluk glanced over at him, then lowered the gun, placing it back in the leather holder on his belt. "As you wish."

"What are you doing?" Kirima said under her breath. "They're going to kill him."

"Trust me," he said quietly, then raised his voice back up. "Lusa, everyone, I left the village in your care, and I come home to find you trying to kill one of our own? What madness is this?"

Lusa began to speak, but Miki stepped forward before she could. "I tried to tell them it was a bad idea. They felt…"

"Oh, that's ridiculous," Seona said. "You came right along with it. We all voted. There were no dissenting voices."

Other voices joined in, but Gabriel raised his to be heard. "I leave to find someone to protect the village, and you turn to murder."

"It's not murder," Lusa said. "It's what the Imakut want. They tried to take the boy and this girl denied them their prize." Kirima felt ice running through her veins when the simuq pointed at her. "We are only giving them what they demanded."

"If you feel so strongly, why don't you tie yourself up out here," Phillip said, the point of his knife aimed at Lusa.

"Phillip, silence," Gabriel said. "We will not sacrifice our own. That is not who we are. That is not what we believe."

"There was a time when we gave our own to the Imakut," Lusa said.

"That time was long ago, far before living memory."

"Perhaps it is time the practice returns."

Kirima watched as Gabriel's eyes narrowed. "Not so long as I am in charge."

"Then perhaps we should find a new leader," Alpin said, spitting in the water. "One who will do what must be done."

Phillip's knife pointed toward him, and Siluk drew his gun once more. "Everyone, stop." Gabriel yelled the words, calling out at the top of his lungs. It worked, as all eyes were drawn toward him once more. "This is not getting us anywhere. We're not going to save out village by fighting amongst ourselves, nor by sacrificing our own. And we're not changing leadership, neither myself nor the Council."

Kirima watched the faces of those in the water, a mix of shame and anger, and in Lusa's case, quiet defiance. She felt her hand go to her necklace, to the jarak pendant, and her thoughts turned to her father. What would he have done here? She felt helpless standing there.

Phillip moved without warning, elbowing his way past those in front to his brother. He brandished the knife as he sliced through Calum's bindings, catching his brother as he collapsed forward. No one moved to stop him as he helped Calum to his feet and walked him toward the boat. She moved to the side as he arrived, helping him into the boat.

"Just like I said," Miki said. "This was never the solution."

"You be quiet," Gabriel said. "We're going back to the town."

"I hope you know, Gabriel, you have doomed us all," Lusa said.

"If you wish to discuss this further, we can do so on the beach," he said as Phillip climbed in after his brother.

Lusa's voice was raising, growing louder as the engine started back up. "I am standing here in these waters trying to save our people, and you thwart these efforts with a misguided sense of mercy."

The boat grew louder as Gabriel maneuvered it around. Calum was resting against the rear, his teeth clenched as Phillip examined him.

Lusa slapped the water before her, spraying some droplets in the direction of the boat. "You only delay the inevitable, Mayor. The boy was doomed already, but now you doom the rest of us as well."

The boat grew a bit louder, and a few others began to churn as well, those who seemed to have only come to watch but not act. Behind them, several of those at the shrine had already begun to make their way to their own boats to follow. Lusa's screeching voice still carried through the damp air after them.

"You don't know, and you never will, Gabriel. The blood is weak in your line. You'll never know."

A crowd was gathered along the beach, no doubt watching the scene unfold at the shrine. Gabriel drew the boat in as close as he could and dropped the anchor. Phillip was the first out, turning to help a hobbled Calum down into the water. Their mother was there as well, not even bothering to beach the boat as she jumped out, the two of them helping Calum up the beach toward their house.

"What's going to happen?" Kirima asked Gabriel as they trudged through the shallows toward the beach. She spoke softly, but the way the people on the beach were looking at the three mercenaries, she probably could have shouted the question, and no one would have paid it any attention.

"We'll see." His eyes turned out toward the approaching boats, the rest of the council coming back from the shrine. "I just hope I can keep my anger in check. I…no, I'm sorry, it's not something you should see."

Kirima frowned, but she said nothing. She glanced at the crowd, all of them looking in wonder, whether at Siluk's skin or Effie's height or Grier's plainness. She caught sight of Yura, a child clutched in each hand, her own eyes gazing off in some direction, her brow furrowed in a frown. Meriwa's eyes met Kirima's and she waved, beaming widely. Kirima waved back but found herself having trouble matching the smile.

Gabriel seemed to have calmed, but as the boats approached, he didn't even wait for them to reach the shore. He stomped through the water, making right for Lusa's boat. Kirima trailed after him, stopping at the water's edge, not sure if she was there to support him or simply to hear what was said.

"Have you all lost your wits?" Gabriel asked. "How could you do something like this?"

"Where did you get that boat, Gabriel?" Sawney said, nodding toward it. "The Company give it to you?"

"No wonder he was able to get to Adhan and back so quickly," Seona said. "In any of our boats, a trip like that would take a week."

"This isn't about me," Gabriel said. "This is about the fact that you were willingly giving one of our own to the Imakut. This is not how we do things."

"Is that so, Mayor?" The volume of Lusa's voice had lowered, but there was no less force behind it as she hobbled down from the boat, supporting herself with her cane, but seeming no more hindered by the water than normal. "There was a time when the mayor of Aliit wouldn't think twice about giving someone young and strong as a gift to the Balance in times of dire need. A time when it was considered the highest honor to make such a sacrifice."

"This is not the way we do things," Gabriel said. "The old ways are old for a reason."

"Your kind could never understand our ways," she said. "No matter how long you live here, how many generations, you will always be wary of our ways."

"My family has tended to the Balance for generations," Gabriel said. "How dare you say that to me."

"Your family was filled with grifters who forced our village into accepting you and your ilk. You came because you were no longer welcomed in the south, and it was our tradition of hospitality that allowed you to settle here. Except you brought change, and you paved the way for the others to come. For that Company to come. All because of your people."

Gabriel was gesturing wildly as he spoke. "The Company harms us all equally, you, me, everyone in this village. I gain nothing from them being here."

She nodded toward the boat. "Only that tiny gift that you chose to hide from us."

"A boat that allowed me to go all the way to Adhan to get help. A boat that has only been used for the benefit of our people."

Miki stepped up next to Lusa. "If you hid this from us, what else have you hidden. What secrets could we find if we tear up your home?"

"What else could we have gotten from the Company?" Seona said. "You never consulted us, perhaps you asked for too little."

"We can't trust you, Gabriel," Lusa said.

"Hold on," he said.

"As the Council, we have the right to put forth a vote of no confidence and decide a new mayor. I think it's time we invoke that right."

"Perhaps instead of a vote, we should give him to the Balance," someone called out.

The entire town seemed to have come out now, and they all seemed to speak at once. The beach was filled with voices, each trying to rise up to be heard over the others. It was only when the gun fired that they stopped, the gun that sat in Kirima's hand. She hadn't remembered taking it from Siluk, but a glance back was met with a smile and a nod.

"Listen to yourselves," she said. "We live in these waters in peace for hundreds of years, and with the slightest sign of adversity, we turn into monsters."

"Don't speak of what you don't know, girl," Lusa said.

"And don't presume to speak to me like I'm a child," Kirima said through clenched teeth, shoving a finger into the old woman's chest. "You speak of the old ways? Well I grew up with the old ways. I row my canoe out to the Narrows, I sing the songs that our simuq once taught our fishers, not a simuq like you, but a real one, with real powers. I do it all as I was taught."

She could see the flush in Lusa's cheeks, either from embarrassment or anger or both. She turned from her, addressing the rest of the town.

"But right now, the old ways aren't working. None of them. Maybe that's because of the Company, or maybe it's because we ourselves have been lost along the way, but what's important is that we're not going to solve this by quarreling like this, and we certainly aren't going to fix it by sacrificing our own. Now we've brought help…"

"Three people?" Sawney sneered, arms crossed over his broad chest. "You may as well have not come home."

"An enchanter, and two experienced fighters," Kirima said. "People who can help us."

"We don't even know what we're fighting," Alpin said. "Or if it can be fought."

"Would you rather leave?" Phillip asked. "Maybe that is what the Imakut are trying to tell us."

"We can't leave here," Sesi said. "Our people have lived here for centuries, working these waters."

"Then you need to stop fighting and we need to work together," Kirima said. "These people can help us, but we need to allow them to."

There were murmurs, some passing between the council members, but none seemed eager to have any real discussion or step forward to refuse. Behind her, in a voice just loud enough for her to hear, Siluk said, "Not quite the warm welcome I was expecting."

"I suppose we should consider ourselves lucky we're not getting run out of town," Grier said.

Effie grunted. "I'd like to see them try."

Siluk stood, adjusting his coat and the waist of his pants. "Well, seems they're not going to run us off, so I suppose we should get to work. And maybe see if anyone's running a still around here."

12

"So tell me, how many of you have ever fought anything?"

The townsfolk had gathered out on the beach once more, the morning mists not yet given way to the light of the day. The mood seemed to be somewhat improved, though there was still a lingering cloud in the general attitude, mostly manifesting in inaudible grumbling and sour looks, either toward her or Gabriel or the mercenaries. It seemed to match the weather, the rain swirling around them, seeming strong enough to dampen even the powerful blaze of the bonfire.

"Not even wrestling contests? Okay, what about hunting?"

Phillip leaned over across her to whisper to Siluk. "We fish."

"Fishing, of course. Fantastic. Just fish? What about whales? Dolphins? Seals?"

Kirima shook her head. "None of that."

"Even my old village hunted." Siluk sighed loudly. "Alright, we're going to have to start with the basics. You have weapons, at least?"

Phillip shrugged. "Some spears for catching flounders. Knives for prepping fish. Axes for chopping wood."

"No swords? No bows and arrows?"

"None."

"I suppose that would be asking too much." He raised his voice over the crowd once more. "Alright, new plan then. Today, we're going to be building defenses and crafting weapons." He motioned with his hand down the center of the crowd, then motioned to his left. "Everyone to this side, you're with me, preparing this beach. Everyone else, go with Effie."

Effie stepped past, her walk uneven on the sand. "Come with me, boy, I want you there in case they give me trouble."

Kirima turned to go with them, but Siluk snagged her by the sleeve. "No, stay here. What I'm about to say is not going to be popular."

"Seems to be the trend."

Siluk stepped toward where the boats were lined up on the beach. "Alright, we know these things come from the sea, so we want to make it as hard on them as possible, and we need to have a contingency. So I want you to place the biggest, most sturdy boats on the far side of the island. We need a way out."

Miki stepped from the crowd as they meandered toward the water's edge. "Contingency? You think this won't work?"

Siluk waved his hand in an absent manner. "Always have an escape plan. Take the rest and sink them in the shallows."

Miki froze, his mouth agape. "But those boats are our lifeblood. How will we fish?"

"You can repair them, or build new ones, if we get past this. If we don't, you won't have much use for them."

Miki's eyes turned to Kirima, seeming almost ablaze. "This man seeks to ruin us."

"He seeks to help," she said.

"This won't even stop them," he said, motioning out toward where some of the boats were already being pushed out. "Do you think they can't swim past them? That they can't climb over them?"

"A barrier rarely keeps someone stopped indefinitely," Siluk said. "All that matters is that it slows them long enough to give you a chance to kill them." He turned to the people setting up. "I want the first line along the beach and the second on the first sandbar."

Miki glared, his arms crossed over his chest, but he said nothing. The sound of axes chopping wood filled the air, the townsfolk hacking away at the bottoms of the boats until the water began to flow, sending them sinking to the sand below. Beyond, Gabriel was in his boat, leading three others past the shrine. A new lamb had been set out there, but Kirima had a feeling that she knew what its fate would be.

By the time the last villager trudged back onto the beach, the barriers were starting to take shape, the boats settling into their new spots on the harbor floor. Some of the boats stuck out while others were hidden beneath the waves, white water breaking over them as each one passed.

"Good," Siluk said. "Now we prepare the beach."

Some were set to dig trenches while others went to gather wood. He set Kirima to the former, so she grabbed a shovel and worked with others at digging. It wasn't long before she grew warm, hot enough that she removed her parka and was still sweating.

As the trench began to take form, the rest soon began to appear with logs and branches of all sizes. They would stack them and return back toward the forest to gather more. Soon, there was a huge pile, larger even than the fire that currently burned.

"Looking good," Siluk said as he made his way toward them. "Dig them a bit deeper and leave two areas to either side for other fires." He turned and began to address the others. "We're going to stack logs for fires here, here, and over there closer to the first buildings. The smallest branches and shavings should be used for kindling. For the larger branches, I want sharp points carved into both ends. Once the trenches are dug we're sticking them in there."

He continued giving instructions, directing people around, but it was lost to her ears behind the wind and waves. Kirima was still digging, but her eyes wandered, first to the others digging to either side of her, up and down the beach, and then to over to where Grier stood, smoking. She paused, placing the end of her shovel into the ground and wiping sweat from her forehead.

"Not helping?" she asked.

Grier gave a smirk, gazing past her to where the others were working. "I'm not much for manual labor."

"Couldn't you just, I don't know," she gestured around, "use your powers and have this all finished?"

That brought a throaty chuckle. "Not quite. My powers don't really work like that. Besides, it takes a lot of effort to move matter like that."

She picked up the shovel and began to dig again. "How does it work then?"

He seemed to consider it for a moment. "Have you ever held your breath?"

"Of course. When I was younger, we used to have competitions to see who could swim the furthest underwater. Phillip used to be able to swim almost the whole way to the shrine."

"Sounds miserable."

"You get used to the chill."

"Well, when you were doing that, I'm sure you noticed that if you tried to do it too soon after a try, you can't hold your breath as long."

"Yeah, I've noticed. I also noticed that I could hold it for longer the next time."

"Right. Enchanting is the same way. It drains you, and some things drain you worse than others."

"Like what?"

"Like levitation, for example." Her face must have looked as confused as she felt, because he said, "Lifting things. It takes much more energy to lift things with your mind than with your body."

"Why is that? I always thought it would be easier."

"Lots of people think that. To be honest, though, I couldn't tell you exactly, and I don't think anyone else really could either."

"Why not?"

He shrugged. "They don't know. Scientists have been studying people like me for ages, but they're no closer to understanding how it works any more than they were a century ago. Everyone has a theory, but I doubt any of them are correct."

"What's your theory?"

He leaned a bit. "Huh?"

"You said everyone has a theory. What's yours?"

Another chuckle. "I did say that, didn't I?" He paused for a moment, exhaling smoke. "I suppose it's because our minds aren't meant to lift matter like that. We can control things like air and fire and water because there's much more of an ethereal aspect to them, but matter is too...real, I suppose. If that makes sense."

"Because it's heavier?"

"Yes and no. It's hard to describe."

"Do you think there's anyone strong enough to do so?"

"Maybe. If you believe the stories, there used to be a lot who could."

"But you don't believe the stories, do you?"

He flicked the paper roll away. "No."

"It's said that our simuq were once enchanters, long ago. It is said that the Imakut grant their blessing on a select few when they are born, more if a town is especially blessed." She paused, both in speaking and digging, her tongue working at the side of her mouth. "I guess we should have seen this coming."

He drew a few steps closer, his thumbs resting in his pockets, his wide brimmed hat tipped back to reveal the weathered face. "Why is that?"

"It's been close to a century since we've had one."

"Your current simuq is not?"

Kirima smirked. "She'd probably tell you she is. Why, can't you tell?"

"Not unless she actively enchants."

"You'll be waiting a long time. Just another one in the long line of powerless simuq." She shook her head and began to dig again. "Perhaps we should have realized that was a sign. Perhaps this was inevitable."

"You said the sacrifice was always taken. How could you have known?"

"I don't know. It seems so obvious now."

"It always does when you have the benefit of looking back."

"Of course." The words passed her lips quietly, enough so that she wasn't sure he heard. She continued digging, pilling the sand on the side closer to the water as Siluk had instructed. She seemed to lose track of time in the task, just as she did while out on the water, the repetition of the motion seeming to take her mind away from the present, but it was whipped back at the sound of Siluk's voice.

"That's deep enough." She looked up to see that people were approaching, their arms filled with branches that had been filed to a point at each end. A boy around her age named Kanut came to her section, depositing his there before turning away, no doubt to fetch more. "You're going to arrange these in the trenches, and then we're going to work on barriers. This beach needs to be as inhospitable as possible to whatever is climbing out of that water."

Kirima filled her area, carefully spacing the stakes, their sharp ends pointed toward the sky. She looked over it once she was finished, thinking that it looked quite deadly. She wasn't given much time to admire, however, as Siluk was already giving instructions for the area behind the trenches. Logs were laid to form barriers, with spikes poking out from the base, and another bonfire was created, left unlit like the ones at either end of the trenches. Once one row of barriers was lain, another was created behind it, further up the beach.

By the time the sun had set and a halt was called to the work, much of the beach was covered by either barrier or trench or bonfire, defensible against whatever may come from the sea. And every muscle in her body seemed to ache.

Some of those not helping had cooked up a meal for everyone, but Kirima felt too tired to even consider eating. She took some fish and seaweed salad, ate a few bites, and then made her way back to the house. Inside, she didn't bother changing or even speaking to the children, instead making her way to her room and collapsing onto the bed, falling into a deep, dreamless sleep.

It seemed as if she had only been asleep for a moment before a loud whistle was sounded, pulling her from her slumber. She blinked her eyes, seeing the light of day filtering through the window. She could hear Siluk in the distance, calling for everyone to wake up.

"We don't know when the attack is coming," he called out. "Time is short, so get moving."

The weapons that the other group had made were laid out, curved sticks, each with a taut string connecting one end to the other, set beside sticks that looked like smaller spears, carved weighted points at one end and feathers at the other.

"This," Siluk said, holding one up, "is a bow and arrow. You notch the arrow like so." He attached the feather end to the string. "Pull back." He drew it back, looking down the arrow. "And release." The arrow flew in a straight line, striking a straw target that had been set up. "I want everyone to practice this. We need to see who can do it and who can't."

Each person there stepped forward in turn, picking up a bow and several arrows apiece. As Kirima moved to pick one of her own, Siluk moved in front of her, stopping her in her tracks. "Not you. You get more practice with the gun."

Kirima felt her eyes light up. "Really?"

"I need someone else who knows how to use one. Come on."

They left the town behind, hiking up into the woods. As they went along the path, she noticed pieces of red cloth marking every few trees. "What are these for?"

"The way to the boats. In case something goes wrong."

"Do you think something will?"

"Let's not talk about that, yeah? I'd rather be ready just in case."

"Okay." Each one seemed to stand out a bit more to her as they passed, her mind thinking of what it would be like to try to follow this at night. Perhaps she wouldn't have to find out.

They followed the path, coming to a wide clearing. Further on, she could see the slope down to the small harbor where the boats were moored. In the clearing, however, additional straw targets had been set up.

"Here." He held out the pistol, and she took it from him. "It's loaded, so make sure you don't point it at anyone. Especially me."

She made certain to keep her finger outside the ring as she gripped it. "Which one am I shooting?"

"Do you remember the lesson from the other evening?"

"I do."

He nodded toward one of the nearer targets. "Show me."

Kirima stood there, squaring her shoulders toward the target. She held the gun out, aiming for the target, bracing herself for the shot, and then fired. The shot caught the edge of the target, sending straw and dust flying at the impact.

"Good, but not great." She turned and only just got her hand up in time to catch the bullet as he tossed it to her. "Eject the case and load that one in."

She looked down at it. "How?"

He nodded toward it. "Figure it out."

She turned over the pistol in her hand, her eyes finally coming across a latch. She pressed it, and a segment opened, a metal casing popping out. She took the bullet he had tossed her and slid it in, closing the hatch with it.

"Good," he said. "But you're going to have to learn to do it much quicker than that."

"That's the first time I've ever done it."

"And you're going to have to learn quickly. The Imakut aren't going to wait around for you to become a master at it." He produced a box, the sound of metal jingling within, and tossed it to her. "Practice without firing for a while, just unloading and loading until you get it down. Then practice with firing. I'll be back to check up on you later."

"You're just leaving me?"

There was no answer, only his back as he made his way from the clearing. She wasn't sure what else to do, so she began to practice.

She worked her way through the entire box, loading and unloading each bullet without firing. She could feel it in her fingers after a while, the ache setting in with each bullet, but she continued on, cursing every time she fumbled one, but not stopping to celebrate when she got it right, only pushing to go faster.

When she finished with the box, she bent down and picked up all the bullets once more, slipping them back into the box. Then she started over, this time firing instead of just ejecting. It felt awkward at first, her fingers hurting from the repetition, her ears ringing from the sound, her arms feeling almost numb from the impact, but she kept going, faster and faster. She would fumble with one, dropping it and breaking her concentration, and then go right back into it.

She didn't stop until the last bullet was gone. She fired it, striking the target not in the center, but close enough, a good way to end. She stood there, breathing heavily, gazing over the targets, now spotted with holes where the bullets had struck, as did several of the trees behind them.

There was the sound of clapping, and she turned to see Siluk standing there, Grier beside him. "Well done," Siluk said. "Not bad for a beginner."

Kirima wiped wetness from her forehead, rain or sweat or both. "Thanks."

"We'll find some smaller targets for you," he said, stepping forward and taking the gun from her. "Your accuracy still needs some work."

"Do you have enough bullets for that?"

"Plenty," he said. "We can try again tomorrow…"

He was interrupted by a massive banging sound, one loud enough that Kirima jumped, turning in the direction of it. "What was that?" she asked. In the distance, she could hear the people of the village reacting as well.

Grier was frowning. "Sounded like an explosion."

"From what, though?" Siluk said.

Kirima turned, running toward the rise that looked over the town, the highest point on the island. Before she even reached the top, she could see the smoke, drifting upward in a great dark cloud in the northern distance. She heard footsteps come to a stop behind her as the other two caught up.

"What's over there?" Siluk asked.

"The Company outpost," she said. "What…what could have happened?"

"Maybe just an accident," Grier said. "A refinery caught fire, perhaps."

"Or something caused it," Siluk said.

There was no mistaking his meaning in that. Kirima watched the plume of smoke for a moment more, then turned and began to walk at a brisk pace away from the rise. "Hey, where are you going?" Siluk called after her, but she didn't respond.

She was almost to the clearing when she saw Phillip coming up from the village, his eyes wide. He ran up to her, then fell into pace beside her, moving backwards as he spoke. "Did you see that?"

"Yeah," she said, not stopping. "We need to go see."

"Go see what?" he asked. "What are you doing?"

"Getting a boat," she said. "Is that not obvious?"

Kirima had started jogging by the time she reached the cove where the boats were stashed. She jumped into Gabriel's, her eyes passing over the controls. She had watched him do this before, which one was it? She glanced back up in the direction of the town, perhaps expecting him to pop up over the rise at any moment, but the mayor was nowhere in sight. Her eyes returned to the panel, resuming her searching.

"You saw that smoke, didn't you?" Phillip said, still down on the beach, looking down at her. "It's dangerous over there. And you don't know what caused it."

"Your uncle is over there, isn't he?"

"I...well, yes."

"Don't you want to see if he's safe?"

Grier and Siluk came scrambling down, both of them sliding to a stop next to Phillip. "You can't be thinking of going over there," Siluk said.

"I agree with him," Grier said. "This is not wise."

"Then come make sure I don't get hurt," she said. "Or try to stop me."

They all looked at each other uneasily. Her eyes fell upon the switch, and she hit it, the engine rumbling to life beneath her. She glanced up at them, all still standing there. "Well?"

Siluk and Grier exchanged glances, but Phillip waded into the water, climbing on the deck next to her. "Last chance," she said.

Siluk threw up his hands. "Fine. Only to make sure you don't get yourself killed."

"Same," Grier said.

They climbed down, much more carefully than Phillip had. Once they were in, she hit the lever and steered it out of the cove, toward the ever-growing plume.

13

The stench of the smoke lay heavy, even at a distance. At the first sign of coughing, Grier removed one of his layers and used his knife to slice it into makeshift masks. Even with the cloth covering her mouth and nose, Kirima could still feel it in the air, thick and warm, stinging her eyes and drying out her airways.

They were still a good distance away when Siluk pointed out the flames, emerging from one of the large buildings, the refineries, Grier said, where they turned the whale blubber into oil. She wasn't sure how long they watched it, but it soon became clear that it wasn't going to go down in intensity any time soon.

"What do we do?" Phillip finally said.

"We should go back and wait for it to die down," Siluk said.

Kirima turned to him. "We can't do that. There could be people hurt over there."

"As I was about to say before being interrupted, I don't think she will allow that."

"Oh," she said. "Well, we should."

"'Should' doesn't always reconcile with the reality of the situation, but we're here." He turned to Grier. "Are you ready?"

"Always."

He motioned toward Kirima. "Proceed."

She pulled the lever, and the boat shot forward, perhaps a bit harder than she intended. It bounced along the waves, drawing up toward the wooden platforms, and it was here that she began to see the extent of the damage.

All of the ships were either sunk or sinking, but not in the deliberate way that theirs had been back at the harbor. She could see the anchor lines still submerged on some, and others still moored to the wooden platforms.

Few displayed their wounds, but the ones she saw looked as if a bear had torn through a thin woolen blanket.

"What could do that?" Phillip asked as they passed one, its shredded nose just poking out of the water.

"I don't know," Kirima said. She looked to the other two, as if they may have the answers, but they appeared just as perplexed as she was. So much for hiring experts.

Up on the beach, it only grew worse. Some of the platforms had been smashed, and it was beyond that where she began to see the bodies.

They were scattered among pieces of rubble, broken wood, dropped guns, and dozens upon dozens of footprints. Much of the sand was stained in either soot or blood. She could see a massive hole in the side of one of the refineries where something had broken through, a colossal blaze visible within.

"Right up there." She could see Siluk's arm from the corner of her eye, directing her toward a clear section of one of the platforms.

"Do you think there are any survivors?" Phillip asked.

"There's only one way to find out," Siluk said. He turned toward Grier. "A clear path, if you please."

Grier stepped up to the front of the boat, waving his hands in a circular motion before thrusting them outward. Right before Kirima's eyes, everything on the platform was pushed aside, even the smoke seeming to spread out around the space. She watched as Grier hopped up onto the wooden platform, holding a hand above his head, and Siluk went after him, glancing around.

"Come on," Siluk said. "Look for survivors, but also look for guns. Anything that can be used to protect the town."

"Okay," Kirima said as she stepped onto the platform. Her eyes were darting every which way, perhaps waiting for the Imakut to come from the sea, perhaps waiting for the dead Company men to stand up and attack them. As it turned out, neither happened, only the falling ash around them, glancing silently off the invisible barrier that Grier provided.

They had moved beyond the refinery before they found the first survivor. He was laying there in the sand and reached out without warning. It took every ounce of strength Kirima had to not jump back, her heart pounding against her chest as she watched Phillip crouch down and tend to him. It didn't take long to see that he was beyond help, his skin badly burned, his face indistinguishable in her mind. She wondered if he was one of theirs or one of those who had come from the south.

Phillip spoke to him in a quiet voice for some time, then stood and turned. "He said there are more in the living quarters."

Kirima turned toward Grier. "Is there anything you can do for him?"

Grier shook his head, but it was Phillip who spoke. "He knows it's too late for him, even for an enchanter. But there are others we can save."

Kirima took one look at the man, laying there on the beach, not moving, perhaps already dead. Phillip lingered as well, but the other two were already moving past, toward those buildings in the rear. She stepped up and touched Phillip's sleeve.

"We should go," she said.

"I know."

"Was he one of ours?"

Phillip shook his head. "No."

"But that doesn't matter, does it?"

"No."

She put a hand on his shoulder. "I'm sorry."

"Oki may still live." He shook her off. "Come on, let's see if he's there."

Kirima drew in a deep breath. She steeled herself, then followed after him, trudging through the wet sand toward the buildings in the rear.

The doors lay open, double doors that had been partially torn from their hinges. Just inside, she could see wooden furniture that had been pushed up against the door now broken into pieces and scattered about, a failed barrier against whatever had come through here. Across some of the debris lay a body, the back of its head a mangled mess that almost made her sick right there.

Siluk stepped up beside her, glanced inside both ways, and then stepped off to the side. "Grier, clear a path, if you would."

Grier nodded, pushing back his sleeves, then thrusting out his hands as if he was physically pushing something. There was a bang, not like before, but the sound of something colliding with something else, and the debris was flung to either side, leaving a clear path for them.

Kirima stepped up beside him, looking down as he leaned forward, his breath heaving. "I thought you couldn't do that."

"On the contrary," he said, drawing in a deep breath, "you can see how hard that was on my body. Lifting is a whole other level of strain."

"Oh," she said. "Are you alright?"

"I will be in a moment." He gestured toward the doorway, which Phillip and Siluk had already entered. "Go on."

She gave him a lingering look of concern, then obeyed, stepping past him and into the hallway.

The ground was covered in a soft surface, not unlike the fur that lined the inside of her parka. Each step sank into it, muddy footprints left behind in her wake. There was a wider entryway that quickly narrowed to a long hall flanked by doors on either side, partially lit by those same powered lights, a few out, some flickering, mingling with the late afternoon sun to cast an eerie glow on the space. The walls were painted white, but there was a viscous blue-green colored slime splattered in places, a fishy stench emanating from it.

Phillip and Siluk were ahead, Siluk with two pistols drawn, Phillip holding one of the spears that the others had made the previous day. They moved slowly, calling out for anyone who may still be alive, Phillip calling out for Oki in particular.

Siluk turned back to her. "Check the rooms. There might be survivors within."

Kirima turned toward the next door, slightly ajar, and pushed it open. Inside, it looked like the area where they prepped fish after everyone had gone through their catches. There was no telling if what was in there came from a person, but she wasn't keen to find out.

Up ahead, she heard Siluk call out. "We found them."

Phillip was nowhere to be found when she reached Siluk, standing at a doorway. She followed his gaze inside and found stairs with more furniture stacked up, creating a barrier. Some of it had been cleared away, revealing a path up, no doubt where Phillip had already gone. There was more of that bluish substance, but what really drew her eye was the body that lay on the ground.

The think on the ground before them wasn't human, but it had the shape of one. Its skin was a dark shade of green, and in many places, she could see the outline of bones through its scaly skin. Its head had a fin running down the middle of its skull, the skin surrounding it smooth and shiny, and its jaw hung open, revealing multiple rows of razor-sharp teeth. It had long fingers and toes, skin stretching between each digit, and each one ending in a claw, just like the hand that she had severed. A long gash stretched across its chest, leaking the same sludge that covered the walls.

"So this is what we're fighting against," Grier said.

"You saw the hand they had, didn't you?" Siluk said.

"Not quite the same."

"No," Kirima said. "It's not."

Siluk nudged her with a bony elbow. "Makes your feat that much more impressive, I'd say."

Kirima felt some bile at the back of her throat and forced it back down. The stench filled the space, and the longer she looked at it, the more certain she was that she was going to be sick. She was staring at it so intently that she almost jumped out of her very skin when she felt Grier touch her on the arm.

"Sounds like Phillip found someone," he said. There was a silence, and she heard voices coming from the floor above. "Let's join them."

"Yes, let's," Kirima said. "Not sure I want to stare at this thing any longer."

Siluk went up the stairs first, having to turn sideways to get past the blockage. Kirima followed, hearing the voices grow louder as they climbed to the next floor. Phillip was the first one she saw, talking to one of the Company folks, still in his uniform, though much more soiled than the ones she had seen the last time.

It was Grier who first spoke. "Survivors."

The man Phillip had been talking to nodded. "The guards told us to barricade ourselves in here. We've been up here since last night."

"How many of you are there?" Siluk asked.

"Thirteen," the Company man said. "At least here. We lost contact with the others, and no one has volunteered to go looking."

"We'll help look," Phillip said. "But you should all come back with us."

"A Company vessel will come within a week. I think we're better off staying here."

"Do you think you'll last a week?" Siluk said. "Do you think they won't come back?"

Another one of the Company men spoke up. "We'll certainly be safer here than in some unguarded village. We held them off once."

"And you're injured, down in numbers, without weapons."

"We have the armory. Nothing is stopping us from rearming."

"But you are not fighting men."

The one Phillip had been talking to glanced back at the others, but none spoke a word. Siluk continued, "I happen to be one, myself, this man here, another back at the village, all of us formerly Company Militia. We were brought to help."

"Only three?" one woman said. "They cut through our entire guard like they were nothing." Others around her voiced their agreement.

Siluk turned his eyes on her and she seemed to shrink a bit before him. "And were any enchanters?"

"Aye, there..." The woman was cut off by the person next to her elbowing her in the side. She glanced over but said nothing more.

"Company enchanters, here or not, are not built for battle," Grier said.

"And you'd know this?" one asked.

"I would," he said. "I was one of them."

There was a silence over the survivors. Siluk stepped forward, rubbing his hands together. "Can anyone direct us to the armory?"

Siluk took a few of the survivors with him, first to raid the armory and then to see if there were any workable boats. The remainder took Kirima, Phillip, and Grier to find the others. The ones in the center building had been overrun, the barriers they had set up torn apart and the space they had been covered in blood, trails leading out the front door and toward the beach. A few of their group ventured inside to check deeper within, but Kirima had quickly turned away, having no desire to see the aftermath.

It was in the next building that they found Oki. Phillip spotted him as soon as they were past the barricade. He called out his name and ran to greet him. Oki seemed apprehensive at first, but when he saw the rest of them approach, he wrapped his nephew in a tenuous embrace.

"You're alright," Phillip said.

"I am," Oki said with a nod, looking over at her and the others. "What are you doing here? You're not supposed to be in here."

Phillip frowned. "After everything that happened, that is your first thought?"

"I…" He rubbed at the back of his head. "I guess."

"What did happen?" Kirima asked.

"They came when we were unloading the boats at the end of the day," he said. "Out of the water."

"The Imakut?" Phillip asked.

"Those creatures. Whatever you want to call them. The soldiers told us to barricade ourselves in, so we did."

"You didn't see anything?" Kirima asked.

Oki shook his head. "No, none of us were brave enough to look out the windows. But we could hear the gunshots. And the screams."

"But they never came here?"

"They tried, for most of the night. Guess our barricade was good."

"Well, I'm glad you're safe," Phillip said. "Come with us, we're taking folks back to the village."

Oki frowned. "Why? We would all be safer here."

"We hired some mercenaries," Phillip said. "They're helping fortify everything, teaching our people how to fight."

Oki shook his head. "That's not going to work."

"Why not?" Kirima asked.

"Those things tore through seasoned veterans of the Company Militia. What do you think they'll do to our people?"

"They weren't expecting it," Kirima said. "The governor ignored our warnings."

Grier shook his head. "No, they would have still been prepared. These people aren't the type to put any kind of warnings aside, not when it affects production."

"Even if that isn't true, I can't imagine expecting it will do any better," Oki said.

Phillip put a hand on his shoulder. "Please, Oki. Come home. People listen to you, they'll follow you if you go, just like they did when you went to the Company."

Oki avoided looking at him, remaining silent for a moment before letting loose a deep sigh. "Very well, I'll come, we all will. We can return when the Company comes to rebuild. If we're still alive, that is."

"Let's get to the boats, then," Kirima said. "No telling when or if they'll be coming back."

By the time they returned to the beach with the survivors, several additional boats had been loaded up with supplies, at least three like the one they had ridden there. The surviving Company workers began to load into the boats, settling in where there was space between crates and barrels and guns that Siluk had collected.

Kirima watched for a moment, her eyes drifting around the ground at her feet. It was mostly rubble scattered around the dark brown sand, but something caught her eye, what looked like a jagged white rock. She stepped through, moving a few other pieces aside and picking it up. It was like a crystal, at once both smooth and jagged, the color a milky white. She pulled out her necklace, the one her father had given her long ago, the tiny stone that was the same color, carved into a small oval.

"Is that what I think it is?" Phillip asked.

"A jarak," she said, feeling the weight. "I've never seen one this large."

"The Company was harvesting them," Oki said from behind her.

She looked up at him over her shoulder. "Harvesting?"

"The ones we find are all tiny like that, small enough to wash onto shore. There are much bigger ones that can be found on the bottom of the sea. The Company uses enchanters to conjure air bubbles for divers to go searching for them."

"What does the Company want with them?" Phillip asked.

"It comes from the whales," Oki said. "It apparently burns longer and hotter than just the oil."

"We didn't know they were taking these," Kirima said. "Did they know they're sacred?"

"No one told them, at least not to my knowledge."

"Why not?"

"Intimidation. Threat of losing a job. Or maybe no one cared to." He shrugged. "Didn't seem important."

"Do you think this is why?" Phillip asked.

"It would make sense," she said. "The Company was operating for years before the trouble started."

"Whatever the case, it's too late to stop it." Oki reached out and took the jarak from her hands. "We can sell this for a lot of money."

"We should put it back," Kirima said.

He seemed to cradle it closer. "It'll do us a lot better being sold than at the bottom of the sea."

Before she could say another word, he strode off, making his way to the boats. Phillip stepped up beside her. "He never was a believer."

"He should know," she said. "He should have said something. Someone should have said something."

"Do you think that would have stopped them?"

"No. I mean, perhaps. Maybe someone would have listened."

"Then you have more faith in them than I do."

"Whatever the case, we need to get back." Above, the light was beginning to fade, the rain continuing to fall. "They may come tonight."

"I almost think it would be better to just be done with it," he said.

"Maybe," she said. "Maybe we should just leave."

"Many would resist."

"We may not have a choice." She began walking toward the boats, the two of them joining the others to return to the town.

14

Nothing happened that night.

The Company workers were welcomed, though the arms and boats were even more welcomed. Kirima and Phillip got a gentle chiding from Gabriel for taking the boat, but any thought of punishment was quickly forgotten as the mayor saw to housing the survivors.

A watch was set that evening, both on the beach and on the outcroppings, rotating through different people every hour, while the fires were kept ablaze. Instructions had been given, with everyone knowing their part should the alarm sound.

Kirima passed the night in fitful sleep, filled with a passing between wakefulness and dreams with seemingly little difference between the two as she found herself anticipating the sound of the warning bell, the sound of the Imakut arriving. When she finally arose with the morning sun, she felt no less tired than when she had gone to bed.

As the morning went on, she found herself standing at the height of the village, Gabriel standing with her as they watched the activity below. A few still practiced with bows on the targets that the mercenaries had set up, but more had shifted to using the guns taken from the Company, the popping sounds and scent of smoke filling the air. Others were working on the beach, bringing more logs to the fires, adding stakes to the pits, and reinforcing the barriers. A new sacrifice was placed out in the shrine, not that anyone expected it to work. Lusa had waded out to the shallows before the first line of sunken boats and was leading a small group in prayer.

"Everyone has their own way of dealing with it," Kirima said.

"Your father used to say that you can tell a lot about a person by how they handle adversity," Gabriel said.

"He'd be right there in the thick of things, probably with the barriers," she said. "Or out fishing. Nothing in between."

Her eyes drifted to the targets where Yura was taking aim with a rifle, her children sitting several paces behind her, cheering her on. When she first lifted it up, Kirima had been certain it would be too heavy for her, especially with the bulge of her belly, but watching her now, she seemed like a natural, firing off shot after shot, each one striking the target, many within the center.

"Can you believe that?" Gabriel said.

Kirima gave a slight chuckle. "I feel like I should be surprised, but knowing her, I can't say that I am."

Her sister was beaming as she lowered the gun. She turned to see Kirima watching and waved with her free hand, pointing. "You see that?"

Kirima nodded. "Now do it again."

Yura's grin turned wicked as she grabbed some more bullets and began to reload the gun. She could hear Meriwa shouting that she wanted a turn.

"I think tonight will be the night," Kirima said.

"Why do you say that?"

"Something in the air, in the water. I don't think the Imakut will wait much longer."

"Perhaps their attack on the Company has sated their desire for revenge."

Kirima's eyes traced to the shrine, where she could see the top of the sheep sticking out of the water. "Somehow I don't think we'll be that lucky."

"Do you think they're ready?"

Kirima shook her head. "How can anyone be ready for something like this? Those Company men, they were trained better than any of our people and they were slaughtered."

A silence lingered in the air. "Are you having second thoughts about fighting?"

She glanced over at him, trying to keep her face straight. "Of course not. But I don't think it helps to be unrealistic."

"A little optimism wouldn't hurt."

"Papa would probably have smacked you for saying something like that."

"Hmm, probably."

Yura had finished with her bullets and put the gun down. She now made her way toward them, picking her way carefully across the rocky path and up the slope. "I can't believe we've never had those before. Firing a gun is so exciting."

"You looked like you were having fun," Kirima said.

"Mama wouldn't let me use the gun," Meriwa said, her bottom lip sticking out.

"I told you, when you're older," Yura said.

"I'm big enough. You'd let me use one, wouldn't you, Auntie?"

Yura shot her a glance, and Kirima wiped her own smile away. "I agree with your mother."

The girl made a frustrated noise, then turned away, heading to a place where she could pout in peace. Yura only shook her head. "That girl grows worse by the day."

"She takes after her mother," Kirima said.

Yura scoffed. "I was never that bad."

"You never stopped being that bad."

"Speaking of which." Yura trailed off as she glanced over her shoulder, then looked back. "What are we going to do with the children?"

"Put them somewhere safe," Gabriel said.

"Obviously, but where? And who is going to watch them?"

"I think an equally important question is what we're doing with you," Kirima said.

Yura frowned at her. "What do you mean? I'll be fighting."

"Yura, you can't fight," Kirima said. "You're pregnant."

"That didn't hinder me down there."

"Fighting is different. We don't know how many there will be, or how fast they can move on land. We can't put you in danger like that."

"That's not your decision to make. This is my home, and I deserve to be allowed to defend it, just like everyone else." She turned to Gabriel. "Tell her."

Gabriel seemed to hesitate, his eyes going between the two women. For a moment, Kirima was certain he was going to take her sister's side. "No, Kirima is right. You need to be with the others."

"I can't believe this. I'm the best shot out there, you both saw."

"It's different when the target is moving," Kirima said. "Or when it's bearing down on you. Siluk will tell you."

"Like you're some kind of expert now." She crossed her arms. "You can't tell me not to fight."

"I will drag you there myself and tie you to the boat if I have to."

Gabriel stepped in between them, using his hand to urge Kirima back as he faced Yura. "You need to protect your children. And if you're with the others who can't fight, they'll listen to you. Just like they listen to your sister."

Yura frowned, looking between the two of them, then let loose a sigh as she threw up her hands. "Fine."

Kirima could see the tension ease in Gabriel's shoulders as he turned so that he was facing them both once more. "That's settled, then. We can put everyone not fighting in my home. If things go bad, there's a path leading up the ridge in the rear."

"Maybe we should put them on the boats," Kirima said.

"No, not unless things go bad. The last place we want them is on water, especially waiting for others."

"We can send them now, save others for the rest of us."

"The house will do, I think," Yura said. "I think it will be safer."

Kirima watched her for a second, but she seemed sincere. "I hope you're right. First sign of trouble, you take them, all of them. Don't wait for anyone."

She could see her sister struggling with the thought, but she finally said, "Alright, I will."

"I'm going to go prepare my home now," Gabriel said. "Yura, it may be good to start gathering people now."

"Alright."

He turned away, leaving the two of them standing together. They exchanged a glance for a moment, neither of them speaking. It was Yura who broke the silence.

"I can't believe you get to fight, and I don't."

"I don't have children to watch over."

"They're almost as much yours as they are mine. If you asked them, the difference wouldn't be so great."

"I'm also not with child."

Yura frowned, even as her hand drifted down to her belly. "Never once has this stopped me from doing anything. I wouldn't have it start now."

"I know, but this decision is bigger than you or I."

"I know. Just…make sure you come out of this alive."

"I'm going to do my best."

A smile crossed her face. "Papa would be proud of you."

"You think so?"

"I know so."

Kirima's hand found the jarak stone at the end of her necklace and her fingers wrapped around it. "I've always done my best to carry him on."

"And you do a wonderful job."

Kirima didn't speak for a moment. Her eyes traced over those below. She saw Siluk instructing, and a few people over, Phillip firing. She saw the prayer group. She saw Grier and Effie speaking about something as they watched more logs get stacked, Calum helping carry a large one.

"Just promise me that you'll go as well," Yura said, placing a gentle hand on her arm. "If things go bad. Don't try to be a hero."

"I won't," she said.

"Are you afraid?"

"Petrified."

"The kids think you're not."

Kirima chuckled. "I guess I'm doing a good enough job of hiding it."

"If you come back for anything, come back for them. They need their

Auntie, especially since they already lost their father."

"I know. I'll do my best. For them."

"I'm going to go help Gabriel. If I don't see you, just know that I'll be praying for you."

"Of course."

Yura left her standing there, still watching the preparations below. It was almost time. She could feel it. Tonight would be the night.

15

The rain was falling harder as the sun set, accompanied by a frigid wind from the north. The fires still burned brightly, but Kirima found herself worrying that the rain would be enough. Perhaps that was by design, perhaps the Imakut were bringing the weather to announce their arrival.

Yura and the children had packed a few scant belongings and some supplies, and made their way up to Gabriel's house, leaving Kirima alone in their own. It felt odd; she had been in the house alone before, but it had never felt so quiet, so empty, so lonely. She lit the fire and cooked herself dinner but found her appetite lacking. She forced herself to eat what she could, though she tasted none of it.

Just like the night before, sleep eluded her, her tired mind in a dreamlike state even as she stared at the ceiling of her room. She thought of Yura and the children, of Phillip and Calum, of Gabriel and the Council, of the ruins of the Company, of the Imakut, and of many more things. She thought of her father, of the days they used to spend together on the beach and on the water. And when she heard the bell ringing, quiet, distant, she wasn't sure if it was real or a part of her mind. As it persisted, something triggered in her mind, and she sat up, realizing that it was real, and she sprang to action.

Kirima pulled the hood of her parka over her head as she stepped out, squinting through the rain. The fires were still burning on the beach, but it looked like some of the braziers had gone out, a few townsfolk working to relight them. The ringing of the bell filled the air, piercing her ears now that it was no longer dampened by the walls of the house. Siluk was moving around, barking orders, yelling to be heard over the sounds.

She fell into stride beside him as he moved down the slope toward the beach. "Where do you want me?"

"Second tier. Find Phillip." He took one of his pistols and put it into her hand. "I left a few boxes of ammo there. But save it for when they get close."

She stopped as he continued on. "Don't you mean if?"

He didn't respond, and she watched his back as he directed a few more people before jumping onto one of the barriers, raising his voice to be heard. "Listen up!" He waited a moment for chatter to die down before continuing.

"It seems that tonight's the night. We don't know how many are coming, but the folks from the Company tell us they're vicious, and they don't seem to stop. So use your cover, get behind to reload, and if they get close, retreat back to the next tier, and make sure to take as much ammo and weapons as you can. Do not cross into this area behind me, no matter what. We have a few surprises set up for them."

He stopped, pausing for a moment. "I know you're all scared. It's perfectly natural to be. But this is your home. You're defending it, defending it for your friends, your families, for all those up in Gabriel's house who can't defend it themselves. May the spirits watch over us."

With that, he went to take his own place at the end of the first barrier. And they waited.

The silence that came with the ceasing of the bell was oppressive. She could hear the pattering of the rain and beneath that, every movement of the water in the harbor, each splash that could be one of the creatures coming onto land. She could hear coughing and sniffling and shifting, but no one spoke, not even a whisper. She adjusted in her place, the noise from that seeming excessively loud, and leaned forward as she squinted past the fires and out into the harbor, barely able to make out the outlines of the sunken boats and the shrine in the distance.

A sound called out from the darkness, low and long at first, a long wail that grew and grew in intensity with each passing breath, like the sound of a heavy wind blowing through an open window. Chills ran down the back of her neck, and she could suddenly hear whispers around her, whispers that became murmurs as people glanced around, seeking out the source.

"What was that?" Phillip said from beside her.

"The wind," Calum said. "Surely just the wind."

"No," she said. It was almost a hallucination, shapes created by the movement of the waves, but the longer she looked, the clearer it was. "They're here."

"Are you certain?" Phillip asked, squinting his eyes through the falling rain.

"Without a doubt," she said.

Phillip shifted his rifle, the stock in the crook of his shoulder, the barrel resting on the barrier. "This is it, then. Are you ready?"

"No," Calum said.

"Not at all," Kirima said.

"I don't think I'd ever be ready," Calum said.

"Guess the Imakut don't care either way," Phillip said.

"Hold steady," Siluk called from up ahead. "Don't fire until I give the order."

Up ahead, she saw him motion to Grier, and the enchanter stood, walking toward the barriers, standing before the blazing fire. His hands began to word, and the flames in each of the bonfires began to grow, as if the motions of his hands were feeding them invisible fuel. Beyond the fires, she could see the dark shapes climbing out of the water atop the sunken boats.

"No bad shots," Siluk said. "Open fire."

The sound of gunshots echoed through the town. Beside her, both Calum and Phillip fired, but Kirima took her time, looking down the sights at a creature as it climbed onto one of the boats. She fired, and the bullet struck, as evidenced by the way its right shoulder kicked back. The creature seemed hardly impacted by it, glancing down before leaping down on the other side of the boats, trudging through the water toward the shore.

"Don't stop and admire it," Phillip said from beside her.

"It didn't even seem fazed by it," she said, her fingers fumbling for another bullet.

"Try hitting it in the head," Calum said, lining up his rifle and taking another shot.

"Easier said than done." Kirima managed to slide the bullet in, then took aim once more. This time, she did aim for the head of another one that had climbed out, but the bullet went high, sailing harmlessly over the creature.

The first ones reached the edge of the water, stepping up the slope of the beach toward the first defenses. Her eyes dropped to where Grier stood, still working his hands. He suddenly thrust them outward to either side, and as he did, flames erupted from either side of the center bonfire, forming columns of fire to connect it with the other two.

Kirima lowered her gun, gaping at the scene before her. It burned so brightly that it was as if day had retuned, and not the cloudy days they were so used to but a bright, warm day, like it had been in Adhan. The heat was so intense that she had to fight the urge to shed her parka, sweat forming beneath.

"Would you look at that," Phillip said from beside her.

"Follow your own advice and admire later," Calum said. "Keep firing."

Kirima did keep firing, but it was impossible not to stare. The fire seemed to flow across like a river, blocking the entire path from the creatures. She saw them hesitate at its edge, giving easy shots for those firing. Some fell, but more came to replace them. She watched as one tried to push its way through the flames, but it was quickly engulfed, a shrill cry coming from its lungs as it staggered into the trench and impaled itself on one of the stakes.

"Keep firing," Siluk yelled, barely audible in the sound of gunfire. "Kill as many as you can."

From her vantage point, Kirima could see the way their blood painted the sand at the edge of the water, the same sludge-like ooze she had seen at the Company outpost. Behind, some of the creatures were dragging the bodies away, making room as more emerged from the harbor. Others began trying to splash water on the fires, but they were burning far too strongly, the splashes sizzling into steam the moment they struck.

"How are you holding up?" Siluk shouted to Grier.

"I can go all night," he said over his shoulder.

From where she stood, it certainly seemed like it. The fire was flowing strong, Grier showing none of the fatigue he had mentioned to her before. It seemed channeling the fire was much simpler than lifting something.

The noise was almost lost behind the sporadic gunshots and the pounding rain. Like when the creatures had emerged from the water, Kirima wasn't sure she had even really heard something at first. But she was certain she had when she saw the glob arching over the flames and landing on the beach just beyond where Grier stood.

He turned, keeping his hands wide, the flames faltering just the slightest as his concentration was broken. "What the hell was that?"

"Don't stop, we'll handle it." Siluk turned toward someone at the front barrier. "Get out there with the shields."

Two people immediately stood, each picking up a large, flat wooden object that strapped to their arm. Another few globs fell around Grier as they stepped in front of him, holding the shields up to block him. More globs fell, many missing completely as others splashed harmlessly off the shields.

"What is that stuff?" Phillip asked, pausing to look down at the spots where it had landed on the beach.

"I don't know," Kirima said, following his gaze down. It lay there where it struck, sticking in the sand, but doing nothing else. "It's splashing like water, but it looks thicker."

A cry drew their attention. One of the shield holders was staggering, stumbling backward, enough that Grier stepped back as well, the flames faltering but not going out. She couldn't tell who it was, but they were giving out cries of pain, looking like they were trying to shake something off their foot.

"What's happening?" Calum asked.

"He was hit," Kirima said. She squinted through the rain. There seemed to be tendrils of smoke rising up from the man's leg, part of it now missing. "It's...melting him."

"It's what?"

"Look at his foot. It looks like a burning candle."

More fell around him, and then one struck him right in the face. The effect was instant. He dropped the shield, hands going to his face as he writhed about, screaming in agony. Grier took another step back as more globs fell, coming now at a frightening pace. The other who had the shield, a woman Kirima didn't know from the Company, had turned now, her shield lowered just enough as her face twisted in horror.

"Shield up, shield up," Siluk called out.

A glob struck her on the side of the neck, and the result was little different. Her cries pierced through the air as she turned and fell to her knees. Kirima could see the way it ate away at the side of her neck, exposing the muscle and tendons beneath. The man had stopped struggling, his body convulsing in its dying throes as he lay face down on the ground.

"Grier, pull back," Siluk shouted.

"I've got it," he said, though he did take a step back.

"You've held it long enough, it's too dangerous."

"I'll be fine, I…"

He was cut off as one struck his outstretched left arm. He instantly recoiled, doubling over, his teeth clenched together, holding his left arm against his chest. Siluk was already running toward him, shouting orders to keep firing. Already, the flames between the bonfires were dissipating, as if sucked right back into the center one. And then, it was as if the floodgates were opened.

"Keep firing," Siluk shouted, trying to get Grier away from the front. Something fell from Grier's side to the ground, and Kirima thought she was about to vomit when she realized that it was his arm. He was not screaming like the others were, but there was no doubt that he was in incredible pain.

"Kirima, what are you doing?" Phillip said from beside her. "Fire!"

She tore her eyes away from the enchanter and looked toward the barriers. The creatures rushed through the space where the flames had once been, pouring forth like ants from a disturbed nest. Some fell, impaled on the stakes, but there were so many pouring from the sea that most just ran over their dead companions. She raised her gun without thinking, taking aim at the first one she saw and firing. She wasn't sure if she even struck it because she was already grabbing another bullet, shoving it into the chamber and bringing it up to fire again.

Within seconds, it was clear that the first barrier was going to fall. She fired again, then glanced around, desperately looking for Siluk. There were no orders being given, only chaos as the creatures descended on the front line.

"First line, fall back," she shouted. She turned to the line behind them. "Give cover, we need to get them out of there."

As she turned back, she caught sight of Siluk, Grier's arm around his shoulders. The enchanter's eyes were partly closed, his clothing and what remained of his left arm hanging in tatters. The feeling in her gut returned, and she forced herself to swallow it down.

"Let me help," she said, moving to take him.

"Not with this," Siluk said, moving away. "Help by pulling them back. Reorganize them. Your town needs you."

He was already moving in the direction of Gabriel's house, half carrying Grier up the slope. She turned toward the beach, where the creatures were advancing. She saw one person get torn apart, and another being dragged kicking and screaming to the sea as more rushed past. One of the fires was completely out, and another was almost out.

"Everyone, get back," she said, running forward. The first barrier was lost, but the second still stood, and she could save them. She tapped at the shoulder of the person nearest the center to the left and then the one to the right. "Retreat. There's too many of them."

People began to pull back, but others remained, either from not being able to hear her or from pure stubbornness. She called out to the most distant, but her voice was lost in the sound of the battle. She saw the creatures reach the second barrier, and she knew it was lost.

Kirima turned to retreat herself, but she felt herself caught, something grabbing onto her ankle. She looked back, seeing a creature with its finned hand gripping her, its massive, toothy jaw gaping, the stench of its breath filling her nose. She pulled against it, trying to separate it, kicking at it with her free leg, but its grip was like iron, its fingers refusing to separate. She felt it pulling her in, dragging her back toward it, and the sand of the beach giving way as she fought.

Her fingers gripped uselessly at the loose ground, gaining no traction. Her gun had fallen out of reach, growing only further away as it dragged her, other creatures running past. She could see the lights of the village seeming to fade through the falling rain.

A large, dark shape suddenly blocked everything from her sight, knocking several creatures aside and leaping right over her. She turned onto her back, watching as it gave a roar and grabbed the creature that had her. She felt its claws tear through her pants and her skin, drawing blood, but she was free. She scooted up the beach, watching as it slammed the creature into the ground over and over, breaking it into pieces before finally flinging the remainder into the beach. It didn't linger, leaping across the beach to attack a group of them.

She felt hands under her armpits, pulling her to her feet. "Come on," Gabriel said. "Get up."

"What the hell was that?" she said.

Gabriel shoved her rifle into her hands. "That was the Giant."

"Effie?"

"She changed right before my eyes," Gabriel said, shaking his head. "I don't know how, but I'm glad she's on our side. Come on, get back to cover."

Kirima's eyes remained on the beach below, the shape of the creature, Effie, she reminded herself, as it tore through the creatures. It drew the attention of many of the others, allowing those still firing to pick several off.

"She's destroying them," Kirima said. "She's got them on the run."

Siluk's voice appeared from behind her. "I wouldn't be so certain."

"Why do you say that?" she asked.

"The Company folks said they don't give up so easily."

As if to confirm, another long wail sounded, this one louder than the initial one. "What was that?" Gabriel asked.

"Reinforcements," Siluk said.

A roar echoed through the harbor, one that did not come from Effie. Kirima's eyes went to the water where something massive was rising out of it, perhaps as large as the whales the company hunted. Even in the dim light, she could see how the body seemed as if it was made from seaweed, the thick head attached to broad shoulders without seeming to have a neck, the way its eyes glowed.

Everyone seemed too shocked to move, too stunned to act. The guns had stopped firing, the people around her stopped moving, even the creatures seemed to have stopped attacking. All eyes seemed focused on the thing that now emerged from the deep.

"What is that thing?" Kirima asked.

"Something big," Gabriel said.

"Don't just watch, fire on it," Siluk shouted from beside her. "Everything you've got."

The shots began to sound once more, all around her, but it didn't even flinch at the impacts. The creature gave another ear shattering roar, and it picked up a boat from the shallows and flung it. It flew in the air over the barriers, and several people scattered as it crashed into one of the houses behind her, raining debris everywhere.

"Look out."

Siluk grabbed her, pulling her aside. She had still been looking at the one behind her, not even aware that another was coming toward them. Siluk was shielding her with his body, the boat kicking up sand and chunks of wood as it crashed into the barrier.

"We have to get everyone out of here," Gabriel said from somewhere nearby.

"No, we have to keep fighting," she said.

"We can't fight that thing."

"Effie can," Siluk said.

When she finally looked, Effie was already moving into the water to meet it, each of them letting loose roars as they met. She grabbed it, and it grabbed her back, the two of them struggling against each other, each trying to throw the other down.

"We can't just stand here and watch," Siluk said. "More are coming."

He was already moving to get behind one of the further barriers, and Kirima scrambled after him. "What about Grier? Is he alright?"

"No telling," he said. "He's with those in Gabriel's house."

"They haven't left yet?"

"Your sister in particular seemed quite adamant that they stay."

She shook her head. "Stubborn."

"Worry about them later. I need you shooting those things."

She took up a place beside him, slotting a bullet into her gun and taking aim. With Effie engaged with the large creature, more of the smaller ones were pouring out of the sea. She took shots, watching the battle in the harbor in between each one. Effie had managed to get it onto its back, but it had reacted by pulling her down and rolling over. It now had a piece of a boat with a jagged end in its hands, trying to stab Effie with it as she held it back.

"Look out!" She felt herself taken to the ground, Siluk on top of her. At first, she felt anger, but that instantly faded when she saw the creature above her, its clawed hand reaching out for her. How had she missed it?

She reached around for the pistol on the ground, finally finding it, aiming upward, and firing right through the creature's head, splattering the viscous blood over both of them. She spit some from her lips, a vile taste reaching her tongue.

"Thanks," she said as Siluk quickly stood, helping her to her feet.

"Pay attention," he said. "I won't always be there to save you."

"Understood," she said.

She picked up her own rifle, but already she could see that they were overrunning the remaining defenders below. More were being dragged out to sea as others died right there on the beach, their bodies lying alongside those of the creatures, indistinguishable in the pouring rain.

"We have to pull back," she said. She looked over to Phillip and Calum, both where she had left them, still firing away. "There's too many of them."

"What about her?" Phillip said, motioning out to the harbor.

Kirima looked out, seeing that Effie had managed to stab the thing in the shoulder, but it seemed to be hardly fazed by the wound, one of its hands holding hers in place as its other struck her in the head over and over again.

"She can take care of herself," Siluk said. Kirima glanced at him, unsure whether he was lying or not, but she saw no indication either way.

"Kirima's right. Fall back."

"Go," Calum said. "We'll cover."

Kirima waited until she saw Phillip nod, but Siluk was already moving, shouting at others to fall back to Gabriel's house. Kirima turned toward others, motioning them back. She had let go of the rifle, her hand now gripping a long blade in one hand, a pistol in the other.

"Get back to the house," she shouted. "There's too many. Retreat."

Most obeyed immediately, others needing more physical coaxing, but they went. One she saved from an instant death when her voice drew the attention of an attacking creature, allowing the woman to slice through the creature's jaw with her blade, sending it tumbling back with a sickening cry.

Kirima reached the end of the barrier and looked back. Only Phillip and Calum were left on her side, the rest drawing back. Beyond them, Siluk was already trailing the others up the slope. She began to run, shouting as she did.

"That's everyone. Go, now!"

Each of the boys fired off a last shot before turning away. Kirima was running down the lane behind them, several paces back as they raced toward the end of the lane. She didn't even see the creature that leapt up from below, not until it was already colliding with the boys. Phillip was knocked aside, sprawling into the rocky wet dirt of the path, while Calum fell beneath the weight of the creature. Phillip was back on his feet immediately, pushing off a nearby wall and launching into their attacker.

Kirima skidded to a stop, her eyes looking over the scene before her as her brain fought to keep up. She could see that it had torn a gash across Calum's belly, his blood covered hands clutching at it as he tried to scoot away, his feet scrambling against the rocky ground. Phillip grappled with the creature, holding his rifle crosswise as leverage against its strength. Kirima raised her own pistol, taking aim, but they shifted position, Phillip blocking her sightline.

"Get him out of here," Phillip yelled over his shoulder. "Get him to the house."

"What about you?" She was already moving even as she said the words, grabbing Calum and pulling him up the slope.

"Don't worry about me, I…"

It seemed instant, the way the creature moved, extending its neck, its jaws wide open as it clasped onto his face. Muffled screams escaped, but they quickly faded into a slurping sound, blood dripping from either side. The rifle dropped from his hands, his body convulsing as it sucked the life right out of him.

"Phillip!" She started to release Calum, to step forward, to do something, anything, but a hand grabbed her arm, pulled her back.

"No." It was Siluk's voice. "We have to pull back."

"But Phillip. I can save him."

"No, you can't."

She tried to step toward him, but Siluk pulled her back harder, wrapping his arms around her and dragging her back as two others came and lifted Calum. She struggled, tears in her eyes indistinguishable from the rain as she watched Phillip's body go limp, as the creature released him and he fell backwards, his face completely vanished into a mess of blood and bone.

She forced herself to look away, but no other direction offered any respite. She could see bodies that littered the beach, lit by the fading light of the bonfires. Some were being dragged into the water by the creatures as more emerged from the waves. In the harbor, Effie lay lifeless atop one of the boats, the Imakut giant using a chunk of wood to bash her head in, over and over.

The rain was still falling, so hard that it was jarring when it suddenly stopped. She blinked at the sudden brightness, the warmth and dryness that surrounded her as the door was closed behind her, Gabriel stepping forward and sliding a thick wooden bar into place to lock it. She blinked and looked around her, seeing all the familiar faces, the fearful looks, some covered in dirt and grime from fighting, others still dry from being in the house.

Her eyes drifted down to where Calum had been placed, the extent of his injury now visible to her in the light, the way the blood stained his parka around the wound, the way he lay there limply, his eyes staring lifelessly into the distance.

Kirima found her strength had fled her. She collapsed against the wall, slid down into a seated position, and began to sob.

16

She wasn't sure how long she wept. It felt like a long time, but it could not have been that long. No one stopped her, and when she finally wiped away the wetness from her cheeks, she finally took note of the room.

They had moved Calum away, somewhere out of sight, though she could still see a trail of blood where he had once lay. There were still many alive, the room filled almost to the brim, but there were so many who were clean, those determined not able to fight, vastly outnumbering those who showed signs of having been on the beach.

She felt warm hands on her cheeks and looked up into her sister's eyes. "What happened?"

"There were so many," she said. "So many of them. So many dead. Phillip, he's dead. Calum too. And Effie. And many others." She choked down another sob and it turned into a cough.

"I know." She suddenly wrapped Kirima in an embrace. "I know. I'm so sorry. But there will be time to mourn later. We need you now."

It was then that she felt the impact, so strong that the entire house seemed to shudder. She sat up straight, her eyes wide open, looking around at those in the room. She saw Gabriel, close, breathing hard, his eyes turned to her. She saw Grier passed out, or perhaps dead against another wall, his missing arm loosely bandaged in tattered wool. She saw Oki standing amongst some of the council members, saying something to them, his clothing remarkably clean and dry. She saw her niece and nephew, embracing each other, both putting on brave faces as they watched her, and she saw Yura, still kneeling before her.

"We need you, Kirima."

She slowly stood from where she had fallen, trying and failing to hide the wince as another bang came. This time, though, it wasn't shaking the house; she could hear it behind her, a blow so hard that she could hear the cracking of the wood, like the door would shatter right off its hinges. They were just outside, and it would not be long before they were in.

She glanced around to those who had fought, trying to pick out those who still could. There was a difference, and she could see it in those stained in blood, those who avoided her gaze, those who still looked back at her with exhausted eyes.

She turned to Yura. "You have to lead them away." Yura nodded. Kirima turned back to the room. "We need to hold them long enough for everyone who can to get away. Who's with me?"

At first, there was no response. It was Gabriel who first stepped forward. "I'm with you."

Siluk was next, not that there was any doubt that he would be. Others stepped forward. She looked toward Oki and the council members, but none stood. Grier, however, did.

"I am with you."

"Can you fight?" she asked.

"Better than most the men here."

"I have no use for idle boasts."

"If I were boasting, you'd know it."

Kirima nodded toward him, then drew in a breath, turning toward the rest. "If you can't fight, or if you won't, go with Yura. You know if you're one or the other. But we need to hold, to allow the others time to escape. We may not live, but we will make sure that others will."

There was another bang on the door, this time, the cracking of the wood clearly audible, the door seeming all but ready to come off its hinges, to burst inward and allow the flood of Imakut creatures to tear them all apart, to drag them kicking and screaming to the sea.

Already, the crowd within the house had begun to separate, to split between those who would stay to fight and those who would go. Kirima looked over, seeing Oki amongst the latter. "Oki, are you not going to avenge your nephews' sacrifice?"

He looked at her and back at the others, and she could see the fear in his eyes. "They need someone to protect them."

"They have plenty to protect them," she said. "Come fight."

Oki glanced around at the others, then slowly made his way across the floor. Kirima hardly looked at him, her eyes focused right on Yura. "Straight down the path to the boats. Make sure you leave one for the rest of us. Get far enough offshore and don't look back. Head south, and just keep going."

"You'll be right behind?" Yura said.

Another crash at the door. She looked back and found she could almost see right through the cracks, the door now braced by two of the larger ones. She turned back to Yura "As close as we can be. Go, now!"

Yura didn't hesitate any further. She pushed open the back door, ushering everyone through. They fled out into the pounding rain, filing out the door as quickly as they could without pushing each other over. The children were the last ones out before Yura, and she threw one last glance at Kirima before leaving herself.

As she turned back, she found Siluk looking at her. "Are you ready?"

"No," she said.

"No one ever is." He raised his voice. "Alright, back away from the door. We're going to let them in and kill as many of these bastards as we can."

The men at the door obeyed, while Oki looked over at him in disbelief. "You're just going to let them in?"

"If we let them overpower us, we're at a disadvantage. Let them pile into a place where we can see, where they can only come in a few at a time. Kill them and let the bodies pile up."

"Remind them of who they are facing," someone called out.

"Until our dying breath," said another.

"Until our dying breath," Kirima repeated.

The men bracing the door moved away from it, and everyone took position, ready to fight. Kirima gripped her blade tightly, the sword in one hand and a knife in another, the pistol shoved into her belt, readily available should she need it. She moved in place, keeping her muscles limber as the banging came again and again and again.

The door split open, and the creatures flooded into the room.

It was several beats before the first one reached her. Every single one that entered before was cut down quickly, by Gabriel or Siluk or someone else. The first one she saw, she sliced down the front of the chest with the sword, following with Grier's blade through its eye. She fought the urge to admire the kill, already turning to the next one.

She killed another, then another, and another. There seemed to be no end. Each one that fell was replaced by two more, then three more. They piled in, first just through the door, then through the windows, widened as the creatures broke through the glass and pulled away at the wooden frames. One defender fell, and then another, their bodies falling amongst those of the creatures.

"There's too many," Oki said from behind her.

"Keep fighting," she said as she watched Siluk kill a pair with his twin blades. A different one fell upon her, its hands grasping her shoulders, its jaws snapping mere inches from her nose, but it suddenly stopped as a blade fell pierced its eye. She stumbled back from it, looking over to see Oki pulling a blade out, the look on his face showing the same surprise that she felt.

"We need to pull back," he said, turning toward the onslaught, holding his blade out toward the door. "They must be far enough by now."

"No," she said. "They need more time."

"And who is going to give us time?" he shouted.

"No one," Siluk said. "We're on our own. Not until Kirima says."

She slashed at another one, watching another fall. She thought she heard a bang, one that may have shaken the house, but it could have simply been her imagination. "Keep fighting," she said. "Give them more time."

"We're going to die," Oki said.

"If that happens, then so be it," Siluk said.

Behind her, she saw Grier, doing his work with only a single arm, seeming to barely be able to stand. Oki was not far from him, his blade held out before him, now covered in the green sludge from the creature he had stabbed. Grier made a motion with his hand, and the flames that emerged were a pittance compared to what he had been enchanting earlier. It did the job, though, slicing like a stream through some of the creatures as they pushed through, scalding some and setting others aflame. Their screeches filled the air, one in particular turning and trying to run back out the door, catching others on fire before finally colliding with the wooden wall.

Kirima watched as the flames began to spread up the wall to the ceiling, the smoke beginning to fill the room. "That may be our cue," Siluk said from beside her. He pulled out his pistol and shot one through the head, the sound even louder in the closed space.

There was a loud crashing sound as a massive fist punched through the side of the house, shaking it enough that Kirima stumbled back, nearly losing her footing. It seemed to sit there a moment, the light of the fire glistening off the seaweed-like skin. Up close, she could see it moving, like there were creatures wriggling within the seaweed. A loud rumbling noise sounded as the fist opened and the palm searched around. Before anyone could react, it grabbed someone, pulling them kicking and screaming through the hole.

"If the flames weren't, that was," she said. "Everyone fall back. We've bought them enough time."

Behind her, Oki was already through the door, though Grier continued to spout flames out. She stabbed at a creature, grabbing someone by the sleeve and pulling them back, shouting at the others, but she quickly saw that they were overwhelmed. Up ahead, she could now only see Gabriel, but there were creatures between the two of them.

She called out his name, and he turned in the slightest, revealing the mix of his own blood from a gash on his forehead and the green sludge from the creatures on his face. "Go," he shouted.

"You need to come too," she said. She could feel Siluk pulling on her, dragging her back toward the rear exit. "Leave it."

"Don't worry about me." He was already turning and slashing at the creatures, slicing through a couple with the swing of one and then stabbing with his knife.

"We have to go back for him," she said as Siluk pulled her toward the door. "We have to help him."

"There's nothing we can do but get ourselves killed. Don't lessen his sacrifice by getting yourself killed."

She tried to protest, but the words stuck in her throat. I didn't ask for this. I didn't ask for him to sacrifice. Not that it mattered what she had asked for.

Gabriel killed another one right as a larger hole opened, the massive seaweed creature crashing through a piece of wall weakened by the flames. She could get a better look at it now, the massive fist, the squirming that covered it, that dripped from it to the ground, the toothless maw and beady eyes on its head. It seemed to look right at her for a moment, then turned down to Gabriel. He saw it as well, stabbing out with his sword as it reached for him. The sword went in, but seemed to do no damage to it, and as it lifted him up off the ground, he struggled to pull it out, to strike again. The last she saw of him was the gargantuan pulling him through the hole in the wall as Siluk pulled her from the house.

As she exited, it was as if a fog had cleared in her mind, perhaps driven away by the rain that was still pouring. Siluk still had one hand on her shoulder, leading her, a blade in his other hand. She could see no one except Grier, leaning against a tree, his hand holding the spot where his arm was missing. He had lost his hat, long brown hair matted to his forehead, his eyes closed, even as they approached.

"Can you still conjure?" Siluk asked as they approached, dropping his hand from her shoulder.

Grier's nostrils flared as he breathed in, his lips remaining a sliver, and he nodded. His eyes opened just a bit, and she saw how bloodshot they were, almost enough that she thought they might start bleeding right there. Any other night, that might have been the most disturbing thing she had seen. Even so, it gave her a strange feeling in her gut.

"Bring it down on them."

Grier nodded. She wasn't sure if he had lost the ability to speak, or if he was just too exhausted or in too much pain. Either way, he looked like he could hardly stand, yet he did, stepping forward on wobbling legs and raising his remaining hand. It shook, his eyes closed, his teeth clenched as he curled his fingers.

The house began to crumple, turning inward on itself as he worked his fingers, closing them in until they formed a fist. Blood was leaking from his nose, his entire body shaking from the effort. The house turned inward a bit further, the screams of the creatures sounding within, and the flames flared up, taking the wooden roof and walls, raindrops sizzling as they struck the flames.

"That won't hold them," Siluk said. "We need to get to the boat."

He took a couple of steps and then turned, placing a hand on Grier's shoulder. The enchanter had dropped to a knee, and in the firelight, she could a darker puddle forming at his feet where blood was dripping from his nose. She watched for just a brief moment, the way Siluk's hand lingered there, the way Grier sat unmoving.

"Is he…"

Siluk nodded. "Too much power used."

"I didn't know that was possible."

"It's possible to take in too much of anything." He removed his hand and began to walk up the path at a brisk pace.

"Shouldn't we do something?" she asked, casting a glance at Grier, still in that kneeling position. "Say something? Take him with us?"

"No," Siluk said. "And he would have wanted it that way."

She hurried after him, not listening to the sounds of the dying creatures in the burning house behind them. She only hoped they couldn't get through, not for a long time.

17

The sound came just as they reached the clearing where she had been practicing. It was just like that first sound, like the sound of a gale passing through narrow crags. She stopped, turning back as she peered through the trees. She could see the flames of the fire, no doubt spreading through the rest of town, and the smoke that rose from it, the blackness blending with the dark sky and pouring rain to seem like a waterfall flowing upward, but she saw nothing of the creatures.

"Listen," Siluk said.

"To what?"

He held up a finger, and they were both silent. At first all she heard was the sound of the rain pattering around them and the wind whispering through the trees, but there was another sound, one that manifested itself beneath the others, growing and growing with each passing second.

She looked at him, feeling her eyes grow wide. "They're coming."

Siluk nodded, already turning toward the inlet. "Time for us to run."

She took his cue, sprinting after him. Behind, she could hear the footsteps as the creatures pursued them, tearing through the trees at frightening speed. She refused to look back, not wanting to see how close they were, how much danger there was right then. The sound was more than enough.

Kirima and Siluk ran down the path, reaching the small inlet that the boats had been in, except there were no boats to be found. There was only Oki, standing at the water's edge, looking out across the horizon. Kirima reached him first, skidding to a stop in the sand.

"Oki, what are you doing?" she said. "They're coming, we have to go."

"The boats are gone," he said. "They're all gone. They didn't wait for us."

She looked back and saw the figures up the slope. She turned back to him, pushing him along the shore. "Come on, we can't just stand here."

"What's the point?" he said. "We're doomed here."

"Come on," Siluk said. "We can't wait. He can die if he wants."

Siluk turned down the beach, and she followed him. As she glanced back, she saw Oki following as well. The sand slowed them, but she couldn't imagine the creatures would fare any better. All the while, her mind worked. He was right, wasn't he? They were gone, and it had taken all the boats for them to get away, it seemed. What choices did they have? Evade the creatures until the morning? Would they even leave in the morning? Stand there and fight? Against those numbers? They wouldn't stand a chance. And if they somehow did, would the creatures not be back the next evening?

"Kirima."

It was Siluk's voice that brought her back. She skidded to a stop and turned, seeing that he was looking back at Oki, stopped himself a few paces back. She stepped toward him, raising her voice.

"Oki, we don't have time for this," she said.

"No, no, time is something we don't have."

A few more steps toward him. "Oki, come on. Let's go."

He shook his head, flinging water about from his hair. "No, it's over. And it's your fault I'm even here."

"Oki, please." It sounded as if the creatures were approaching quickly, as if they were right on the other side of the trees.

He pointed his knife in her direction. "I could have already been on the boat, safe from these things, but I'm here because you forced me to."

"I didn't force you to do anything. I'm not staying around for this."

She turned away, but he lashed out, grabbing onto her arm with a heavy grip. She pulled and pulled, but he was much stronger than her, the days and days of fighting against the whales that the Company hunted ingrained in his very bones and muscles.

"Hey, what are you doing?" Siluk was on them in a flash, and Oki's knife was on him just as quickly, the point driving right through his belly. He gasped, his hands gripping it, pulling it from Oki's hand as he stumbled back. Kirima found herself gaping, watching as he fell to the ground.

"No." The word just escaped her lips.

"We're not prolonging the inevitable," Oki said, turning to face the oncoming creatures, turning her with him, his arm around her throat. "We will die sooner instead of waiting. Let's eliminate a few minutes or hours of pain and paranoia."

"No, we can survive," she said. She focused on him, not wanting to look at Siluk's body bleeding out on the ground. She managed to throw her weight enough that she caught him off guard, causing him to stumble toward the water. She dug her foot in and pushed again, this time throwing her weight downward. It worked just as she hoped, taking them both into the surf.

The cold water sent a shock through her system, her mouth drawing in a sharp breath as she felt it seep through her clothing to her skin. She recovered quickly, pushing away from Oki and scrambling through the water. She only made it a few steps before she felt him grab her legs, sending her sprawling face forward into the water. Her eyes stung, and she felt the salt go up her nose and into her mouth as her breath was driven from her lungs. She pushed herself up, gasping for air, but she only caught a bit before she was struck from behind, the force driving her back beneath the water.

She struggled, pushing up against him as he held her down, but even her strength from rowing the canoe through the Narrows day after day faltered against his years of hunting whales. Already her lungs struggled, burning as they sought out a breath of air. She saw black, but she was unsure if it was because she was about to pass out or because of the dark night above. Her hands flailed, no longer pushing but instead seeking out some sort of purchase or perhaps even a last-ditch effort to foil her assailant. Except they only grasped air and water, neither serving her much good in escaping.

Suddenly, the pressure was gone, his weight no longer planted on her back and head. She couldn't have been in more than a few inches of water, but even so, it felt like she was rising up from the bottom of the sea, her burning lungs seeking air until she broke the surface and they found it. She sucked in a deep breath, not even sure it would be enough, but then came another and another. She spat up water, coughing and breathing in more as her body recovered.

The water cleared from her eyes, the world slowly coming back into focus as the salt drained out. She could see two figures grappling, their hands held together, a knife in one of them. As her vision cleared further, she could see Oki, his teeth gritted, that crazed look in his eye, and Siluk, his white skin seeming almost like a wraith in the rain, his clothing stained with both his own blood and that of the creatures he had killed.

Kirima tried to stand, but it felt as if her muscles did not want to obey. She coughed again, spitting out more water that she didn't think she had. Up ahead, Siluk and Oki had separated, the knife in Oki's hand. He slashed at Siluk, who just barely avoided it. Oki slashed at him again, this time off balance, and Siluk grabbed his arm, pulling on him, using his momentum to send him flailing into the water.

Siluk was slow to turn, his hand holding the wound on his side. He brought his hand up, looking at the blood that covered it, then lunged himself at Oki. Oki was only pushing himself up, shaking water from his hair, and the impact drove him back into the water. They tumbled around, splashing water about as they fought. Siluk ended up on top, and he punched him once, twice, again and again. She thought he would go until Oki was dead, but he stopped suddenly, his mouth open in a silent scream of pain.

Oki was climbing to his feet, his teeth clenched as he pressed both thumbs into Siluk's wound. He pressed until Siluk collapsed backward, and still kept one hand on the wound as the other grabbed Siluk by the neck, driving his head beneath the water. Kirima tried to rise, to give any help she could, but it felt impossible, like her limbs were refusing to work. It was such a helpless feeling, as if she were trapped in her own body, only able to watch as Siluk was slowly drowned.

There was no sound when the creature appeared. It seemed to emerge from nowhere as it stepped through the rain, moving smoothly as it came up beside Oki. It grabbed him and tore him away from Siluk, lifting him into the air into the air with one arm. She saw his eyes widen, as if his mind was still trying to figure out what had happened as the creature ripped his throat out with its free hand.

Siluk managed to rise, but another emerged from the darkness, driving him back to the ground. She could see him thrashing in the shallow water, his legs kicking and his arms flailing, but she could not see what was happening. All she knew was that he was not likely to escape. And neither was she.

She allowed herself to fall back, the water lapping against her cheeks, her eyes gazing upward. The rain was still falling, though the clouds had parted just in the slightest, giving her a view of the stars above. The last stars she would probably ever see. Her mind turned to Yura and the children. She hoped they had gotten away, that they were already far from the island, far from the north, heading toward a better life.

A dark figure appeared before her, and she closed her eyes, preparing to meet the same fate as the others. When nothing happened, she opened her eyes again, seeing the figure standing before her, only its outline visible in the dark night, an outline that showed a human-like figure, one missing the right arm beneath the elbow.

Her heart beat faster as she stared back at it. Did it know who she was? Did it have something special planned, revenge for the loss of its arm? Or did it only know that she was the cause of other deaths, that she and her companions had sent so many to their graves? Would it kill her now or drag her into the cold, dark depths, where she would drown before any of the real horrors began?

She did not hear the shot, but she saw the impact. The creature recoiled, its head jerking back with sudden violence, the viscous blood spraying into the air. She heard sounds, but they were quickly drowned out by more shots firing one after another. Another creature fell, then another, while others scattered, scared off by the sounds.

Kirima didn't move. The water lapped at her, the rain continued to fall, perhaps a bit lighter, she thought. Something bumped her, one of the bodies, no doubt. A figure appeared above her, but the shape was different, not the sharp features of the Imakut creatures, but soft, familiar. She thought she heard her sister's voice beneath the sound of the churning water, but it seemed distant, a figment of her imagination.

She saw another figure and felt strong hands grabbing onto her, lifting her from the surf. The voices felt less distant now, more clear, almost real. She heard her sister speaking.

"Kirima? Kirima, are you alright?"

Her mind was still in a haze. "I don't know. Is this real? Or am I dead?"

She could see her sister now, see the way she frowned, even in the dim light. "Of course this is real. Now come on, get to the boat before more of those things come."

"What are you doing here?"

Yura had slid beneath her arm, supporting her with her weight. "I came back for you. Is that not obvious?"

"You shouldn't be here, not in your condition."

"Pregnant? I've done much more strenuous work while with child. Now come on. Quickly."

She allowed Yura to lead her, to support her as they moved toward the awaiting boat. A light shone from the top, guiding their way. She watched the waters around it, expecting the creatures to appear, to burst from the waters and climb onto it and slaughter the rest aboard. She so expected it that even when they reached Gabriel's boat, when those aboard helped her and Yura up, that when the engine was started and it began to move away from the island, she still wasn't sure she believed it.

18

When the sun rose, the island was nowhere in sight, but there was still a lingering cloud in the distance, the black soot from the flames not yet faded into the atmosphere.

They made no stop, no time for camp. Kirima had not realized how exhausted she was, not until Yura led her to the small cabin below and made her lay down on the bed. Even when she finally awoke, when the next day was coming to an end, she could feel the fatigue in her body, enough that she needed help to get back onto the deck.

None of the adults outside of her sister seemed eager to speak to her, or even acknowledge her, but the children kept her occupied and cuddled next to her when she returned to the cabin a while later. The next morning, she felt a bit more refreshed, if still a bit sore, actually able to help around the boat.

The weather warmed around them, and the waters grew clearer and bluer beneath them. She watched as they passed the islands with the towering ruins that were being reclaimed both by the crashing waves and by the plants that were rapidly creeping up their walls. Perhaps that was what her own town would look like once the fires had been extinguished and the land had time to recuperate.

Soon, she found herself once again looking upon the wall of mountains that surrounded Adhan. She moved to the front of the boat when they appeared, watching as they passed by, the wind whipping around her hair. They had said that the mountains offered protection, but there would be no protection from the Imakut, not if they came this way. And she was certain that sooner or later, they would.

Navigating to the city itself had been accomplished using the old maps Gabriel had stashed on the boat, but as they approached the city, it was her experience that guided them. She directed them toward the same docks they had moored at only days ago, and when the boat was tied up and the official paid, she led them to the temple.

Walking was still painful, the aches from the night of battles still weighing on her body, but she was no longer tired, not like she had been. She led them down the dock and through the market, seeing the same looks of wonder that she had felt on her own face when she had first arrived. Now, everything here seemed almost insignificant, the sense of wonder faded with time. Or perhaps that night had dulled her senses that much.

A few seemed resistant to leave the boat, particularly Lusa, but Kirima insisted that everyone come. The boat would be safe, especially without the small piece of metal that Gabriel had taken the first time, the one that allowed it to run, and besides, there was no telling when they would come back to it. Perhaps their luck would be good, and they would be back within a day, but she did not think that would be the case.

Even as they made their way through the market, her and her sister keeping a close eye on those who were particularly taken with the surroundings, there were those who suggested staying, finding a place where they could make a new home in Adhan. But that was not what they were there for, and she did not think that was wise either. No, Adhan was much too close to their home, and she had a feeling that it would not stop there.

The same woman with the shaved head was at the temple, Catriona, her name had been. Kirima could almost see her face drop when she laid eyes upon them, when she saw the ragged group that had come so far, all of them in the same cold weather clothing that Kirima had worn that first day, bundled up despite the heat that the city held. It was a look of pity, of understanding, of empathy, of sadness. They had failed, and she knew it. So she helped.

The room she put them in was fairly small. Not as small as Kirima's room had been back home, but small nonetheless. Mats and blankets were laid around the edges and in the center, close enough to each other that movement was hard, but it was better than nothing. It was certainly better than sleeping on the boat had been.

Once they were settled in, Kirima approached the priestess. "A word, if I may?"

"Certainly," she said. "Come, this way. I have a private space where we may speak."

She led Kirima to a small chamber, her own, it seemed, decorated with the same kind of imagery that the main hall held, but on a smaller scale, and perhaps in a way that was not so violent. There was a small bed, a desk, and something that contained numerous rolls of what looked like paper, though Kirima could not be certain in the dim light.

She waited for Kirima to enter, then turned and closed the door. "What can I do for you?"

"Our fears were realized," she said.

The woman's face remained stoic. "I see. And your companions, the two men who were with you? Did they…"

Kirima breathed in deeply and let it out in a long sigh, the only way she could stop from letting her emotions get the best of her. "They didn't make it."

The woman gave a quick bow. "I am sorry to hear of that. They seemed like good men."

"They were," she said quietly. "They truly were."

"So the Imakut did come?"

"They did. They destroyed the town and killed almost all of our people. I was on a boat that survived. We had at least three more that got away, but I'm unsure what became of them. As far as I know, those in that room are all that remain."

"You chose to fight?"

Kirima nodded. "We did."

"And you failed."

Kirima watched the woman for a moment. There seemed to be no malice in her statement, but that didn't prevent it from feeling like she had just been punched in the gut. "We failed."

"I am sorry for your losses, for your suffering. Truly I am. But it is still a blessing. We now know that fighting is not the right choice." She put a hand on Kirima's shoulder, one that was probably meant to be comforting, but was too hard, too unyielding to be. "I wish I could have given you the same advice when you came."

"I do too."

"Is there anything else you want to know?"

"I just…" Kirima paused. Right then, all she wanted was to go to sleep, her mind so exhausted from that night, from the trip on the boat there, from everything. But at the same time, so many questions filled her mind that she wasn't sure that she could go to sleep if she tried. "How much do we really know about the Imakut?"

The woman frowned. "Have you not been contributing to the Balance your entire life? Were you not raised in the faith?"

"I was," Kirima said. "But all we were ever taught was that we must give to them, and that there may be retribution if we take without doing so. There was never much reason given to the how or why."

The priestess folded her hands, walking over to the bed and taking a seat. "Our worship of the Imakut dates back generations, longer than we have tracked time. In the early days, when our people were first fishing the waters of these islands, it was discovered that many were taken. It was first attributed to bears, but soon it was discovered that the creatures of the deep were truly the ones to blame. It was then that the Balance was established, a gift when the moons both show full to placate those in the depths and to restore the balance for that which we take. It was known that the first gifts were successful because the jarak stones were given in return, a small token of acceptance."

Catriona looped her finger through her own necklace, showing a smoothed gem of milky white, a bit larger than Kirima's own. "Just as we all wear."

"Just as the Company was taking from the deep."

The woman frowned. "They are?"

Kirima nodded. "We discovered this when the Company outpost was destroyed. We went to see if there were any survivors, and I found a large one, bigger than I'd ever seen before. One of the workers said it burned even better than the whale oil they take." The words had come from Oki, and she closed her eyes as she tried to push him from her mind.

"But how could they get this? These stones only exist in the deepest depths."

"Enchanters were creating air pockets for men to dive down and search. I know nothing more than that."

The woman stood, pacing the small space. "This is disturbing indeed. They know not what they do."

"And if they were doing it in your waters, no doubt they are doing it elsewhere," Kirima said. "Tell me, I knew the stones were sacred, but not much beyond that."

"Sacred, yes, perhaps more than that. It is said that the jarak hold the souls of all life that passes through the seas. We've known the stones burn, of course, but to burn even a piece is a mortal sin, one worthy of being given to the Balance."

"Like a human sacrifice?"

"Yes, precisely. Burning a piece of jarak is destroying those souls, a transgression the Imakut cannot forgive." She paused, her fingers running over one of the paintings that adorned the walls. "I'm sure you saw the ruins spread throughout the islands on the way to Adhan?"

"I did."

"A civilization that existed long before us. It is said that back then, the seas were lower, that these islands were a continent instead of an archipelago. A state like ours, vast, prosperous, scientifically advanced. But they angered the Imakut and were thus destroyed. Their people slain, their valleys and cities flooded, their entire way of life dashed to bits because they did not heed the warnings. All that remains are those remnants that you see. Perhaps more lies beneath the water."

Kirima was silent for a moment. "Do you think that will happen here?"

"I think it could." She turned back to Kirima. "Were you able to speak with your Assembler?"

Kirima felt her eyes drop. "No. We were almost kicked out, but someone took pity on us and helped us as much as she could. An aide, I think she said."

"Do you think you could find her if we go back there?"

"I don't know," she said. "Maybe." She thought for a moment. "I remember her name. Iona."

"We can at least try. Maybe she can help us." She was already moving past Kirima toward the door. "Come, we should go immediately."

They rode the same contraption along the metal lines that she had with Gabriel and Phillip the last time. This time, it seemed that the wonder was lessened, perhaps by having seen it before, or perhaps simply from her state of mind. There seemed to be less of a sheen to the city, as if the cracks that had been hidden were starting to become clear to her mind. She saw the splendor and opulence, yes, but she also saw other things, rundown buildings and derelict homes, people covered in grime living in crowded alleys and begging on the corner. Had they been there before? Had things changed that much since she had been there, or were her eyes just a little more open?

They crossed the bridge over a wide expanse of blue water, ships large and small passing beneath, ships larger than her town had been. They rode up the hill on the island, the Assembly building before them, dwarfed by the towering buildings of the individual representatives and the Company. The cart stopped before the one she had visited before, and they both stepped off, Catriona leading the way into the building.

It seemed little different from before, perhaps a bit less bright. It was still bustling, every single person looking as though they had somewhere to be at that very moment, barreling through the lobby as if whatever mission they were on was the most important thing in the world. Perhaps it was. But she doubted it.

"Let me do the talking," the priestess said. She walked right up to an open spot at the front desk, a young woman with dark hair tied into a long, tight braid, almond shaped eyes, rosy cheeks, and a wide, dimpled smile. Kirima's eyes ran up and down, looking for the man they had dealt with last time, but if he was there, she either couldn't see him or did not recognize him.

"Can I help you?" the woman behind the desk asked.

"I am High Priestess Catriona from the Imakut Temple," she said. "I would like an audience with..."

"I'm sorry," the girl said. "His Honor is of course very busy. I can deliver a message."

"I would like to speak to Iona," Catriona said. "Is she available?"

Kirima could see the woman falter just the slightest. "I can certainly check. One moment, please.”

She began tapping at something in front of her, a loud beeping noise emerging from it. She stopped after a moment, waiting until more beeps came back, this time without her tapping. She listened intently for a moment, scribbling something on a piece of paper before her, then finally looked back up at them.

“She is available for you, High Priestess.” She held out her hand to the left. “Take the elevator to the eleventh floor.”

Kirima’s stomach dropped at the thought of getting back on the elevator, but Catriona did not hesitate in the slightest. She followed the priestess into that same hallway she had entered the last time, and into an open elevator. Catriona was pressing a button as Kirima settled into the back corner, already gripping the railing before the doors closed.

She could feel her heart still racing as the elevator came to a stop and she stepped out onto the ground with wobbling legs. Iona was standing there, a frown on her face, followed by her eyebrows raising when she looked at Kirima.

“You’re back,” she said. Her frown deepened. “But the others?”

Kirima only shook her head.

“I see,” Iona said. “Come with me.”

She led them to her office, closing the door behind them. The view was still there, but the lack of a sun that day diminished it, just as it had the rest of the city when they were on their way. The office seemed even more cluttered than last time, papers and books and scrolls lying around. Cold air filtered through the opening in the ceiling, almost making it feel like home, if not for the underlying heat that permeated the windows around them.

“What brings you back, Kirima?” she asked. “And with a High Priestess, no less.”

“We failed,” she said, the words pouring from her mouth. “We tried to fight, and we failed. And we don’t think it’s the end of it.”

“What do you mean?”

Catriona removed her pendant, placing it on the desk between them. “Do you recognize this?” she asked.

Iona reached over and picked it up, turning it between her fingers, examining it. “Of course, I do. This is oilstone. The Company presented it to the Assembly several months back, saying they discovered a way to extract large quantities of it. Half the city runs on it now.”

“In our old language, we called it jarak. It is sacred to the Imakut.”

Iona’s eyes were still focused on the stone in her fingers as she spoke. “Assembler Blair did not say anything about it. Is it not something that all your people find sacred?”

Catriona folded her arms over her chest and nearly spat the words out. “Blair speaks as if he follows the old ways, but he never has. He would not have known what it was or why it was sacred."

Iona flashed her a look but said nothing on the matter, turning her focus back to Kirima. "You think them harvesting the oilstone is what caused this?"

"Without a doubt," Kirima said.

There was a silence for a moment, broken by the priestess. "I understand as a nonbeliever it may seem extraordinary, but there is a real danger here. She and her people can attest to that."

"This certainly isn't something the Assembly will want to hear," Iona said.

"But it is something they must hear," Kirima said.

Iona gave her a smirk. "You're not familiar with politicians, not where you're from. If you bring them a truth they don't care to hear, they'll make the conscious choice to not believe it."

It didn't sound all that different from the Council in her mind. "Be that as it may, they still need to hear."

Iona leaned back in her chair, seeming to consider it for a moment. "I cannot get you a private audience, but they are holding public hearings today. I can get you to the front of the line."

"That will have to do," Catriona said.

Iona stood. "Come, the session will be starting soon."

19

Even though the Assembly Hall had been dwarfed by the surrounding buildings, its lavish interior brought on more wonder than even the towering structures could.

The entry hall rose high above her head, supported by columns of white stone. The ceiling was covered in paintings, much as the temple had been, but here, the paintings were of people in different poses, most of them seeming to be leading in some respect or another, some from pulpits and some from battlefields or upon boats. Sunlight filtered through large windows, cast upon smooth, hard floors of stone with inlaid patterns.

Like the other building, there were people of all shapes and sizes filling the space. Iona walked with purpose, her heeled boots clicking loudly with each step. The crowd did not part, not like it seemed it should have, but she still led through, her vision picking out a clear path through with practiced precision. It was all Kirima and Catriona could do to keep up, the path seeming to close just as quickly as it opened.

Massive doors stood at the far end, but Iona steered them away from them, walking up to one of many smaller doors on the side, guarded by a man in a colorful uniform with a hat shaped like a short spearhead, the barrel of a rifle sticking up over his shoulder. He said nothing as they approached, his eyes focused on Iona. She pulled back the neck of her coat, revealing a golden badge. The guard took a close look, then nodded and stepped aside, allowing the three of them through the door.

She led them through a dark hallway and out into a wide space. Here, Kirima could see the dome above, light seeping through the curved glass that filled the spaces between iron supports. It rose above a circular room, the edges supported by the same white columns that had been in the foyer. In the center was a long table upon a tall dais, eleven people in fine clothing seated in evenly spaced intervals. Before the dais was a single wooden platform, partially surrounded by a wooden railing. Someone stood at the railing now, saying words that were lost in the cavernous space, directed toward what she could only imagine was the Assembly.

"Come, this way," Iona said.

They followed her down a short set of stairs, walking toward a wooden barrier with a small gate, where more guards stood by. Her eyes traced around the barrier, taking notice of the scribes taking notes on one end, and the line of people waiting to be heard at the other. Iona walked up to the guard standing by the front of the line and said a few words to him. The guard nodded and Iona motioned them toward the gate.

As they reached the barrier, she could hear the crowd stirring behind them. "They're not going to jump the line, are they?" someone said. "I don't care who they are, we've been waiting days for our turn, they should wait like the rest of us."

Neither they, nor the guard, turned to acknowledge the voice. Kirima felt her cheeks start to flush, but she reminded herself that what she was going to say was important.

"Hey," the man said. He reached out and tapped the guard on the shoulder. "Hey, you're not going to let them go before us, are you?"

"Good luck stopping that," another voice said. "Just like always, the rich get put in front."

"Well they don't look rich to me, least not that one. Looks like someone from up north who was pulled right out the water."

"Smells like one too."

"I hope you're ignoring them," Iona said from beside her.

"I'm trying," Kirima said, her fingers gripping the sides of her parka.

"Anyone can come as part of the general hours. People wait in line for days to be heard, and most bring either trivial matters that are not worthy of the Assembly's time or massive things that are beyond the scope of our government's capabilities. Some have suggested doing away with the general hours, but most feel like it would have a detrimental impact on the public's view of the Assembly."

One of the Assembly members banged a wooden hammer on the table, and loudly called for the next in line. The person at the platform stepped down and was ushered out the far side by one of the guards.

"Come on," Iona said as the guard opened a gate in front of them, motioning them through.

Kirima obeyed, hearing the shouts and boos of the people behind her. Iona led her toward the wooden platform, helping her up to it. Catriona stepped up beside her, and they both stood, their hands on the railing as they looked up to the men and women who made up the Assembly.

It reminded her of the Council back home in a lot of ways. They were all older, most of them showing grey hairs and wrinkles. Even the ones who appeared the youngest had been weathered by the years, or perhaps by the weight of rule weighed down upon them. The hammer sounded on the table once more, and the one with the hammer called for order.

The guard stepped forward. "Kirima of Aliit, and Catriona, high priestess of the Imakut temple."

The table was struck once more before the hammer was placed down, and the Assembler motioned toward them. "Proceed."

At first Kirima said nothing. It was only when Catriona nudged her with an elbow that she managed to find her voice.

"We're here because my town is no more."

"What do you mean?" asked one of the Assemblers, a woman on the right side.

"We were attacked by creatures sent by the Imakut from beneath the waves."

There was a silence, a different look on the face of each Assembly member as they tried to process what she had said. She looked across all of them, and she all it took was a single look of each to tell their thoughts on the matter. It was one of the men in line behind her that voiced what was no doubt the same opinion.

"That's what I got skipped for? She's insane, get her out of here and let those of us with real problems be heard."

His words were met with a mix of laughter and jeers as others in line took up his cause. She fought the urge to look back, feeling the heat in her cheeks grow. Why did they not believe her? Was it really such a strange possibility? Of course, many in her own town had been skeptical, but she had seen everything with her own eyes. Beside her, Catriona took her hand and squeezed it.

The leader of the Assembly took up his hammer once more and banged it loudly, calling for order. When everything finally quieted, he turned to one of the Assemblers to the left. "Assembler Blair, this seems to be one of yours."

"Indeed." The man who spoke seemed to have a kind face, one that was currently furrowed, showing wrinkles on a wide forehead beneath thinning grey hair, his hands clasped and resting against his chin. "Iona, I'm sure you have a good reason for bringing this woman and the high priestess before us, but the possibilities currently escape me."

"Yes, Your Honor," Iona said. "This woman came to me two weeks ago with two companions, speaking in fear of an attack on her home. She now returns with detailed tales of what transpired, the others who had accompanied her now dead."

He cleared his throat and leaned forward a bit. "And you believe her?"

Iona nodded quickly. "I do."

Blair turned back to the platform. "And you too, High Priestess? You believe her story to be true?"

"I would not be here if I did not," Catriona said.

"I see." Blair gestured toward Kirima. "Tell us your story, then, girl. Speak clearly and truthfully."

There were some more grumbles behind her, but Kirima cleared her throat and began to speak. "I do speak truthfully, Assembler. These creatures started taking our people several weeks ago, which was when we came here looking for help. After we returned, they attacked the Company outpost and destroyed it."

Blair glanced over to one of the others, a woman with straight white hair hanging to her shoulders and a puckered face. "Moyra, can you confirm that the Aliit outpost was destroyed?"

"I cannot, no," she said. "Our last supply run was two weeks ago. Another is due to leave port here in Adhan in a week, but we will not know until then."

"I see," he said. "Can an advance team be sent?"

"I can speak with President Ramsay."

Blair nodded and motioned to Kirima to proceed. "We found out when we went there that the Company was harvesting jarak," she said.

"Harvesting what?" one of the Assemblers asked.

Kirima hooked her thumb through her necklace and pulled it up to show the stone. "Jarak. It is sacred to our people."

"She means oilstone," Moyra said.

Blair glanced across the table to her. "And that is true? The Company has been harvesting it?"

"Of course it's true," Moyra said. "Oilstone is the most potent fuel per gram in the known world. Much of this city and Omak run on it, and plans are in place to expand its usage across the country."

"We believe that the harvesting of it is what brought about the attack from the Imakut," Kirima said. "If it is not stopped, then they will not stop."

There was silence for a moment, then Moyra gave a sharp laugh. "You must be insane, girl. Oilstone is what makes this city run. It is the highest grossing product that the Company put out this year by a long shot. Its power has enabled the expansion to the barrier islands and the distribution of electricity in poorer districts. The very idea of stopping harvest on it is absurd to even consider."

"Perhaps it can be paused until an inquest can be made," a younger woman at the end said. "Just temporarily to see if what this woman believes is true."

"Just finding that the outpost is destroyed would give some credence to the tale," Blair said, rubbing at the whiskers on his chin.

"If production stops, then power in many parts of the city will be interrupted," Moyra said. "Do you want to answer to a crowd of people who have lost their power?"

"Many did not have power a few years ago," someone said.

"And many have grown used to having it."

Iona leaned in closely. "As I said, the drug of comfort."

Blair turned back to them. "Is there any definitive proof you can provide stating that the farming of oilstone is directly related to this phenomenon you're describing?"

"The Company has been there for years," Kirima said. "None of this happened before they started taking the jarak."

"Perhaps you missed leaving a goat out?" Moyra said.

That drew some laughs, both from the line behind them and from a few members of the Assembly. Kirima looked around, glancing over her shoulder, then back to the Assembly. "They think we're a joke," she said quietly.

"The truth is on your side," Catriona said.

"But they will not act without proof," Iona said.

"The proof is back in Aliit," Kirima said. "If they choose to leave their own dead behind. And I'm not going back there."

Blair cleared his throat, drawing their attention. "If you do not have anything for us to go on, then we have a lot of others to get through."

"Wait," Kirima said, louder than she intended. She watched as all eyes of the Assembly turned toward her, all of them waiting for her to speak. She licked her lips, drawing in a breath before continuing. "I understand this may seem hard to believe, but there is a danger coming. The Company outpost is destroyed. My town is destroyed. What other places have suffered the same fate that we don't know about? I only just escaped with my life, and I still have the wounds to prove it."

"Your wounds could have come from anything, young lady," Moyra said. "I see no reason to disrupt the lives of hundreds, maybe thousands of people on such a fantastical tale."

"Your Honor," Iona said, raising her voice from beside them. "Assembler Moyra, have there been other outposts that have been destroyed?"

"I don't see what that has to do..."

"Assembler, she asks a good question," the Assembly leader said. "Is that information readily available?"

Moyra seemed to pause before straightening in her chair, her chin held high. "There have been some problems, particularly in the northern islands, but that is to be expected. Company operations carry a high risk by nature, and we all know that elements in your district, Assembler Blair, are particularly challenging. Even with all the lengths we go to, we cannot eliminate the risks, particularly when winter comes."

"Of course," Blair said. "I would still like an inquiry into Company operations in my district."

"That can be arranged," Moyra said. "And certainly without interrupting operations."

The Assembly leader held up his hammer. "Then we shall vote. The issue at hand is whether to cease harvesting oilstone while an investigation can be made, or to have a basic inquiry made into problems at Company outposts without disturbing production. No action is a valid response. Any for ceasing harvest?" No one moved. "For basic inquiry?" Ten hands raised at once. "And no action." Nothing. The hammer banged. "The motion for a basic inquiry carries. Next."

Kirima could feel her head swimming with how quickly it had all happened. "What does that mean?" she asked Iona.

She could see the way Iona's shoulders sagged. "I'm sorry. We failed."

The guard was motioning her off the platform. "Madam, please."

"No, wait," Kirima said, turning back toward the Assembly. "Please, you don't know what you're doing."

The hammer fell a couple of more times. "You will restrain yourself, young lady or you will be forcibly removed."

Iona took her by the arm, but she shook it off. "They're coming, and they'll be here sooner than you think. If you think the barrier islands or any of your weapons or army or anything will stop them, then you're completely mistaken. They don't stop. They don't stop coming."

One more bang, then a motion with the hammer. "Guard, escort her from the building. We have far too much to do to listen to this nonsense any further."

"No, don't do this." The guard had come behind her and physically lifted her off the platform, holding her arms to her sides. She kicked, but he was big, strong, handling her just as she would Meriwa or Hanta. "You don't know what you're doing. All these lives will be on your hands."

She was unable to see or hear the response. The words were hardly past her lips when the guard carried her into a hallway, the door shutting loudly behind them. He did not stop, carrying her down the hallway, through a door, and out into the warm day. She was still kicking, but it seemed more out of principle than anything else, and it quickly ended when she felt herself falling, landing hard on the ground.

The thought of attacking the guard filled her mind, but it quickly fled when she saw Iona and Catriona emerge, the guard already closing the doors behind him. The anger fled with a sigh, as if it had attached itself to her breath and flowed right from her body.

"I'm sorry," she said. "I did not intend to react like that. I couldn't stop myself."

"I'm sorry nothing more could be done," Iona said. "But as I told you, the Assembly will not be able to bring itself to break anyone from the comfort the Company provides. So long as that exists, the Company will control the Assembly."

Kirima shook her head. "Surely there's something more we can do."

"You should return to your people," Catriona said. "Surely some rest will help clear my mind."

"And I need to return to my work," Iona said. She paused for a moment, staring off at one of the towering buildings around them. "You really think they'll come here?"

"I have no doubt in my mind," Kirima said.

"I see." Another silence. "I've always dreamed of moving somewhere quiet. Perhaps this will be a good time to do so."

"You could come with us," Kirima said. "We'd have you."

"I appreciate the offer, but this will be something on my own." She turned to Kirima and smiled. "I wish I could have helped more."

"You did all you could."

"I suppose. Goodbye. I hope you stay safe."

"You too."

"May the Imakut bless you.," Catriona said.

"Perhaps," Iona said. "Or perhaps I would prefer if they ignored me."

She turned away, leaving the two of them alone in the street.

20

Kirima was not sure how long she had slept in that dark room, but she awoke to the sound of quiet voices. She sat up, blinking away the sleep as if it would make the room any brighter. Instead, her vision slowly cleared to the small candle that was lit in the corner, the source of the voices. She could see the high priestess there, and Yura as well. Alongside them were Lusa and Miki, the two council members who had been on their boat.

She heard movement around her, other whispers, grunts, coughs, but it was those around the light that drew her, as if she was a moth. It was Yura who saw her first, a slight smile on her face, her hands resting on a belly that seemed ready to burst. The others slowly realized, their conversations turning as they turned to look at her.

"Tell me," she said, her whisper matching their own tone. "What are you all talking about?"

"What comes next," Miki said with a shrug. "What else is there?"

Kirima sighed. "It shouldn't be such a difficult decision."

"Yet it is," Lusa said. "No decision like this should be taken lightly."

"Perhaps you do not see the same life and death choice that the rest of us do," Yura said. "I cannot imagine an easier choice."

"Is it truly such an easy choice?" Lusa said. "We don't know what's further on. Even the priestesses don't know what's beyond Omak. There could be nothing for all we know, just miles and miles and miles of sea until we run out of fuel and starve to death."

"Traders come from lands to the south to Omak," Catriona said. "There is something there."

"Do you know how to get there?" Lusa asked.

"We can speak to those traders," Yura said as the priestess shrugged. "They can tell us how to get there."

"And what then?" Lusa asked. "Even if we do find these mythical lands, what are we going to do? How will we survive? Here, we at least have the temple to help us. We can make a life here. And the navy and army can offer protection, just as it does to all the rest of the people here."

"Until the Imakut come and take it from us," Yura said.

"How do we know they won't come south as well? Sooner or later, we have to stop running."

"Maybe once they destroy those farming the jarak, they will stop," Kirima said. "Perhaps even Omak would be far enough."

"The further, the better," Yura said. "As close to the edge of the world as we can get."

"Can we even afford more fuel?" Lusa asked. "How far can we even get on what we have?"

"Far enough, I'm sure," Yura said.

"Can the temple help?" Kirima asked.

Catriona seemed to consider it for a moment. "Yes. And I think we'll be accompanying you."

Each person around the candle had a different look, but it was all some degree of shock. "But what of the temple?" Lusa asked. "Are you just going to abandon the people here, the believers?"

"I'm afraid there are few believers here and fewer by the year, it seems," Catriona said. "Even for those who worship, it is a secondary part of their lives. The traditions are rooted in people like you, who must live off the sea, who have not made themselves a part of this society."

"But those who are," Lusa said. "You are abandoning them. How can you? It is your vocation."

"The temple has never been about the priests or priestesses," she said. "It will still stand for as long as the people will have it. Or for as long as the Imakut will have it. Besides, these events have made it clear that we don't know what it means to properly worship them. Or whether they care."

"And the Balance?" Kirima asked.

Catriona closed her eyes for a moment, breathing in through her nose. "We have upheld the Balance for as long as we could. When we reach a new place, we shall continue the practice, but I fear it is no longer sustainable in a place that the Imakut have already doomed."

"This is madness," Lusa said. "How do we even know that they are coming to Adhan?"

"Word came last night from a Company vessel that passed Ota," Catriona said. "The town is gone."

"Where is that?" Yura asked.

"Northeast of here. A day's boat ride or so, two islands away."

"They grow closer," Kirima said.

"Which means we must leave soon," Yura said. "Is there any doubt remaining."

Lusa shot her a glance. "I still have doubts, young lady. And last I checked, I am still the simuq. With Gabriel gone, the power defers to the Council."

"And you stand alone," Kirima said.

"Do I?"

Lusa looked over to Miki. He frowned, looking between her and the rest, his mind seeming to work so hard that she almost expected smoke to pour from his ears. He took a deep breath. "I think we should go."

For a moment, Kirima was certain Lusa was going to smack him with her cane. It seemed Miki thought the same, because he seemed to draw away, his eyes refusing to look at the scowl that Lusa cast in his direction.

There was a heavy silence between them all, neither side willing to budge on the matter, neither side willing to give even an inch. Finally, it was Kirima who spoke.

"If you wish to stay, then stay. Those who wish to go will be leaving."

Lusa's gaze turned toward her, then Yura and the priestess, and back to Miki before finally looking down to her lap as she heaved a sigh. "You leave me no choice. I will not abandon my people. I will go with you all."

"This is the best decision for us," Yura said. "For all of us."

"What of the others?" Miki said. "Should we not wait for them?"

It has been two days since we arrived," Kirima said. "And it will take us some time to prepare provisions for the trip. If they do not arrive in that time, then I do not think they ever will."

"How long do we dare wait?" Yura asked. "Is it safe for another night? Two nights?"

"It will have to be," Lusa said. "We have people who need more rest, and we must get provisions."

"She's right," Kirima said. "It will take at least a day. Perhaps if we're quick, we can finish before sundown."

"Kirima, dear," Yura said. "It's already past sundown."

"Oh." Kirima rubbed her eyes. "Is it truly that late? I thought it was just the room."

"It does play tricks with the mind, but she speaks truly," Catriona said. "The market will be open at dawn. We can go then."

"We need to know what to get," Miki said.

"Food, fresh water, fuel," Kirima said. "That is what is important. How quickly can we get it all?"

"An hour, perhaps two," Catriona said. "It should all be available in the market. If we go early, we can depart by midday."

"Then we leave tomorrow, once we have what we need," Kirima said. "Are we all in agreement?"

There was a chorus of affirmatives. The priestess was the first to rise, making her way from the room to go tell the other members of her clergy, a pair of priests and a trio of priestesses. The two Council members moved off to the side, speaking quietly between themselves, leaving Kirima and Yura alone.

"I thought she would put her foot down," Kirima said, her voice low, her eyes watching Lusa and Miki. "I was afraid that if she refused, the others would too."

"She wasn't going to," Yura said. "She knows you hold the power now."

"Do I? It doesn't feel like it."

"You see how the others have reacted to you. You're in charge now. For better or worse, we're all following you now."

"Can't help but feel like it will be for the worse."

"Father would have disagreed with you on that."

"You think?"

"I know." She patted Kirima's leg. "Get some more rest. Tomorrow will be busy."

Kirima lay awake for a while, listening to the quiet conversation around the room. Sleep came surprisingly easily, but it was not a good sleep, her dreams filled with the sights and sounds of that night in the village. She saw Phillip and Calum and Gabriel, the three mercenaries and all the others. All those who died that night, the young and the old alike. It was when she saw Siluk jumped that she awoke with a cry, sweat clinging to her skin. After that, she slept no more.

When dawn broke, the priestess came and collected her and Miki. A cool wind coming off the water, mingling with a light fog that lingered in places, but the rising sun was already beginning to warm the air, a harbinger to the heat the day would bring. The priestess walked at a bring pace, across the park that surrounded the temple and through the towering buildings to the market.

Catriona moved rapidly through the stalls, stopping every so often and dealing with the keepers in rapid succession. With each purchase, something was handed to Kirima or Miki until their arms were both full, carrying sacks filled with all sorts of items: dried meat and cheeses, fruit preserves and jarred vegetables, flattened bread and nuts and herbs, and several varieties of medicines. By the time they emerged from the other side, Kirima was not sure she would be able to walk even the length of the dock to the boat, but she somehow managed it.

They loaded everything onto the boat, filling every compartment they could find and stacking the rest in a corner below the deck. While Kirima and Miki worked, Catriona left them, returning after a short time followed by men driving a cart filled with several metal barrels, the stench of whale oil drifting from it. It made Kirima's stomach churn, the thought of being sick filling her mind, but she forced it down. They would not get far at all without it, she knew, so she would endure it.

Once the boat was stocked, Miki remained behind to watch it while Kirima and the priestess went back to the temple to collect everyone. It was about midday before they had everyone on the boat, the sun beating down on them with no cloud cover in sight.

When the last one had stepped onto the boat, Kirima began to untie it from the mooring. Out of the corner of her eye, she caught sight of the priestess standing at the boat's railing, gazing off toward the city. Kirima followed her gaze to where the temple stood, visible in the gap between the taller buildings.

"We're all leaving something behind," Kirima said.

The priestess nodded. "I've lived here almost my entire life. My entire adult life, for certain."

Kirima finished untying the rope and tossed it onto the boat, climbing up after it. "Maybe one day we'll be able to return."

Catriona gave a sad smile. "I'm not optimistic that will be the case."

"You never know."

Kirima made her way to the wheel and started the engine. She began to ease the boat away from the dock. Yura had stepped up beside her, leaning against the railing.

"Everything you bought, all the supplies, will it be enough for us?" Yura asked.

"It will last us some time," Catriona said, turning away from the city. "There is still money for us to restock in Omak."

"And for beyond that?"

"We can't know, not unless we find someone who knows," Catriona said. "But no doubt we can find a trader in Omak who can tell us. Or perhaps a cartographer who has mapped the places beyond. Or even our own temple there. Even that far south, there are still those who follow the old ways."

"I wonder what we'll find beyond Omak," Kirima said.

"Hopefully a new home," Yura said.

"Are you both afraid?"

"Of course," Yura said.

A slight smile crossed the priestess's mouth. "Were you afraid when you faced the Imakut?"

Kirima suppresses a shudder, the goosebumps feeling strange in the heat of the day. "Petrified."

"I'm certain no one here is any less frightened, but we all show it in different ways. It's there, you just have to learn where to look."

"The one thing we know," Yura said, "is that our only way is forward. There's no going back."

Kirima nodded. "Forward. Together."

"Together," Catriona said.

Kirima turned the boat away from the docks and headed for the exit, for the space between the barrier islands. Behind her, the city grew smaller, fading into the distance in a way that seemed impossible, cast in shadows by the setting sun.

"This is it," Yura said. "Further from home."

"Further from home," Kirima said. "A home we'll never see again."

"Do you think we'll be safe?"

No. The word sounded over and over in her mind, but her lips and tongue rebelled, pushing back against it. "I think we will."

A chuckle. "Papa always said you were a terrible liar."

"He always knew me best."

She felt Yura wrap her arm through hers. "Whatever it is, at least we have each other. All of us. Us who remain."

Kirima nodded. "And we'll do it together."

She navigated through the strait and out onto the open ocean, heading south. Somewhere in the distance, she thought she could hear the wailing of the wind, but perhaps it was nothing.

I hope you enjoyed this novel. If you did, I would greatly appreciate it if you took a moment to rate it on Amazon or Goodreads.

If you'd like to receive updates on future works and other news, feel free to follow me on Facebook (drewmontgomerywrites) or Twitter (@dmontgomery008).

ABOUT THE AUTHOR

Drew Montgomery is a graduate of Texas A&M and the author of books such as <u>The Darkest </u>Corners, <u>The Last Dragonkeeper</u>, <u>The Burial</u>, <u>Taika Town</u>, and <u>The Elder Gods</u>. He currently lives in Houston, TX, where he moonlights in tech. When not writing, you can often find him reading, playing video games, drinking craft beer, and occasionally watching and complaining about the local sports teams.

You can find him in many places on the web:

Website: https://www.drewmontgomerywrites.com/
Patreon: https://www.patreon.com/drewmontgomery
Twitter: https://twitter.com/dmontgomery008
Reddit: https://www.reddit.com/r/drewmontgomery/
Facebook: https://www.facebook.com/drewmontgomerywrites

9 798882 850629 3